TURNING THE TIDE

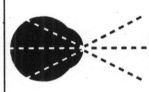

A QUAKER MIDWIFE MYSTERY

TURNING THE TIDE

EDITH MAXWELL

THORNDIKE PRESS
A part of Gale, a Cengage Company

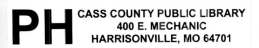

GALE
A Cengage Company

Farmington Hills, Mich • San Francisco • New York • Waterville, Maine
Meriden, Conn • Mason, Ohio • Chicago

LIBRARY OF CONGRESS CIP DATA ON FILE.
CATALOGUING IN PUBLICATION FOR THIS BOOK
IS AVAILABLE FROM THE LIBRARY OF CONGRESS

ISBN-13: 978-1-4328-5375-4 (hardcover)

Published in 2018 by arrangement with Midnight, Ink, an imprint of Llewellyn Publications, Woodbury, MN 55125-2989 USA

Printed in Mexico
1 2 3 4 5 6 7 22 21 20 19 18

*I dedicate this book to
the feminists of the nineteenth
and twentieth centuries.
Thank you for fighting for the rights
of all women, those in your day
as well as those to follow.*

AUTHOR'S NOTE

This book takes place during the national election week of 1888. I was fascinated to learn the history of the candidates, the issues being discussed, the customs surrounding elections — including Election Cake! — and more. I read accounts of events taking place locally in the *Newburyport Daily News* on microfiche at the Newburyport Public Library and the *Newburyport Daily Herald* on microfiche at the Amesbury Public Library.

As the book has a sub-theme of women's suffrage, I studied whatever I could find in the library and online. I took the liberty of paraphrasing a few sentences from Elizabeth Cady Stanton's essay, "The Solitude of Self," which was not published until 1892, for her to speak in person in this book (at Bertie and Sophie's evening gathering). I couched it as Stanton developing her thoughts on the topic, and I trust her departed soul will approve. The song "Daughters of Freedom," which the women sing in this book, was a women's suffrage rallying piece copyrighted in 1871, with lyrics by George Cooper and music by Edwin Christie. Thanks for supporting the movement, gentlemen. Alas, my schedule didn't permit visiting the Women's Rights National Historical Park in Seneca Falls, New York.

I want to thank Peter Bryant of the former Salisbury Point Railroad Society for checking my train details. I cribbed the three things a detective needs from *A Good Month for Murder: The Inside Story of a Homicide Squad* by Del Quentin Wilber. KB Inglee again read for historical details and corrected several of my errors, and Alison Russell checked my facts for that election season.

I'm always on the lookout for intriguing authentic names from the period. My writer friend Nancy Langmeyer mentioned her great-great grandfather Hilarius Bauer over wine one evening. I asked if I could use his name and she said, "Sure!" Mystery author, independent editor, and good friend Sherry Harris wrote a Facebook post some time ago about discovering interesting names of some of her ancestors. I borrowed her paternal grandmother's first name for the character of Zula in this book. I know nothing about Ursula Gates Novinger, and am quite sure any negative characteristics and behavior of my Zula have no connection to the real Zula of the past.

I used the wording of a couple of letters and invitations that I found in this resource: *The American lady's and gentleman's modern letter writer: relative to business, duty, love, and marriage,* University of Pittsburgh, Digital Research Library 2002. I attended the Strawbery Banke Harvest Festival in Portsmouth while writing this book. The festival features craftspeople and artisans in period dress making their arts, doing their crafts. I was delighted to encounter Rose Carroll's own bicycle among a display of vintage cycles. I was able to put my hand on the split leather seat and learn that cycles of the time even featured a small headlight.

The menu for the dinner for twelve at the Dodges' is taken nearly verbatim from Miss Parloa's Bills of Fare, found in *Miss Parloa's New Cook Book And Marketing Guide,* 1880. Note: the fictional Dodge family bears no relation to the ancestors of my good friend from Newburyport Anne Dodge and her West Newbury cousin John Dodge — although I did borrow their name, and their forbearer did, in fact, own a successful shoe business in that town.

I'm also always looking for sources of how people, particularly women, spoke in the era. For this book I perused several of Louisa May Alcott's books for dialog, plus I gleaned bits from Sarah Grand's *Ideala,* George Egerton's (Mary Chavelita Dunne Bright) *Keynotes* and *Discords,* and *The Wing of Azrael* by Mona Caird, all books written by women in the late 1800s.

Susan Koso is not only on the Board of Directors of the Amesbury Carriage Museum, she is also a fount of limitless knowledge about carriages and carriage driving of the period. While I was writing this book she took me riding in her own antique runabout, pulled by her mare Hope, on a former carriage road through Appleton Farm in Ipswich, Massachusetts. While we drove, I asked endless questions, all of which she answered, and she offered invaluable tips on everyday life. Susan also read an early draft of this manuscript, and corrected a few of my errors, but I'm sure more remain, which is no reflection on her expertise. The Amesbury Carriage Museum is also an invaluable resource with their collection of carriages from the period in which I set this series.

I continue to train as a docent at the John

Greenleaf Whittier Home and Museum. In this book I quote one stanza of Whittier's poem "The Lakeside." Whittier's comments on not remembering his own work are paraphrased from a quote in the November 1, 1888 *Newburyport Daily Herald.* The Whittier Home Association, along with the Amesbury Public Library, generously starred *Delivering the Truth,* the first book in this series, as the All-Community Read for 2016, and they staged a reading of the scenes from the book featuring Rose and Whittier at the Amesbury Friends Meetinghouse. I was honored and delighted. Chris Bryant, President of the Association, continues to be endlessly supportive of my work and stocks my books for sale in the home's gift shop.

I continue to refer to the following historic references, among others: Marc McCutcheon's *Everyday Life in the 1800s* (1993), *John Greenleaf Whittier: a Biography* by Roland H. Woodwell (1985), the *Sears, Roebuck & Co. Consumers' Guide* for 1894, *The Massachusetts Peace Officer: a Manual for Sheriffs, Constables, Police, and Other Civil Officers* by Gorham D. Williams (1891), and *A System of Midwifery* by William Leishman, MD (1879). I consult the Online Etymology Dictionary endlessly to see if I can use a particular word or phrase, or if its first attested occurrence was after 1888, and often check Pinterest and other sites for examples of clothing from the era.

I traveled to New Orleans for the Bouchercon mystery convention while I was working on this manuscript, and I happened across the Pharmacy Museum in the French Quarter. I discovered an entire room upstairs devoted to midwifery and childbirth from the 1800s. It was set up like a bedroom, complete with historic tools and medicines, with well-curated explanatory signage. Bliss.

I very much enjoy reading the novels of my fellow historical mystery writers who set their books in close to the same period, especially those of my friends Jessica Crockett Estevao, Nancy Herriman, Alyssa Maxwell (no relation), Ann Parker, and Anna Loan Wilsey, and of course the long-running series of both Victoria Thompson and Rhys Bowen. You should check out all these well-written books. I hope I have absorbed only a general feel for the era from them and not subconsciously lifted anything too specific.

Obviously, any remaining errors on anything historical are of my own doing.

ONE

Rowena Felch stood tall and graceful on the podium in the Free Will Baptist Church hall. "In this election season of 1888, we must work with ever more diligence to gain women the vote!" She sliced the air with her fervor. "We must convince our Massachusetts lawmakers to act. It is past time."

The Saturday-night meeting of the Amesbury Woman Suffrage Association was jamfull. I'd arrived a bit late with my friend Bertie Winslow, and we'd found places to sit near the side of the hall. I could see easily, being at least as tall as the speaker, but petite Bertie craned her neck to catch a glimpse of Rowena. It was my first suffrage meeting, although not Bertie's, and I'd met Rowena only once before, at Bertie's house. The full room was warm with female bodies and smelled of women: floral aromas, breast milk, and yeasty hints of sweat. Scents integral to my world of midwifery. The gas lamps on all the walls gave a welcoming aura and highlighted Rowena's face glowing with fervor.

"Do not lose heart, ladies," Rowena went on. "We shall gather on Tuesday across from the main polling place in the new Armory. Frannie will hand you each a sash on your way out tonight." She gestured toward the back of the room. "Please wear them proudly on Election Day."

I turned to look. Frannie Eisenman, the grandmother of a baby girl I'd delivered just last week, held a sunflower-yellow sash in the air and waved it for all to see.

"Does anyone have a question?" Rowena asked.

An older woman with hair the color of iron stood. It was Ruby Bracken, a member of the same Friends Meeting as me. "What is our plan if we're met with opposition from the gentleman, as we surely will be?"

A teenage girl with curly black tresses sat next to Ruby. The girl's eyes widened as if in fear at the thought of opposition, but I was glad to see females of all ages at the meeting. An older lady with a comfortable corset-free figure and soft white sausage curls framing her face emerged from a side door at the front of the hall and walked to the podium. Rowena took a pace back, beaming at the newcomer.

"If this comes to pass, we shall link arms and stand tall," the woman proclaimed, her flat black lace headdress falling like a veil and accentuating her snowy-white hair.

Bertie's mouth fell open. "That's Mrs. Stanton!"

"*The* Mrs. Stanton?" I asked, shifting on the hard wooden chair.

"Elizabeth Cady Stanton herself. Why, I never." Bertie's eyes were bright. "Right here in Amesbury. Let's go greet her after the meeting finishes."

Murmurs of the name rose up all around us. My mother, an ardent suffragist in her own right, had gotten to know Elizabeth Stanton at the International Women's Conference in the spring and had sent glowing tales of Elizabeth's courage from Washington City.

"Be not afraid," Elizabeth continued. "We are in the right and we shall not be intimidated. Please stand and join me in song." She waited until all rose, then began.

Daughters of freedom arise in your might.
March to the watchwords Justice and Right.

The women's voices singing the inspiring lyrics in unison raised goosebumps on my arms. I hummed along since I didn't know the words.

15

Why will ye slumber? Wake, O wake.
Lo, on your legions light doth break.
Sunder the fetters custom hath made.
Come from the valley, hill and glade.

The song went on from there until the hall filled with applause.

"Come on." Bertie tugged my arm as the clapping ended.

"Won't we be intruding?" I asked, pulling back a little, even though of course I wanted to meet the famous and tireless advocate for women's rights. I allowed Bertie to pull me to the front until we neared Elizabeth and Rowena. Rowena's skirt was hemmed shorter than many and I glimpsed a pair of red leather shoes underneath.

We waited while a mother with two young daughters spoke with the women. Elizabeth bent down and gave the children warm greetings, but Rowena was cooler, merely smiling and shaking their small hands.

After they turned away, Rowena smiled at Bertie and extended her hand. "Hello, Miss Winslow, and Miss Carroll, isn't it?" She shook first Bertie's hand and then mine, with a firm smooth grip. "Thank you for coming to our gathering," Rowena said. "Mrs. Stanton, may I present Miss Bertie Winslow? She's Amesbury's postmistress." Rowena, about five years older than my twenty-six, wore her smooth flaxen hair gathered into a low knot under a flat-top hat decorated with only a single green ribbon and feather. Her well-cut green dress was fashionable without being frivolous. I knew she was a lawyer and I didn't believe she had children of her own, at least none whom I'd delivered either during my three-year apprenticeship or in the last year and a half since I'd taken over my mentor's midwifery practice. Our bustling town of well over four thousand held many residents whom I knew either slightly or not at all.

Elizabeth Stanton extended her hand. "I'm pleased to make your acquaintance."

Bertie shook her hand and said, "I'm much honored to meet you, ma'am. This is my midwife friend, Miss Rose Carroll."

"I am humbled to meet thee, Elizabeth." Friends didn't use titles, as we believe we are all equal under God. It sometimes shocked people of a certain social status when I called them by their given names, but I was well accustomed to their reactions by now. I waited, but this luminary of the movement didn't bat an eyelash.

"It's my pleasure, Miss Carroll." Elizabeth gazed at me for a moment. "I met a Mrs. Dorothy Henderson Carroll at our meeting in the capital in April."

I smiled. "She's my mother, and she spoke very highly of thee."

She laughed out loud. "And you're the Quakers."

"Indeed, we are."

"Like our dearly departed Lucretia Mott, gone these eight years now." Elizabeth's smile was a sad one. "Finest Quaker I ever met and my own mentor in this effort of ours."

Lucretia Coffin Mott had been in the forefront of the abolitionist and suffrage movements for many years, always in her Quaker bonnet and plain dress.

"She was a model for us all." Rowena nodded.

Someone hailed Elizabeth from the other side of the room and she excused herself.

"Rowena, I thought thee spoke with power and elegance," I said.

"Thank you." Her deep brown eyes looked directly into mine. "Let us hope and pray our increasing numbers will make an impact on those in power."

"We'll both be there on Tuesday," Bertie said. "Let's go get our sashes before they run out, Rose."

I caught deepening lines on Rowena's forehead as I turned to go. I followed the direction of her gaze toward the back of the

18

hall. A young woman in a dark dress with her hair pulled into a severe knot, a black trilby topping it, stood staring at Rowena, arms folded across her chest. I glanced back at Rowena, but her back was to me now.

My calling as a midwife makes me alert to small changes in expression. Often a pregnant woman will harbor worries to which she isn't able or willing to give voice about the birth. Part of my job is to ease her fears. A body rigid with tension during labor can prolong and complicate the birth itself. What was the reason for the tense exchange I'd just witnessed? And who was the other woman?

Bertie twirled her sash with one hand as we walked away from the church hall. "Do you think we'll ever see women get the vote, Rose?"

The full moon bathed the world in its bright white light as if God shone his approval on our suffrage movement, but clouds lurked on either side.

"I certainly hope so." I glanced to my right, glimpsing a movement. Two women walked in the opposite direction. When they passed under a street light, I noticed it was Rowena strolling with the woman I'd seen staring at her. The other woman threw her hand in the air. I couldn't see their faces, but her gesture looked like an angry one.

"But we seem to lose as much as we gain," I went on, turning back to Bertie. Women in the Washington Territory had gained the right to vote five years earlier but the Supreme Court had struck down the law only last year, and a similar law in Utah had been reversed. I gestured to two posters plastered to the front window of a cobbler's shop we were passing, one with President Cleveland and A.G. Thurman, the other showing Benjamin Harrison and Levi P. Morton. "It's a pity Belva Lockwood didn't see fit to run for President again. Wouldn't that have been fine, to see campaign posters featuring a woman instead of these?"

"Without a doubt. With the Senate voting against the suffrage amendment two to one in '86, though, the prospects seem bleak for the foreseeable future." She twirled the sash again. "But we shall link arms and stand tall. Isn't that what Mrs. Stanton said?" She tucked her arm through mine.

"She did, indeed."

"What's your betrothed going to think of you demonstrating for the vote on Tuesday?" she asked.

The word *betrothed* brought a blush to my cheeks. "David will be in favor of it, I'm certain." The handsome and delightful Newburyport doctor David Dodge was indeed my betrothed, as he had proposed marriage to me in the summer and I'd happily accepted. We faced a few obstacles yet in our path, his society-minded Episcopalian mother being primary among them, along with my own Friends Meeting frowning on marrying outside the faith. "David is an open-minded man who supports equality between the sexes."

"And you wouldn't be with any other kind of man." She squeezed my arm. "How soon is the midwife going to have children of her own, by the way?"

"What is thee thinking, Bertie! Not until after we are wed, certainly." When I thought of the children I was very much looking forward to having with David, it made me remember Rowena's cool greeting to the little suffragists in the meeting. It was almost as if she didn't like children. "Bertie, does Sophie know Rowena Felch?" Bertie lived with her friend Sophie, a lawyer, in what many called a Boston Marriage, but I knew it was a deeper relationship than two unmarried ladies simply sharing a house.

"Yes, Sophie and Mrs. Felch are friends as well as lady lawyers. Mrs. Felch came to tea one day and told us she is about to leave

Oscar, her husband."

I halted under one of the new electrical streetlights at the corner where our paths would diverge. "Oh? Why?"

"Apparently Mr. Felch is eager to start a family and she's having none of it. She wants to continue her profession in the law."

I nodded. Whether she did or didn't like children was irrelevant in her case to not wanting to bear any. "And the only way to absolutely ensure not having babies is to refrain from intimate relations with her husband."

"Exactly. Which is hard to do if you're sharing a bed." Bertie shook her head. "When she first married him, she thought she could do it all — have a career and raise a family. Once she got into it, she realized that wasn't going to be possible for her."

"Where's she planning to move to, does thee know?"

"She said Miss Zula Goodwin offered to share her flat," Bertie said.

"Who is this Zula, and what kind of odd name is that?"

"She's a young suffragist and a writer. I think Zula is short for Ursula. Her family has a lot of money, and bought her an elegant flat not too far from my house. She was at the meeting tonight. She has a severe appearance about her. Not plain, like certain Quakers I know, but severe." Bertie elbowed me with the jest about my habit of dressing without ornamentation, after the manner of Friends.

"I think I saw her," I said. "She didn't look very happy with Rowena."

"Interesting. I can ask Sophie when I get home. She might know. Maybe Mrs. Felch decided not to share Miss Goodwin's flat after all."

A carriage clattered by on the cobblestones even as the clouds bumped over the moon, darkening our path. I pulled my cloak closer around my neck as I sniffed the chilly air.

"I hope we're not getting an early snow," I said. "I have a woman overdue to go into labor. Her husband is a factory worker and they don't have the funds to send a conveyance for me."

"It wouldn't be the first time it snowed on November third. But I'll admit snow would make riding your bicycle to a birth a messy prospect."

Bertie had suggested I purchase a bicycle last spring and I'd been glad ever since I'd followed her advice. But I hadn't yet gone through a winter with it, and I suspected my cycle would be spending several months stored in the shed at the back of the house I shared with my late sister's husband and my five nieces and nephews.

"Be well, my friend. I'll see thee soon." I detached her arm and squeezed her hand.

"Stay out of trouble, Rose." Bertie grinned. "See you Tuesday morning at the polls, if not before."

I waved and turned toward home. I prayed my sole trouble would be finding a way to attend a birth in a snowstorm. After becoming involved with helping the police solve several murders over the last six months, I longed for my town to stay peaceful, and for me to solve only the miraculous mystery of babies being safely born.

TWO

I cycled home at dawn the next morning. I had been called to the birth last night, after all, and had chanced taking my bicycle, its clever oil lamp mounted on the front illuminating my way in the darkness. Grateful that snow hadn't yet materialized, I yawned as I bumped slowly and carefully along the planks temporarily paving Greenwood Street. They ran parallel to the sides of the road and, if I wasn't careful, my wheel could become trapped in the slot between planks.

The baby had emerged after only a few hours of labor. It had been my new apprentice's first birth observation, and Annie Beaumont had done wonderfully. She possessed a quiet presence, which is essential to fostering a feeling of comfort and security in a laboring woman. The newborn and his mother were blessedly both healthy, and the father had proudly paid me my fee. With any luck I'd be able to snatch an hour or two of sleep before Friends Meeting for Worship at ten o'clock.

I was halfway down the hill and in front of a well-appointed residence when I gasped. I pulled the spoon brake lever and pushed back on the pedals to stop the cycle. A shoe stuck out from where no shoe should be. Its red color echoed the frost-burnished leaves of the lilac bush above it.

I let my bicycle fall and hurried to the shrub growing to the side of the home's front door. Pulling back the branches, my heart athud, I let out a moan. The shoe was on the black-stockinged foot of Rowena Felch, still wearing her lovely green dress from last night. I pulled off my glove and knelt to touch her neck. Her skin was cold and yellow, and not from the chilly fall air, either. Poor Rowena.

I grieved for her even as my mind raced. How had she died? Surely it wasn't from natural causes, not with her ending up under a bush. I ran my gaze over her body. I saw no bullet hole or stab wound. I wanted to investigate further — perhaps she had an injury on her back or her head — but I knew from my previous encounters with him that Detective Kevin Donovan of the Amesbury Police Department would need to see her *in situ.* I glimpsed a slip of paper tucked into her far hand. I tried to make out the words but couldn't from this angle, although I did see that the handwriting was in an unusual upright style.

I stood. I narrowed my eyes when I spied the two arched glass panes in the door. A gaping hole split the one nearer to the latch, with sharp shards lying on the granite stoop. A sudden shiver ran through me as questions roiled in my brain. Had someone broken in? Then why were the shards on the outside? It was a fine house, not as large and elaborate as those of the carriage factory owners two blocks away on Hillside, but still a very nice abode. It certainly contained items worth stealing. A matching carriage house stood back from the street to the right. Was this property Rowena's home? Maybe Rowena had surprised the burglar and been killed in the process.

I wanted to see if someone was inside the house. At the same time, I feared the criminal was still within. I peered through the hole in the glass, anyway. I couldn't see any lights.

"Hello? Is anyone home?" Silence answered me. I grasped the door handle but it didn't turn. When the door wouldn't budge, I was relieved of the need to venture into a possibly dangerous situation.

The house was built on a slope and the front windows were too high for even my five feet eight inches to peer into. I hurried along the side of the house to a sash low enough to see that it looked into a dining room. No lamps were lit, no maid set out breakfast or cleaned the hearth. I cupped my hands on the glass to look closer and gasped again. The room had been ransacked. Drawers from the sideboard were pulled open, with one lying on the floor. A portrait on the wall hung akilter and a dining chair lay on its side. I imagined this had to be Rowena's house, which must have been broken into and robbed. Maybe she'd tried to escape and had been killed by the thief. But where was her husband? I made my way to the back door. I pounded on it.

"Oscar Felch," I called out, and continued to pound. "Anyone? Help, please!"

When I heard no answer, I returned to Rowena's body and made a scan up and down the street. No one seemed to be about. It was too late for the milkman and too early for the postman. I was about to set out for one of the neighboring houses when I perked my ears. Clopping along the planks, a horse approached pulling an open buggy. I stepped into the street in front of the house, signaling the driver to stop.

"Can thee please hurry to the police station and ask for Kevin Donovan to come?" I asked in an urgent tone.

He frowned. "The police, eh? What's happened?"

"A lady has died."

"And why not the funeral parlor, miss?" asked the portly gentleman in a great coat and bowler. "If she's dead, as you say."

How much to tell him? "Please, I believe the police are needed in this case." I clasped my hands in front of me. Despite being half his age, I used my most authoritative voice and stood tall. "Tell him Rose Carroll sent thee."

"Are you sure you don't need my help?" He made as if to climb out of the buggy.

"No, please." I held up my hand. "The help I need is for thee to notify the detective."

He shrugged. "Very well." He clucked to the dark horse and clattered away.

I returned to Rowena's side. I knelt and closed my eyes, holding her released spirit in the Light of God. I also held my own, still very much of this world. I'm a midwife, not a detective, and am accustomed on occasion to witness the demise of one of my mothers or newborns. Those were natural deaths, though. Tragic but unavoidable despite my best efforts. Unless I was seriously mistaken, Rowena's was not a natural end to life. Why did I keep encountering cases of violent demise?

THREE

Kevin Donovan squatted next to Rowena's body twenty minutes later, the silver buttons on the detective's blue serge uniform straining. He narrowed his eyes as he examined the still form without touching it. He glanced up at me. I shivered from waiting in the cold for what had seemed like hours but had been more like thirty minutes. It had been a sad vigil, but I wasn't about to leave Rowena's side.

"So you say you saw Mrs. Felch last evening, Miss Rose? About what time?"

"I was at a meeting from seven to eight thirty or so, I'd say."

"What kind of meeting would that have been?"

"It was the Woman Suffrage Association."

He rolled his eyes. "You're getting yourself involved with those radicals now, are you?" He took off his hat and rubbed his wispy carrot-colored hair, then replaced the hat.

"Indeed I am. But women's suffrage is not the business of this morning." *Or was it?* Perhaps she'd been killed because of her political activities.

"How can you be so sure? I'll need to talk with you later about who else was at the gathering and what took place there."

"Regardless, this was not a natural death, Kevin. Look at those marks." I gestured to two wide indented lines in the dirt near Rowena's feet. "I very much doubt she put herself neatly on her back under a lilac to die. Someone dragged her to that spot."

He nodded. "I think you're right. Gilbert," he called to Guy Gilbert, the young officer who'd come in the police wagon with him, "help me move her out from here." Kevin boosted himself up with an "oomph."

"Make sure you keep that note in her hand." I pointed.

His eyebrows went up. "I should say we will. Could be an important clue."

A minute later they'd shifted the body onto the path leading to the front door. Rowena's upper body was stiff, but her legs and feet flopped. Kevin leaned over and turned her onto her side facing away from him. Her left arm stuck up in a sadly grotesque fashion. Kevin pointed.

"Whacked on the back of the head, from

all appearances."

I gasped and brought my hand to my mouth. Rowena's light hair was matted with dried blood. Guy took a step back and stood somberly, hands clasped behind his back.

"It'll be up to the coroner to figure out if the blow killed her, or something else." Kevin gently rolled her onto her back again.

"What a terrible thing," I said. "To hit her and then leave her here in the cold all night." My heart went out to Rowena. I prayed she hadn't regained consciousness to realize she was dying. I shivered and pulled my cloak closer around me. My lack of sleep was taking its toll. My nerves buzzed and I was slightly sick from exhaustion. But at least I was alive.

"Murderers don't have a care for such things, Miss Rose." Kevin stood.

"But her death might have been an accident." I moved toward the house and beckoned for him to join me, then showed him the broken glass in the door. "I peered in a window toward the back and saw the dining room in great disarray, as if it had been robbed. Maybe she came home from the meeting to find a robbery in progress and the criminal hit her so he could escape."

"Possible."

"Except the broken glass is on the outside.

33

Wouldn't it be on the inside if someone broke in?"

"Good observation, Miss Rose." He peered into the hall on the other side of the door. "There are shards of glass in there, too. It must have fallen both ways."

"I suppose."

"Show me the ransacked room, would you?"

I led him along the side of the house and pointed to the window. "In there."

He pursed his lips. "Looks like a robbery, all right. Where in blazes is her husband, is what I want to know."

"Maybe he's traveling. I'm not certain this is her house, but if not, why would she be under that particular bush?"

With a great clatter another wagon pulled around the corner onto the street, bells ringing, hooves clopping. The ambulance pulled to a halt.

Kevin strode out to greet the driver, shook his head, and pointed to Rowena. I returned to the front, too, pausing at the lilac. I narrowed my eyes, spying something white where Rowena's body had laid. I knelt to see a fine lady's handkerchief edged in lilac-colored thread, its white linen now stained with blood. I picked it up by a corner and turned it in front of my face, but I couldn't see a monogram or indication of whose it was. I sniffed, thinking I detected a scent on it, but I couldn't identify what it was. The handkerchief could be Rowena's. Or it could belong to the killer.

At a soft wet touch on my nose, I looked up. The snow had arrived, falling in gentle sparse flakes all around.

I sat in the police wagon with Kevin in front of the house after they'd taken away the body. He'd offered to give me and my bicycle a ride home, which I gratefully accepted. The snow now blanketing the world, combined with my fatigue, had made the decision easy. A church bell tolled nine times. Guy stood watch in front of the house until such time as the summoned police reinforcements arrived to investigate the burglary. White flakes speckled his dark blue police great coat.

I handed Kevin the handkerchief. "This was under the lilac. It must have been hidden beneath Rowena's body."

He took it and examined it as I had. "No initials. Ever seen one like it?"

"No. All ladies carry one, though."

"Not all as fine as this one." He thanked me for finding the handkerchief and pocketed it. "Now, I need to know more about this meeting and about Mrs. Felch. What can you tell me?"

"Rowena led the meeting, which was held at the Free Will Baptist Church. They're organizing a demonstration for Tuesday in front of the polling place —"

"The devil you say!"

I stared at him over the top of my spectacles. "The devil has nothing to do with it. We have every right to show our displeasure with being shut out of the electoral process. Half the population, Kevin. Half the adults in this country are forbidden to decide who our lawmakers will be. It's simply not right."

"All right, go on, go on." He waved a hand.

"Rowena chaired the meeting. She discussed logistics for the demonstration, but it was also a sort of rally to raise the women's spirits. Elizabeth Cady Stanton made an appearance, too."

"I've heard of her."

"I should hope thee has." Elizabeth was famous nationally for joining with Lucretia Mott forty years earlier to hold the first women's rights convention in Seneca Falls. My mother had told me the story as a bedtime tale since before I could remember. She'd proudly pointed out that all the organizers except Elizabeth were Friends.

"Did you see anyone disagreeing with Mrs. Felch at the gathering? Any arguments?" Kevin asked.

"I didn't hear them talking, but a young woman named Zula Goodwin was looking very unhappy with Rowena. I don't know why."

He nodded. "I know of a Mr. Goodwin. Prosperous gent. Must be her father. Think Miss Goodwin would know the whereabouts of Mr. Felch?"

"Possibly. Bertie told me Oscar is a physician. I'll be seeing David Dodge later today."

"Your doctor fellow?"

I nodded. "I can ask him if he knows. Perhaps a medical convention is underway somewhere to which Oscar might have traveled."

"Leaving his wife alone to stir up trouble with you and the suffragettes."

"May I remind thee that it's a good and right trouble she was stirring up, Kevin?"

"Be that as it may. I'm just not sure if all this change is good for the world, for our country." He tapped the dashboard in front of us. The horse stomped a hoof and made a whoofing sound. Kevin spoke soothingly to it.

"What if the killer is someone who is adamant about women not getting the vote and wanted to silence her?" I gazed at the horse, thinking aloud. "I hope he doesn't plan to pick off the protesters one by one, starting with Mrs. Felch, and make them all look like burglaries. He'd have to kill a lot of people, in that case. The numbers of women — and men — in favor of enfranchisement are only growing."

"I suppose. But it could just be an interrupted break-in, plain and simple. Let's think about what else we know."

Because I'd assisted Kevin in several murder investigations, by now he welcomed rather than rejected my thoughts and the pieces of information collected. I traveled in circles and to places he never could — women's bedchambers and suffrage meetings, for a start — and he knew it.

"Mrs. Felch was alive at least until, say, nine o'clock last evening." He ticked off the facts on his fingers. "You happened across her at seven thirty this morning and her upper body was already stiff, so I'd venture a guess she was killed pretty close after nine. Rigor mortis can take up to twelve hours to completely set in, especially in the cold."

He had educated me on the process of the muscles contracting after death. "So the delay would explain her floppy legs." I glanced at him. I probably shouldn't have mentioned a woman's legs.

Kevin shifted, in fact looking uncomfortable. He cleared his throat. "Exactly. And we know someone broke into the house. I'll have my men round up the motley crew of locals who make a practice of common thievery. They don't usually resort to murder, though."

"I wanted to tell you something odd about the break-in. I tried the front door and it was locked. If the robber broke the glass in order to unlock the door, why wasn't the door open?"

"Could he have come in the back door?"

"Then why break the glass in the front door?"

"Good question. You did observe that most of the shards were on the outside, which fits with breaking the glass from inside. What else?"

"Bertie told me Rowena was leaving her husband. Bertie said he wants to have children and Rowena didn't."

Kevin opened his mouth and then shut it again. In my experience with him, I knew he often expressed the typical opinion of men about women's place. On the other hand, I'd also grown to know that, when it came right down to it, Kevin was fair and only wanted to ensure justice was done.

"I'd certainly like to know where the husband is now," Kevin said at last. "Could be he was furious about his wife's moving out. They got into a fight and he hit her over the head."

"Then faked the burglary? A fake would explain why the front door was locked."

"Indeed it could."

"Bertie also said Zula Goodwin had offered to share her flat with Rowena," I went on.

"The unhappy Miss Goodwin?"

"Just so. Possibly Rowena refused her offer and Zula was unhappy, or even irate. But surely she wouldn't kill Rowena over it." The tragedy of Rowena's life being cut short dragged down my heart like a millstone.

"Nothing is sure at the moment, Miss Rose. You more than anyone should know that."

FOUR

My niece Faith stood at the wide soapstone kitchen sink in the welcome warmth of the Bailey kitchen when I walked in. After my sister Harriet's death the prior year, my moody brother-in-law hadn't known what to do with five children. He'd invited me to use the parlor of the modest home as my bedroom and office, and I'd gladly accepted. The brunt of the housework had fallen to the eldest child, seventeen-year-old Faith, and myself. But Faith had taken over her mother's job in the Hamilton Mills and I had my thriving midwifery practice. It exhausted us to cook and clean on top of our daily exertions, and I was away at births for hours, sometimes days, as well. I'd convinced Frederick last summer to hire a kitchen girl on weekdays, and we sent out the laundry, which greatly relieved our burden.

I hated to have to give Faith the news

about Rowena, but I knew I wouldn't be able to hide it for long.

Faith turned, her hands still in a pan of sudsy water, and smiled at me. "Welcome, dear Rose." She took another look, dried her hands, and hurried over to me.

I set down my satchel and removed my bonnet and gloves. "Good morning, Faith. Or not such a good morning, as it turns out." I squeezed her hands in mine.

"Thee looks distraught. Did a baby die?"

"No, but a fine woman did. I came across her body as I cycled home a while ago after the birth."

"What terrible news." Faith's eyes, brown like mine, drew down in concern. Escaped tendrils from her light brown braid framed her slender face. "It was someone thee knew?"

"I'd met her only last night." I filled Faith in on the suffrage meeting. "And then I spied Rowena, lying under a lilac bush."

"How dreadful for thee." She took my cloak and hung it on a hook. "The police must have come."

I washed my hands and then sat at the table. "Yes. In fact, Kevin Donovan gave me a ride home."

Faith stared. "Does thee mean this woman was killed?"

"It appears so, I'm afraid. She seemed to have been dragged under the shrub."

"What's happening in our town? Will it be unsafe to even go out soon?"

I blew out a breath and steadied my voice. "No, it will not. Thee mustn't fear, Faith. I'm sure Rowena's death was at the hands of a troubled person with a grudge against her. Most are."

"If thee says so," she said, but it didn't sound as if she quite believed me. She glanced at the stove. "The family has already had breakfast but we have plenty of porridge left. Has thee eaten?"

In response, my stomach gave off a loud gurgle.

Faith laughed. "Is thee planning on attending Meeting for Worship? I can give thee coffee unless thee plans to rest."

I checked the clock on the simple pine sideboard and groaned. "I have not slept since yesterday morning." It was already after nine o'clock, and Meeting for Worship began at ten. "But I believe God would want me to join Friends in silent worship today, and I know it will do me good. So thee'd better pour me coffee." Friends gathering in quiet expectant waiting held a power that still surprised me. The experience was far different from when I spent an hour of silent worship alone in my room. It was if the Spirit joined us and multiplied our prayers in a greater unity than simply a collection of individuals.

Christabel, the fluffy gold and white kitten Faith had adopted as a mouser last summer, rubbed her back against my leg. I reached down to stroke her head. She was now six months old and still small, but she'd already shown talent at chasing down vermin in the house. Any murders she committed were perfectly legal and quite welcome. The world of humans was a different matter, though, and nowhere near as simple.

Two minutes later Faith set a blue bowl brimming with oat porridge, milk, and bits of chopped apple in front of me. She brought over a spoon, the sugar crock, and a full tin mug of milky coffee, then sat at a right angle to me.

"Thank thee." I took her hand and we both closed our eyes for a moment of silent blessing. I opened my eyes and tucked into the porridge. Its warmth and hearty chewy texture were just what I needed. Somewhat revived, I thought of the next meal of the day.

"Faith, dear, what shall we do about our First Day dinner? I was to help thee prepare it this morning. I'm so sorry I was absent."

David was joining the family for afternoon dinner today. I hadn't seen him in several days and was looking forward to spending time in the company of his sweet blue eyes and irresistible smile.

"Don't worry, Rose. I made a potato casserole earlier, and we have a dozen pork chops in the ice box. It'll all be ready by one o'clock."

"And we have the apple pies for dessert." Faith and I had spent yesterday afternoon making pies with the apples her steady beau, Zebulon Weed, had picked and brought over.

"Zeb's going to bring sweet potato fritters, too."

"Good." As I sipped the coffee, also perfect, my gaze was drawn again to the sideboard, on which sat a pale green envelope.

"Is the letter from thy grandmother?" I asked. Mother always used stationery and envelopes in unusual colors.

She rose and brought it to me. "Yes, it's from Granny Dot. Thee must have missed yesterday's afternoon post."

"I suppose I did. Bertie invited me for supper before the suffrage meeting. I guess I'd already left." After I perused the letter, I stared at Faith. "Mother is coming on the

45

evening train tomorrow." My parents lived on the outskirts of Lawrence, a mill city some twenty miles to the southwest, on the farm where Harriet and I had grown up. The train trip was not an overly long one, but Mother had plenty of obligations at home and in the suffrage movement, so she didn't visit often. On the other hand, I hadn't seen her in months. I would welcome her stay. "What a nice surprise."

"Why is she coming?" Faith asked. "I love Granny, but what is the significance to her coming at the beginning of November?" She blinked and snapped her fingers. "I know why. Because it's thy twenty-seventh birthday this week! That must be her reason."

True, I was about to turn a year older several days after the election. "But thee knows we don't make a fuss about birthdays in our family."

Faith was nearly bouncing in her chair. "But she is thy own mother. I would do the same with my children. To celebrate the day they came into the world."

I gazed fondly at Faith. It was looking very much as if Zeb would end up the father of her children eventually, and I couldn't think of a better match for her.

I held up the letter. "Actually, no. Mother says she wants to support us in the Election

Day demonstration." I smiled my first smile of the day. "Says she wouldn't miss it for anything."

"Then I'm coming to the demonstration, too. Thee knows I want to support the suffrage effort. And I can write an article about it for the newspaper." Faith had a great interest in becoming a writer, and had had several short articles published already. Her real goal was to leave the mill for a job as a journalist, but the family still needed her income from her Hamilton Mill shift.

"Thee will have to inform thy supervisor at the mill."

"I will." Her expression was determined and her eyes glowed. "I'm not going to miss this event. Maybe Annie and Jasmine will come, too."

Annie Beaumont was now my apprentice, but I'd met her only because she and Faith had worked at the mill together and had become fast friends.

"We shall welcome thee, Faith, and thy friends. Thy grandmother, as well."

I awoke with a start. I'd decided to rest my eyes in my room for just a moment after breakfast. Despite the coffee, I must have fallen fast asleep. The house was quiet and I was dismayed to see my grandmother's clock read nine fifty. The family must have already left for the Friends Meetinghouse only half a mile distant.

Groggy rather than refreshed, I hurriedly splashed water on my face and tidied my hair. If I cycled, I could make it to worship on time. The elders frowned on members arriving late. Depending on the greeter, if one came too much after ten o'clock, one was forced to sit in the cold hall until worship had finished, which could be more than an hour. I knew no dispensation would be given even for a Friend who had been up all the night long — and found a body on the way home.

Cloaked, bonneted, and gloved, I mounted my metal steed and rolled down the path from the house. The earlier snow had been just a flurry, as it turned out. I'd made it around the corner onto High Street when I braked to a stop. The police wagon was pulled to the side of the road and police officer Guy Gilbert held a man by the collar. The fellow, a wiry clean-shaven man in his forties, struggled to get away.

"Hilarius Bauer, the detective just wants to talk with you," Guy said. "Calm down, now."

To my surprise the man with the curious name relaxed and laughed. "Oh, sure. And

48

then he'll pop me in the clink. Just like last time."

"If you had anything to do with breaking and entering a home on Greenwood Street last night, he certainly will."

The smile slid off the man's face and pearls of sweat popped onto his forehead despite the chilly morning. "Now why would you say a thing like that?"

"Detective Donovan will explain everything. My job is to get you to the police station." Guy opened the back door of the wagon. "Now, in with you." He ushered the man in and fastened the latch.

I hailed him. "Guy, does Kevin have reason to believe this man is our culprit?"

He shrugged. "Dunno. He just asked me to go find Mr. Bauer."

"What an unusual name he has."

"I'll say. But a Saint Hilarius lived a long time ago, you know. I learned about him from the nuns when I was young. Too bad this one doesn't act so saintly. He's known for being light-fingered around town." He tipped his hat. "Good day, Miss Rose."

I cycled on, bumping along the cobblestones. Now I would be even later to Meeting for Worship, but I hadn't been able to help myself from watching. What if this so-called light-fingered Hilarius had killed

Rowena while committing a burglary? He'd certainly looked nervous when Guy had mentioned Greenwood Street. At least then it would mean the killer was not targeting suffragists.

Five minutes later and breathless, I hurried up the granite steps into the Meetinghouse. I was relieved to see the greeter in the front hall today was the usually kindly Ruby Bracken, the gray-haired woman who'd asked the question about men interfering with the Election Day demonstration at the suffrage meeting last night. She frowned at my tardiness but moved silently toward the worship room entrance on the left. When she opened the door for me, I mouthed my thanks. I slid into a slim space in a pew at the back. The mother of the large family occupying it, Charity Skells, scooped a toddler onto her pregnant lap that already held a one-year-old and urged the other four young ones to scoot over, making room for me. I spied the Bailey family sitting together in the room on the right, the two large rooms currently divided only by a waist-high wall.

John Greenleaf Whittier, one of the designers of this large but simple building nearly four decades earlier, sat at the far end with the other elders on the pew facing the rest of the congregation, about two hundred in number. John opened his eyes for a moment and raised his snowy eyebrows at me before closing his eyes again in prayer. I'd consulted with the famous abolitionist and poet before on the murder investigations in which I'd been involved. His wise counsel had helped me, but I was surprised he was here in Amesbury today. Even though his home was just down the street, of late he'd spent weeks at a time at his cousin's home in Danvers. He must have returned to cast his vote in the election Tuesday. It was just my luck he'd caught me coming in tardy.

I folded my hands and closed my eyes. The room was filled only with the small noises of people settling into worship: a rustle of petticoats, the creak of a bench, a soft cough, a whisper from a child to a parent. The air smelled of wool and leather, old wood, and gathered living bodies. The sunlight streaming through the eight-foot-high windows painted wavy shadow pictures on the broad pine floorboards, reminding us of the Light within as well as without.

It was always hard for me to calm myself enough to allow God's presence to fill me. I found stilling my thoughts especially difficult today, both from arriving in a rush and from the events of earlier this morning.

51

My heart slowed at last, and I breathed deeply and evenly to try to slow my brain, too. But I couldn't. I saw Rowena's deadly still form under the bush. I thought about Zula's glare the night before, and about her walking with Rowena after the meeting, a matter I had forgotten to relate to Kevin. I pictured the ransacked dining room. I heard Guy telling Hilarius he had to come to the station. I wondered about Oscar Felch's whereabouts. And most of all, I asked myself, had any of these people killed Rowena?

This would never do. Friends came to sit in gathered worship to wait for a message from God. We were to empty our minds in expectant waiting. How could I empty myself of these thoughts and images? I blew out a breath.

John stood, supporting himself with his cane. "Walk cheerfully over the world, answering that of God in everyone." He sank with care back onto the bench.

He'd received a message to share the words of George Fox, one of the founders of our faith. Fox's command, over two hundred years old, still rang true for me. It was one of the basic premises of the Religious Society of Friends: there is that of God in each of us. Thus we are all equal and we must refrain from violence against each other.

But where was that of God in the person who had taken Rowena's life?

Ruby touched my elbow as I filed out after Rise of Meeting. "I'd like to speak with thee for a moment, Rose," she said in a quiet voice. "Let's go upstairs where it will be private."

What did the new clerk of the Women's Business Meeting wish to speak with me about? Ruby had taken over for Althea, the previous clerk, earlier in the fall. Surely this conference wasn't related to the Woman Suffrage meeting. I had no responsibility in the group. Last night was the first meeting I'd ever attended, and anyway, she'd been there herself. Faith, who overheard the exchange, cast me a glance.

"Go on home without me," I said. "I'll be along soon."

Ruby waited with me at the bottom of the narrow spiral staircase leading to the balcony until it seemed people had stopped descending. The seating area upstairs at the front end of the building held more pews overlooking the two worship rooms. Our congregation was flourishing such that we needed the additional seats to accommodate the many Friends who streamed into the Meetinghouse on First Day morning.

I followed Ruby up and perched on a pew next to her. Above us was the trap door to the attic, where a giant wheel controlled a mechanism to raise and lower the central divider. The divider was kept raised except for the monthly business meetings, when it was lowered to allow the women to conduct their own business without the counsel or interference of men. I wasn't in the habit of attending business meeting, as I was neither the clerk of a committee nor an elder.

Ruby faced me, hands laced in her lap, her expression a serious one. "As clerk, I have been delegated by the Women's Business Meeting to speak with thee. We are aware of thy betrothal to a gentleman from Newburyport."

Oh. So that was what this was about. The Women's Business Meeting was in charge of overseeing marriages. I was about to be eldered, admonished for my choice of a partner. My heart sank.

"A gentleman who is not a Friend," she continued, "a man who worships at the First Religious Society of the Unitarian Church while his mother is a well-known Episcopalian."

"True. His name is David Dodge." Also

54

true that David displeased his mother, Clarinda, by attending services with the Unitarians in Newburyport. He'd told me he didn't care for the trappings and beliefs of Clarinda's church.

"We have been waiting for thee to bring this matter to the attention of our monthly meeting for worship with attention to business, but thee has not."

Oh dear. Had my choice to wait offended the women?

Ruby went on. "We want to be sure thee knows thy marrying this man will result in thee being read out of Meeting." She sat with an erect back, her black dress severe against the pale, lined skin of her face.

I swallowed. I knew being essentially expelled from Meeting was a possibility, but I'd hoped the women would be lenient with me. Weren't times changing? And if I had spoken to them earlier, would they have been more understanding? I considered my words.

"I'm aware of this practice, yes. And it's why I've been slow to bring the matter to thee and the rest of the women. I intend to remain faithful to my Quaker values and to the teachings of our community, despite marrying out."

Ruby opened her mouth to speak, but I

held up my hand. "If I might finish? David is a good soul of the highest integrity who believes in equality and embodies a simple, peaceful way of life despite his wealthy upbringing. I hope he might join us in worship one First Day soon." My hands were damp with sweat despite the cool temperature up here.

"Be that as it may. We are obliged to follow our long-established custom." Her expression was cast in iron, perfectly matching the color of her hair.

Were the women harboring resentment against me I wasn't aware of? Did they think it was unseemly I had helped the police solve more than one case of murder? "If this comes to pass, may I not appeal to be reinstated?" I'd heard of this possibility.

She dipped her head once. "After a period of time passes, thee may write a letter making amends and we shall consider it." She stood. "It's highly irregular, what thee is considering, Rose. Thee must search deep in thy heart, and sit with this choice in prayer to discern whether this is God's plan or thine." She edged past me and disappeared down the staircase.

I thought I'd searched deeply enough already. How could a love as strong and true as ours not be God's plan? I could no longer

56

imagine life without David.

But could I also imagine life without my spiritual anchor, my lifelong faith, my community? If I were read out, my First Day mornings would be spent in solitary worship, and I'd be banned from this graceful structure that was so much more than a building. I'd always felt the walls themselves were infused with the Light of God. I'd likely not be called to deliver any Quaker babies during my expulsion, and I would have to hold my head high in the face of widespread disapproval. Even after David and I wed and I'd spent the requisite months on the outside, my letter of amends had no guarantee of being accepted. I doubted appealing to John Whittier independently for help would be taken well by the women. He was a liberal soul, not overly strict in adhering to practices that made no sense in these modern times. But marriage, for Friends, was the business of the women. Maybe there was a more sympathetic female elder I could ask for support.

I closed my eyes and sat in prayer, per Ruby's instruction. After several minutes I sighed and yanked them open again. It was no good. I felt I had waited for discernment long enough and my way was clear. Or was it? It was a way that would diverge from two hundred years of practice. Was I strong enough to brave the coming expulsion? Would David still want me if I was shunned from my faith? I'd been positive he would, but now I felt sure of nothing. My stomach churned, and my heart and mind were even more turbulent.

I gazed down at the now-empty room, at the wooden pews polished by Quaker cloth, at the sixteen-foot-high ceiling. This edifice, now nearly two-score years old, had been built to last. Were both my faith and my love as sturdy?

FIVE

I let David in the front door of the Bailey home at a few minutes before one o'clock, smiling at his handsome face and cheerful expression. It lifted my spirits just to cast my eyes on him. I'd tried to put my cares behind me after I'd cycled home from Meeting, helping Faith with the dinner and enjoying the simplicity of a life with children in the house. But my concerns about the eldering as well as the murder loomed heavy in the background.

David was about to kiss me when eight-year-old Betsy skipped into the hallway holding Christabel in her arms.

"There you are, little miss," he said, reaching out to tousle her blond hair.

"Good afternoon, David." Her eyes gleamed. She reached out her small hand, which David shook, and the kitty jumped down.

"Betsy, run help Faith set the table, please.

I need to speak with David in private for a moment."

"Must I?" she asked plaintively.

"Yes, you must," David said. "And make sure you seat me next to you."

She brightened and skipped away.

"First this," he said, leaning in for a luscious kiss. "How's my beautiful intended?" He asked, laying a hand on my cheek. "You look a bit weary." He didn't look at all tired. His deep blue eyes sparkled and his curly dark hair framed his face just right.

"I am, at that. I was at a birth all night, and on my way home I discovered a woman dead. And then I was taken to task after Meeting for Worship."

"A body?" He turned serious. "This is serious news, Rose, and surely upsetting to you. I know you've seen death before, but it's never easy."

"So true. I can tell thee the details after dinner, but I wanted to ask if thee knows an Oscar Felch from Amesbury. I believe he's a physician." His hearing the news of the body must have overshadowed my saying I'd been scolded, natural for a doctor. I could tell him about that later.

"I am acquainted with him, yes. He lives on Greenwood Street here in Amesbury. Why do you ask?" When Christabel purred and wound herself around David's legs, he reached down to pet her.

"It was his wife, Rowena Felch, whom I found. And hers was not a natural death."

"You don't say!" He straightened. "Another murder, Rosie?"

I nodded. "She appeared to have been hit on the head. She was dragged under a lilac bush and left to die. Thee is certain the Felches live on Greenwood Street?"

"Yes, it came up in conversation one time, I can't remember how."

"So she must have been at her own home. The thing is, Oscar was nowhere to be found. I wondered if there's a medical convention going on somewhere he might be attending."

David thought. "I don't think so, but I can ask around at the hospital tomorrow."

"Thee will let me know? Or better, tell Kevin Donovan, please. He's looking for the husband."

"Of course. I'll call him." David's family, as well as the hospital and the police station, had installed telephones. The devices were becoming more and more common, but my brother-in-law Frederick hadn't seen fit to acquire one for this house.

"Rose," Faith called from the back of the house. "Dinner's ready."

61

I had been about to tell him the details of my being eldered by Ruby, but that could wait.

"Shall we?" David crooked his elbow for my hand and we passed through into the sitting room.

My brother-in-law, Frederick Bailey, stood when we came in. The two men shook hands and greeted one another. I left them and hurried into the kitchen, which doubled as dining room in this modest house. It was fragrant with the smells of fresh rolls, the rich casserole, sizzling meat, and cinnamon from the pies. Thirteen-year-old Luke stood talking with Zeb. Zeb, also a Friend, was tall, with dark intense eyes, and lived only a few blocks away. His brother Isaiah had tragically been killed in the fire of last spring, but Zeb hadn't let his deep sorrow overtake his love for Faith or his caring manner for all.

"Luke, look at thee," I said. "Thee is nearly as tall as Zeb now." It was true. Luke seemed to grow overnight these days, and both he and Zeb were on the skinny side.

Luke flushed as Zeb measured the level of his head at Zeb's shoulder. "It won't be long now," Zeb said with a smile.

"Rose, can thee call the little boys," Faith asked. "They're outside."

"Matthew, Mark," I called out the back door. "Dinner."

A moment later the ten-year-old twins clattered up the steps. "Come and wash," I urged.

"We're hungry," towheaded Mark said, standing in the open doorway.

"Thee is letting the cold air in," Frederick snapped. "Get in and do as thy aunt says."

When Matthew lowered his head and closed the door silently, my heart broke for the boy. Would his father ever learn to be kind to his sons?

"I'm glad thee is hungry," Faith said in a bright voice. She brought the potato casserole, steaming and covered with bubbling cheese, to the table.

"I think I'm going to *die* if I don't eat right this minute," dark-haired Matthew added with great drama from where he and Mark stood at the sink.

"Not until thy hands are clean," I said. "Faith, I'll get the chops."

"My mother's fritters are in the oven, too, Rose, keeping warm," Zeb said.

After we were all nine of us seated in close quarters around the table, with Betsy happily on the other side of David, we joined hands and bowed our heads, as is our custom. A few moments of blessed silence passed before Frederick spoke.

"May God watch over us and lead us in peaceful ways," he said.

May God lead me to peace with both David and Amesbury Friends, I added silently. And may we have no more murders in our fair town.

The four younger children had finished their meal and gone off to play, or, in Luke's case, to study for an examination. The table still held small plates with crumbs of pie and coffee cups.

"Those apples were perfect, Zeb," I said. "Thank thee so much for bringing them to us."

"The pies themselves were outstanding, too," David said. "Excellent crust. Nice and short, as it should be. You'll have to teach me how to make it, Rose."

I cocked my head. "I will be happy to. It takes a little practice, and requires a light hand so the dough doesn't toughen, but it's not too hard to learn. Faith is also quite accomplished in the pastry-making department."

Frederick frowned at David, which accentuated Frederick's heavy forehead jutting out over his eyebrows. "Doesn't thy family have a cook for that kind of thing?"

"We do, of course," David replied. "But I rather enjoy preparing food. So far I have only attempted savory dishes, but I'd like to learn to bake sweet dishes, too. You never know when it might come in handy."

Of course his well-off Newburyport family had a cook, and a driver, and several maids. I felt his hand cover mine under the table. A man wanting to cook despite all the comforts of his life. He was a prize seldom seen in our world. How I longed to marry and set up housekeeping with this most unusual of men. That rosy thought was slammed into a dark cellar by the memory of Ruby's warning. I stared morosely at the table.

"If we are to be equal in all ways, then not only should women have the right to vote," Zeb said. Zeb was another gem, but he was at least a lifelong Friend, immersed in notions of equality from a young age. "But men should also be free to make meals for their families, should they choose."

Faith beamed at him. "I'm going to the woman suffrage demonstration at the polling place Tuesday with Rose."

When David turned to me with raised eyebrows, I nodded, trying to shake off my gloom.

"Truly?" Zeb asked Faith. "I'm proud of thee."

"I'm not so sure I am, Faith," her father said. "It could be dangerous. And thee must perform thy job."

"She said she'll inform her manager," I said. "I support her standing in solidarity with the women of Amesbury. She's not a little girl any longer, Frederick."

He pursed his lips. "Our family needs Faith's pay. Thee knows we do, Rose."

It was true. I contributed what I could to the household expenses, but feeding and clothing five children, all but Faith growing nearly as fast as Luke, was a costly enterprise. At least my mother sewed them each new pieces of clothing when the children visited the farm every summer for a month.

"But Father, Granny Dot is coming for the demonstration, too." Faith looked earnestly at him.

"What? How did I not know of this news?" Frederick folded his arms.

"I only learned about it this morning when I opened a letter which arrived yesterday," I said. "She'll be in on the evening train tomorrow." I was even gladder now. I couldn't wait to discuss the eldering with her, and imagined my independent free-

66

spirited mother would be incensed at the news.

"She can share Betsy's bed," Faith said. "They'll both like that."

"Now then," Frederick began. "Of course I am in favor of ladies being able to vote. But this demonstration business is a sham. Nothing will be accomplished. You'll only get in the way of the legal voters."

"All men," Faith muttered.

"And if the men get it in their minds to turn violent, why, quite a few ladies could be hurt," Frederick went on. "I won't have Faith going, and I'd advise thee not to, either, Rose. Not to mention my mother-in-law."

I set my coffee cup down with a bit too much force, glad it was empty or the table-cloth would have been stained by the dark brew sloshing out. "Listen, Frederick. Thee knows Friends have long been in the forefront of the suffrage movement. We women must show up in great numbers for this kind of event." I was starting to sound like my mother. "It makes a bold statement to the local community and to the world at large. I heard at the meeting reporters from the Boston newspapers will be present taking photographs and reporting on the gathering. Faith needs to be there, too, if she wants to be."

He glowered and shook his head, slowly, three times. "No."

I nearly bit my tongue. I was too tired to keep the peace, though, even though I knew silence was the wiser path. "Harriet would have wanted her to be there. Thee is dishonoring her by not letting Faith go."

Frederick stood so fast he knocked his chair over backwards. "Don't thee dare." He pointed a shaking finger at me. "Don't thee dare invoke my dead wife's name. And don't thee dare think to tell me how to raise my daughter." He grabbed his hat and stormed out of the house.

SIX

Faith sat slumped in her chair, Zeb's arm around her shoulders.

"I'm sorry, Faith," I said. "I shouldn't have pushed back so hard." Frederick was justified to be concerned about Faith's safety, although he had a lot of nerve telling me not to invoke my own sister's name.

"Of course thee should have," she said. "And thee was right. Mother would have wanted me to go. It's Father who should apologize. But he won't. He never does." She straightened, chin in the air. "I'm going Tuesday, anyway. He can't stop me."

"Perhaps your grandmother can talk sense into Mr. Bailey," David suggested. "She's a forthright character, but also has a soothing effect. At least I felt that when I met her last July." He'd traveled to Lawrence to formally ask my father for my hand in marriage, even though he'd already asked me and I'd said yes.

69

"A good idea." I nodded. "She does have a calming effect, doesn't she?" I could use a bit of calm right about now. Anger at Frederick vied with sorrow at the way he often let his temper flare up at his own children, especially his sons, who were really quite well behaved and did not deserve such treatment by their only remaining parent.

"I look forward to being able to vote when I turn twenty-one next year," Zeb said. "Surely women will have the vote by the next presidential election."

"And we can go to the polls together to cast our ballots," Faith said, tucking her hand through his arm.

"David, who will thee vote for on Tuesday?" Zeb asked.

"I'm in favor of keeping President Cleveland in office," David said. "I agree with him that high tariffs are unfair to working folk."

"Yes," I said. "Benjamin Harrison's looking out for his rich industrialist friends."

"At the Parry Carriage Factory, a number of my fellow factory workers support Harrison. But if I could vote today," Zeb said, "I think I would also vote for Grover Cleveland. Our economy prospers and the nation is at peace. Those are important factors."

"I'm glad we're at peace. It would be horrible if thee had to go to war," Faith said to Zeb.

"I'm glad, too." He patted her hand.

"But thee wouldn't go if called, would thee?" I asked. Friends were quite clear about refraining from participating in the military for any reason.

"I expect I wouldn't," Zeb said. "Would thee, David?"

"I would feel obliged to." He cast me a glance. "As a physician, of course, my skills would be in great demand. Let's just hope it doesn't come to pass."

I closed my eyes for a moment. I was sure even being a doctor in a war was terribly dangerous. I couldn't imagine having found love with David and then losing him to a violent conflict. Although countless wives had experienced the death of their husbands in the War for the Union only a quarter century ago.

I opened my eyes again when Zeb spoke.

"Rose," he said, "Faith tells me thee found a woman dead this morning, and the cause was murder. I know thee has worked with the police before. Does thee have an idea of who might have done the awful deed?"

"No, and neither does the detective, at least so far. The victim was Rowena Felch, who would have been leading the dem-

71

onstration on Tuesday. She was very active in the suffrage movement. It could be that a man vehemently opposed to women having the vote killed Rowena, and that he might target other leaders, too." Because this was my family, and only because, I added the details about Zula and the missing husband, and I mentioned the possibility of an ordinary burglar having struck her so he could get away. "In fact, I saw Guy Gilbert, a policeman I know, detaining a man named Hilarius Bauer today on High Street as I cycled to Meeting for Worship."

David stared. "I know this man. There couldn't be two by such a curious name."

"I agree," I said. "Where does thee know him from?"

"He did a few days' work at my parents' home. He's a decent carpenter."

"And he didn't run off with the silver?" Faith asked.

"Not that I'm aware. I wonder if I should put in a good word for him to the police. I believe he's honest. Or he was with my father, at least."

"Kevin said something about collecting the possible suspects in town," I said. "The motley crew of common thieves, was how he put it. I had the impression Hilarius's reputation was why Guy put him in the police wagon this morning, not from any actual evidence. But when Guy mentioned Greenwood Street to him, the man suddenly looked frightened. Or nervous, more like."

"I do know his mother is quite ill and Hilarius supports her as well as his own family," David offered.

"Pertaining to the idea of the killer being against suffrage, I'm on the same shift with a man who never stops talking about why women's place is in the home," Zeb said. "He's quite clear in his mind on matters of who should vote and who shouldn't."

"Are there many like him?" Faith asked.

"A few. But he's the most vocal. Others who aren't even Friends support universal suffrage."

"It isn't necessary to be a Quaker for members of our sex to believe women should have equal rights." David smiled.

"Of course, of course." Zeb went on, "Sometimes this fellow gets into quite the argument on the topic."

"What's his name?" I gazed at Zeb. Was this man Rowena's murderer?

"Leroy Dunnsmore." Zeb tapped the table. "And he's quite the hotheaded fellow."

"Does he seem like a murderer?" David

asked. "Although I suppose that's a foolish question. What would a murderer seem like, after all?"

"That I cannot answer," Zeb said.

"Does thee mind if I pass his name along to Kevin?" I asked him. A yawn escaped me now my anger at Frederick had subsided. I was going to need to sleep, and soon. I took off my glasses and rubbed my eyes before replacing them.

"No, although I suppose to keep the peace on our shift I'd prefer the detective not tell Leroy who gave him his name."

"I think he would honor thy request. I thank thee for telling me."

"If it helps to catch a killer, why wouldn't I?" Zeb stood and gathered the plates and forks. "I'll do the washing up."

David also stood and picked up the coffee cups. "I must get home. I have a patient in need of a home visit before sundown." He set the dishes in the sink.

"I'll see thee out." I walked with him to his waiting doctor's buggy. His mare Daisy, secured to the hitching post, waited patiently in the traces, her roan coat sleek and shiny in the afternoon sunlight. "I want to tell thee about another unfortunate occurrence from this morning."

"Yes?"

"After Meeting for Worship I was eldered by one of the women."

"What does eldered mean?" he asked with furrowed brow.

"It means being admonished about acting wrongly. She made it clear that when we marry I'll indeed be read out of Meeting."

The corners of his eyes drew down in sympathy. "Truly? When I proposed to you in July, you thought maybe you wouldn't be expelled."

"I was wrong." I set my fist on my waist. "It's a stupid custom, not allowing Friends to marry outside the faith. Especially when thee already lives like a Friend, almost!" My ire rose again until my cheeks burned. I wanted to throw something, anything. "Aren't we living in modern times? I can't understand why the women feel they must adhere to this archaic custom."

"Are you doubting your decision to marry me?" He peered into my eyes.

"Not at all." I shook my head, hard. "Not at all."

"Good. What about Mr. Whittier? He and thee are friendly. Could he put in a word for you?"

"I don't dare ask. The Women's Business Meeting is quite clear on what is in their domain and what the men handle. Among

Friends, marriage is very much under the women's supervision. Ruby did say I could write a letter making amends after several months' time had passed, and she said they would consider reinstatement. But it's not a sure thing at all."

"You are a committed Quaker." He touched my hot cheek. "I know how much it means to you. This will be difficult."

"I know." I tried to calm myself. "Has thy mother come around at all?" Clarinda Dodge was completely opposed to our engagement. She'd been so bold as to lie to me last summer about his feelings. She wanted David's marriage to cement her — and his — place in society, which she valued greatly. He'd told me she was also worried about what her peers in the Episcopalian Church would think of her son marrying a working woman and a Quaker.

"My father and I are both working on her. It helps immensely he likes you so much."

"I like Herbert, too. I wish I could think of a way to become friendly with Clarinda. Is there any common ground between us?"

"Besides me, you mean?"

"Yes, and besides John Whittier." I'd arranged a meeting between Clarinda, who was an avid fan of John's poetry, and the man himself, which had pleased her greatly.

"She doesn't knit, does she?"

He tilted his head to the side and regarded me. "Are you clairvoyant? She took up knitting just last year."

"Then perhaps I shall find a few skeins of the most beautiful wool in the world and send it to her as a gift."

"Bribery! I like it." He grinned. "But it might help."

"At the very least we'll have something else to speak of besides poetry when we next meet."

He dropped his smile and took my hand. "Rose, dearest, you know how I feel about you, how much I love you. But I can't bear the thought of causing you pain at being expelled from your faith." He straightened his shoulders, his expression as somber as I'd ever seen it, and swallowed. "It rips me up to say this, but if you need to choose the Quakers over me, you must." He clenched his jaw and rubbed the back of his neck with his free hand.

I stared at him, my own hands suddenly icy, even the one he held in his. "What? Why would I do that?"

"I only wanted to offer you a choice. I think it will be terribly wrenching for you to be separated from your church and I hate to see you be forced to go through such a cleaving." His eyes searched my face. "I would be devastated if you decided to avoid the pain of expulsion by letting me go, but I would understand."

"I never want to let thee go." I extracted my hand from his. This was the last straw for me on a day already full of drama and pain. "Thee needs to leave." My voice shook.

"But Rosie . . ."

I turned back toward the house, my eyes swimming. How could he even suggest such a thing? I didn't lift my skirts enough, and I tripped on the first step, crashing onto my knees. David rushed to my side. He lifted me up and turned me toward him, enveloping me in his arms.

"I'm sorry," he murmured into my hair. "I'm so sorry."

SEVEN

I awoke in the dark to the sound of wailing. Sitting upright, I found my spectacles and lit the lamp. The clock read six. Had I slept through until the morning, or was it six at night? I was still fully dressed, but being clothed wasn't a clue, as I had laid down after David's departure. The memory of our last words flooded back. He'd apologized for offering me a way out of our engagement, saying he was only thinking of my feelings. But now he'd planted a seed of doubt. Had he really been offering himself a way to extricate himself? I would not blame him if he had. He had many reasons not to marry me. His mother's approbation. His much more elevated position in society. His thriving professional life. Even our own differences in faith. Having an odd-speaking Quaker for a wife, a wife with her own business — delivering children, no less — and one who somehow kept enmeshing herself

79

in murder? None of these would further his career or his relationship with his mother. He might be feeling more outside pressure than he had let on to me. I knew he loved me. But that was the only thing I was sure of.

I sighed deep and long, then shook my head to clear it. I ran my tongue over my teeth, hoping to clear it of the taste of fatigue and stale dinner. When the crying I'd heard started up again, I made my way into the sitting room. Betsy sat weeping on Faith's lap. Both were clothed as they were at our First Day dinner, so it must still be the same day. The three boys were likely upstairs.

"What's the matter, dearest Betsy?" I knelt in front of her.

"I want my papa," she cried, rubbing her eyes with her fists.

Faith stroked her hair. "Father hasn't returned," she whispered.

Poor Betsy. She'd already lost her mother. She must live with the fear her father might die, too. So Frederick hadn't come back from his impetuous storming out four hours ago?

"I'm sure he'll be back soon. He must have had matters of business to attend to," I told my little niece. "Dry thy tears now."

She sniffed and swiped at her eyes, her downturned mouth trembling.

"Does thee have any idea where he could be?" I asked Faith.

She beckoned to me. I pushed to standing and leaned over so my ear was close to her mouth.

"The tavern."

I rose and stared at her. Frederick Bailey, a Quaker father and teacher, at a tavern? What in the world was he doing at a drinking establishment?

"He's been going down there of late," she murmured. "I don't know if he imbibes or not. Can thee go find him and ask him to come home?"

I blew out a breath. "I will." It was not an errand I wanted to do, but Betsy needed her father at home. And Frederick needed to stop acting like a pouting boy the age of the twins. Running off to the tavern, indeed. How had I missed Frederick's absences? Maybe he only went out when I was at births or visiting with Bertie. Surely he knew I would be most unhappy with him if I found out.

As I went into the next room, Betsy asked, "What's imbibes mean?"

The kitchen was redolent with moisture and a delicious smell. I lifted the lid on a

81

big pot to see a rich pork broth quietly bubbling. Faith must have set the chop bones
to simmer. With carrots, onions, and potatoes, we'd have a nice soup for supper.

"I'll finish the soup when I return," I
called to her as I donned my outer garments. I drank a cup of water and went
outside to relieve myself, then headed down
the path on foot. It was too dangerous to
bicycle in the dark. I could barely believe I
was walking to Hoyt's Tavern. Visiting a
saloon on a First Day evening was entirely
the last thing I wanted to do. My ire with
Frederick began to rise again, but I banished
it. If I were to have any luck bringing him
home, I'd have to stay as calm and reason-
able as I could. Maybe I should have
brought Luke with me for male company. I
didn't want him to know his father was in a
saloon, though, and he was only thirteen,
with a cracking voice and no hint of a beard
as yet.

I thought of swinging by the police station
and leaving Kevin a message about Zeb's
fellow factory worker. But a message could
wait until tomorrow. Family came first.

Luckily, the tavern was only a few blocks
distant, on Water Street near the Boston and
Maine Railroad depot. I took a deep breath
and pushed open the door. A cacophony of

boisterous voices and clinking of glasses filled the lamplit room. The fumes from alcohol and pipe tobacco nearly overwhelmed me. A polished bar ran the length of the space on the right, with stools in front and a mirrored wall behind. Tables spotted the rest of the room. The noise quieted as the people inside spied me.

I scanned the faces of the drinkers, which were almost completely male, but didn't spy Frederick. A rosy-cheeked matron behind the bar dried her hands on her apron and waved me over.

"Are ye after lookin' for someone, then, miss?" she asked in a heavy brogue, her green eyes taking in my bonnet. "Because I'm thinkin' yer not here to drink."

"No, ma'am, I'm not. I need to find my brother-in-law, Frederick Bailey." The noise in the saloon returned to its previous level. I was relieved to be able to speak with a woman, whose presence likely kept the rowdier customers in their place. I didn't feel at all threatened, and it was a brighter and cleaner environment than I'd expected.

"Ah, Freddy."

Freddy? I'd never heard a soul call him by a nickname.

"Aye, he's off in yon corner where he makes a custom of sittin'." She pointed.

83

A custom. So Faith was right.

"He's got a right brick in his hat again."

A brick in his hat? "Pardon me?"

"Yeh know, three sheets in the wind. Soused. In his cups."

"Ah, I see. He's inebriated. I thank thee."

She grinned. "Thought yeh was one o' them Quakers. With the bonnet and all."

"Frederick is, too."

"Well, I'll be." She whistled. "I guess that makes him some kind of a snollygoster."

As far as I knew, the term referred to a politician guided by his own interests rather than moral principles. I supposed it could apply to a Friend whose own interests included drowning his sorrows in drink instead of refraining from intoxicating substances so he could be clear to await God's help for his concerns.

The woman smiled fondly. "If I didn't have me own mister, I might think of setting me hat for old Freddy. Said he's a widower with wee ones at home. I can tell he's got himself a good soul under his loneliness."

I took a deep breath and made my way across the room. My brother-in-law sat alone at a small table, a tankard in one hand and a book in the other. When he didn't look up, I cleared my throat.

"It's time to come home, brother."

He lifted his head slowly. His eyes were bloodshot. "It's the high-and-mighty suffragette, is it?" He squinted. "Care to join me in an ale, Rose?"

"Come along, now. This is no trifle. Betsy's crying, wondering where thee is."

His shoulders slumped. "My little motherless girl." His gaze seemed to plead with me. "Does thee even know how much I miss my Harriet?" He slurred his words.

"I miss her, too. But she's gone, and right now thy daughter needs thee." It sounded heartless, but it was true. Nothing would ever bring Harriet back. "All the children need thee."

"Faith doesn't need me. Saying she's going off to your women's demonstration. What if she's hurt, Rose? What then?" He coughed. "I shouldn't have gotten so angry with thee earlier. But I would die if something happened to any of my precious little ones."

I'd never heard him express emotions like this. It must be the drink. "I'll watch out for her." I pried the tankard out of his hand and took the book from him. I held out my hand. "Let's go."

"Thee is a regular rouser, Rose," he protested. Still, he placed both hands on the table and pushed to standing, but listed to the side. I grabbed his arm. He was a stocky man and had to weigh eighty pounds more than me. How was I going to get him home if he was this unsteady on his feet? A wiry fellow hurried over and took his other arm.

"Whoa, there, Freddy," the man said. "Steady on."

"Thanks, Bauer." Frederick gave the man a wan smile. "This is my sister-in-law, Rose Carroll. Midwife and guardian angel. Rose, Hilarius Bauer."

I took another look. So it was, the man Guy had taken in for questioning. The police had obviously released him.

"Good evening, Hilarius," I said. "I don't suppose thee would be able to help me walk this man home? It's only a few blocks."

"Certainly," he said. "And I'm pleased to make your acquaintance, miss." He tipped his cap.

"I, as well." We made our way to the door. "Thank thee, ma'am," I said to the matron.

"We'll see ye next time, you old rascal," she called.

I certainly hoped there wouldn't be a next time for Frederick at this establishment. The night air was bracing, with bright stars peeking out between scudding clouds. It was a welcome change from the stuffy tavern. After we'd walked a little way, I said, "I heard thee has worked for the Dodge family in Newburyport, Hilarius."

"That I did. Made them a set of shelves for their kitchen and did a few other bits of carpentry. Nice folks, pleased with my work. And Mr. Dodge paid me promptly, unlike certain others I've had occasion to be employed by."

"David Dodge is . . . a good friend of mine. He mentioned thee." I made a quick decision. "I happened to see a policeman take thee in for questioning this morning."

Hilarius fell silent. The only sounds were the shuffling of Frederick's feet and the clop-clop of a horse plodding by as we moved through Market Square.

"It's true. He did," he finally said. "I've had a few minor run-ins with the law in my past. I fell in with the wrong crowd and had engaged in a bit of thievery. But not anymore." His voice was gravelly. "The detective accused me of breaking into a house and killing a woman. I told him I did no such thing."

"And thee has a witness to affirm thy whereabouts elsewhere during the time of the crime?" I glanced over at him.

An electric streetlight illuminated his face

as he stared straight ahead. Moisture dotted his forehead again and his nostrils flared above a mouth clamped in a grim line.

EIGHT

With a cup of coffee into Frederick and Betsy happily ensconced on his lap in the sitting room, I set to chopping onions. The routine activity set my mind to simmering along with the soup stock. The bar matron had spoken of Frederick being lonely. Of course he must be, with Harriet no longer in his life. It hadn't occurred to me he might seek out a new mother for his children, a new love to take into his arms. So far it seemed all he was doing was dousing his woes with alcohol. Maybe there was a way I could search out a suitable Quaker widow his age or even a younger bride not afraid of taking on a ready-made family of five children. I wasn't sure how the older children in particular would react to Frederick replacing their mother with another, but we could cross the Remarriage Bridge when we came to it. If it came to pass at all.

Then my thoughts turned to Rowena's

murder and the many events of this day that had begun so long ago in a tragic way. Hilarius was certainly lying about last evening. Kevin must not have any actual evidence to link him to the crime, though, or he would have kept him in jail. David had vouched for Hilarius's character, and Hilarius had been very helpful tonight. But he'd alluded to a shady past. Maybe it had come back to haunt him. As my new doubts about David were now haunting me.

I blinked away the tears the raw onions had brought. I melted butter in the skillet and cooked the onions until they were translucent, meanwhile chopping a half dozen carrots and dicing eight potatoes. I fished out the pork bones from the stock and stirred in the vegetables. Would that I could fish out the truth as easily. Oscar Felch being missing was disturbing. I hoped Kevin had managed to track him down.

We were getting low on bread, and we'd eaten all the rolls for our afternoon meal, so I mixed a half cup of sourdough starter into warm water from the kettle always sitting on the back of the stove. I stirred in handfuls of flour until it was a thick slurry called a sponge, and beat it with a hundred strokes of the wooden spoon. After I replenished the starter with a few dollops of the slurry, I covered the sponge with a damp cloth and set it in the entryway where it would have a slow cool rise all night.

My thoughts kept rising, too, and not slowly. There was the Leroy character Zeb mentioned, with an apparent hatred for the suffrage movement. I shook my head. I needed to write all this down. I headed for my room in the front of the house and passed through the sitting room. Faith sat with her feet tucked up writing in a journal while Frederick read a book to Betsy, apparently enough in control of his faculties again to not slur his words.

He glanced up. "I thank thee, Rose." He lifted his chin.

This was no time to discuss his inebriation, so I merely nodded. At least he'd thanked me. I noticed a little smile played on Faith's lips. She had to be happy at his return and at his apparent reconciliation with me. The children, no matter their age, wanted only peace in the family.

My hand was on the door to my parlor when a rapping sounded on the front door. My heart sank. Who could it be but someone calling me to a birth? I quickly scanned through my clients who were due within the next month. Lyda Osgood was the most likely. Her due date was in two weeks, as I recalled. I desperately needed a good night's sleep, but I couldn't not go to a labor in progress. I'd never had back-to-back labors before. Another reason to continue Annie's training. Annie had left her mill job and was working as a companion to an elderly dowager in town. She'd told me several months ago she very much wanted to become a midwife, and I'd agreed to let her apprentice.

With a heavy sigh I went to the door. A young man with a cheery smile greeted me.

"I have a message for a Miss Rose Carroll at this address, and I'm to wait for a reply." He handed me an envelope.

"I'm Rose." I took the note. Reading it, I exclaimed. Not a summons to a birth at all, it was an invitation to come for tea and cake with Mrs. Stanton at Bertie's this very night at seven thirty. What a delight.

I smiled broadly. "Please tell her I shall be there. Let me find thee a coin for thy troubles."

"Oh, no, miss, but thank you. Miss Winslow has already paid me." He touched his cap. "I'm to come back with the carriage and fetch you in half an hour's time, if the invitation is agreeable to you."

"Very much so. I thank thee."

I thought I'd sup on a quick bowl of soup

and put on a fresh dress for the tea party. My notes could wait. I looked forward to clearing my mind of murder and of my personal problems, and I was relieved I'd be able to come back to my own bed in a few hours. Spending an evening in the company of intelligent women was just what I needed.

Half an hour later I was happily sipping tea in Bertie and Sophie's parlor. The warm air smelled of sweets and women's perfumes. My spectacles fogged up at the difference in temperature between outside and in when I first came in, requiring me to take them off and wipe the lenses. Bright lamps lit up a colorful array of fine art on the walls of the room, with paintings by Mary Cassatt, Berthe Morisot, and others I didn't recognize.

After I came in, I thanked Bertie for the ride.

"He's a very nice young man thee found for a messenger boy," I said. "Polite, well-spoken."

Bertie laughed. "He's the son of a friend. I like the kid, and he wanted to earn pocket change. It was Sophie's idea to send the carriage for you. We didn't want you to miss the gathering." My friend was closer to forty than to thirty, but the fine skin on her face was almost completely unlined, perhaps because of her cheerful spirit and optimistic outlook on life.

"I appreciate it, and I'll tell her. I was already out once tonight on a less-pleasant mission, so I was glad not to walk over." At her look of inquiry, I added, "I'll relate the story to thee later, but it involved Frederick acting distinctly unQuakerly."

About half of the guests sat in a circle, with Elizabeth holding forth on her views about the world. The desserts were displayed on a narrow table at the side of the room, next to the tea service. I spied a raspberry-topped cheesecake, a trifle, a plate of sugar cookies, and bite-sized chocolate cakes. Bottles of liqueurs were lined up on the table, along with small etched glasses. While it looked like a party, any laughter was muted and the air tasted somber, as befit a group whose leader had died in the last day. What a pity Rowena herself could not be a part of this.

As I looked around the room, I saw many of the invitees were partaking of spirits, including Bertie and Sophie. The latter stood speaking with Frannie Eisenman, so I headed in their direction. I hadn't seen Sophie in a few months, and I wanted to thank her for the ride as well as inquire of Frannie about her new grandbaby.

Unconventional Sophie, who favored the loose soft silks of the Aesthetic Dress Movement, tonight wore an unwaisted embroidered robe in muted shades of green and orange. About my height, she wore her dark hair in a messy knot atop her head.

"Rose, come join us," she said, extending her hand. "Do you know Frannie?"

I said I did. Frannie and I greeted each other. "How's thy granddaughter?" I asked.

"She's perfectly thriving. Gaining weight already." Frannie's frizzed hair was surprisingly unsilvered for her age.

"I'm glad to hear it." I turned to Sophie. "I thank thee for sending the conveyance. It was a treat not to have to walk here."

I'd forgotten what a deep throaty laugh she had.

"It's my pleasure. Bert and I both wanted you here." She took a sip from her glass. "Can I offer you a drink?"

"No, thank thee." Surely she knew Friends didn't imbibe? Then I thought of Frederick at the tavern only an hour earlier. Maybe there were others who indulged in alcohol and I just wasn't aware of them.

"Well, help yourself to whatever you'd

like." She smiled and moved on to another guest.

I heard the name Leroy Dunnsmore behind me and turned to see who had uttered it. It was Ruby Bracken from Meeting. I hoped she wasn't going to continue with her censure of me here at a social event.

"That man should be put in his place," Frannie said, obviously having heard the same remark.

Ruby glanced over. "You know him, too?" she asked.

Frannie nodded. "Spouting off like it's the Dark Ages."

"He's my neighbor up Whitehall Road," Ruby said. "I never hear the end of it."

"I just learned of him earlier today, from my niece's beau, who works with him at the Parry factory," I said. "Does thee think he'll make trouble at the demonstration, Ruby?"

"He might." She shook her head. "Wouldn't put it past him."

Bertie beckoned me to where she stood with Zula Goodwin near the door, so I excused myself and walked over to them. Bertie introduced us. Zula was taller than me and looked a couple of years younger, now I saw her up close. She wore a mannish jacket over her black dress, with her auburn hair tonight pulled back into a

96

tightly coiled braid.

"Zula, I'm awfully sorry about thy friend's death," I said.

"Rose Carroll." Zula stared at me. "I heard you found my dear Rowena. Was it a terrible sight? Do you think she suffered?"

I took her hand in both of mine. "I'm afraid I cannot say. But the detective told me she had a grievous wound on the head, so perhaps she lost consciousness immediately." I hoped my words would console her.

"Who would harm such a graceful and brilliant person?" she whispered. "Such a loving soul?"

"My friend Rose here is a bit of a detective, you know," Bertie said.

"Are you?" Zula looked surprised.

"No, I'm a midwife. In fact, I am caring for thy sister, Emily. She mentioned thee during an antenatal examination last month."

"That's right, she said so." Zula nodded. "I'd forgotten. I can't wait to meet my new niece or nephew." A little smile played over her face.

"But I did have something to do with solving a couple of murders in Amesbury over the past year," I went on. "And the police detective now welcomes my modest input."

"Are you working on Rowena's case, then?" She blinked several times.

"*Working on* isn't quite right," I said. "I'm certainly thinking about it."

"I understand Mrs. Felch was going to be living with you," Bertie said.

"As a matter of fact, no." Zula took a deep breath in and let it out. "She couldn't tolerate that husband of hers any longer. Mr. Felch is an ogre, and I invited her to share my flat so she could get away."

An ogre seemed like an extreme description. Could it be true? "What does thee mean, an ogre?"

"He wanted to control every aspect of her life," Zula said. "Tie her to babies and housekeeping for the next thirty years."

"When had you thought she going to leave him and move into your apartment?" Bertie asked.

"She planned to leave him soon." Zula looked intently first at Bertie and then at me. "Rowena wanted only a platonic friendship with me, and I . . ." Her voice trailed off. "It was what she wanted, and even her friendship was so rich, so full. Yet she refused my offer of refuge." She pressed her lips together and shook her head, fast. "I mustn't dwell on it any longer. The suffrage movement needs me. And I have my memories."

"Have the police spoken to thee about her death?" I asked.

She snorted. "The detective wanted to, but my father wouldn't allow it."

I found it passing odd this ardent suffragist with an apparent romantic interest in Rowena was letting her father make decisions for her.

"Ladies?" Sophie called out and clapped her hands a couple of times.

I turned to see her standing behind Elizabeth, whose lace collar set off her round rosy cheeks and intelligent eyes.

"Mrs. Stanton wants to say a few words about our common cause. Please find a seat and lend your ears. Mrs. Stanton, we are so very pleased and honored you could join us tonight."

I perched on the arm of the upholstered easy chair Bertie landed in. I pushed up my glasses and caught a whiff of a scent. I didn't use perfumes. It must have been from when I took Zula's hands in mine. I put my hand to my nose and inhaled violet, I thought, or perhaps lavender.

Elizabeth waited a few moments while the women got settled. "I'm gratified to see Amesbury fosters a spirit of independence and forthrightness in its ladies, and I've been pleased to meet each one of you. I know the demonstration on Tuesday is on everyone's mind, but I wanted to share a few thoughts with you beyond the single question of universal suffrage. First, though, let us take a few moments to hold the departed soul of our dear friend Rowena Felch in our hearts — and prayers, for those of you who believe in such matters. She was taken too soon, and with violence, and I hope it was not at the hand of an enemy of our movement." She bowed her head.

All followed suit and the room fell silent, with only the creak of a chair and someone quietly clearing her throat breaking the peace. Before I closed my eyes, I caught sight of Zula with silent tears rolling down her cheeks. I welcomed the moment of silence, holding Rowena's spirit in the Light of God. *May her killer be found soon and dealt with justly,* I prayed. And if I could help solve the case, so be it. I opened my eyes when Elizabeth spoke again.

"I have been much in mind recently of the need to guarantee individual rights. We are each alone, men and women alike. I believe nothing strengthens the judgment and quickens the conscience like individual responsibility. Nothing adds such dignity to character as the recognition of one's self-sovereignty and the right to an equal place. Each of us needs a place earned by personal merit, not an artificial attainment by inheritance, wealth, family, or position." She gazed around the room, meeting each of our eyes before going on.

"We must work to give woman all the opportunities: higher education, the full development of her physical and mental faculties, the most enlarged freedom of thought and action. The strongest reason for giving her a complete emancipation from all forms of bondage — of custom, dependence, superstition, and all the crippling influences of fear — is the personal responsibility of her own individual life."

She sat erect, with a calm clear look on her face. "Go forth, ladies. As I said at the meeting, we shall link arms and stand tall, and we *shall* effect change. There is no other way to proceed."

What a beautiful, stirring speech. I wished I'd brought Faith to hear it, too. As every one of us clapped, I stole another glance at Zula. She applauded even as she still wept. She had truly loved Rowena. Had she killed her because her deep love was spurned? My thoughts flashed to David. His offer today had initially felt like a rejection until I understood his motivation. How would I feel if he'd truly spurned my love? I knew both that I would not be moved to murder him and that my tears would also flow. As had Frederick's after my sister had died. Perhaps he still cried in the privacy of his room, not from the rejection of a living wife but from losing her to death. When he learned of his wife's death, would Oscar Felch weep in the same way?

NINE

I made my way to the police station at a few moments past eight the next morning. I had matters to discuss with Kevin, but I needed to be home by nine to see several scheduled pregnant clients for their antenatal visits. Frederick had been his usual moody self at breakfast. Luckily I'd managed to stay out of his way. Sharing a house with his unpredictable temperament was like treading on eggshells. I never knew what would cause him to blow up in a fit of temper. Harriet had been a saint to put up with him, and that was a fact.

Faith had loved my report on the tea party. "Granny Dot's going to wish she'd been there," she'd said.

"You'll meet Elizabeth Stanton tomorrow, and Granny will introduce you." I'd hugged her and nudged her out the door to her job, lunch pail in hand.

On my way to the station, the rising sun

painted the clouds in the east a shade matching my name. Now I paced in the anteroom waiting for Kevin to appear, but my mind remained with the gathering at Bertie and Sophie's. Elizabeth's words about going beyond merely the vote had moved me deeply. I expected Lucretia Mott and the other women Friends in the forefront of the suffrage movement had influenced Elizabeth's thinking about equality and integrity. Jane Hunt, Mary Coffin Wright, and Mary Ann M'Clintock, along with Lucretia and Elizabeth, were the team who drafted the Declaration of Sentiments presented at the First Women's Rights Convention forty years ago.

I liked that she spoke to the condition of both women and men. I reflected that I, myself, had been well-blessed with a Quaker upbringing. We were taught to act with personal responsibility from a young age.

I checked the wall clock. Eight twenty. Where was Kevin? He was always at the station by eight. Was he already so busy this morning he didn't have time to speak with me? He was going to want to know about the outspoken anti-suffrage hothead Leroy Dunnsmore, and I wanted to speak to him about what Zula had said last night, too. I'd hate it if she were the killer, but justice was more important than my feelings. And she was an odd bird, no doubt about it. I also wanted to tell him what David had said about Hilarius. But I couldn't wait here for much longer.

David. I worried at a stray thread on my sleeve. I couldn't stop thinking about Ruby's message to me from the women, and David's reaction before he'd left yesterday. Was he simply trying to be lovingly generous, giving me an escape hatch from having to leave my Meeting? Or did he want to escape our union himself? I hadn't slept well last night, tangling myself in my sheets as I searched my heart for a solution.

I paced to the door and peered out the glass, then paced back to the waiting bench. The young officer at the reception desk had said he would let the detective know I was here, and then he'd vanished into the interior of the station and not returned. I knew it might behoove me to sit in silent prayer and wait for discernment on whether I should wait any longer or not, whether I should even be helping the police at all. But I had a strong feeling — whether from God or from my moral compass — that God would want me to act for justice. So I waited. And paced.

I perked up when the outer door pushed

open. A weary Kevin let it slam behind him.

"Miss Rose." His words slid out with a sigh. "What can I do for you?" He had dark patches under his eyes and his uniform jacket was misbuttoned, with one corner of the collar sticking into his neck and the opposite bottom corner hanging below the other side.

"Kevin, is thee well? Thee looks terrible."

"I'm fine, but my boy's sick. Fever. I was up all night with my six-year-old lad. Wife is feeling a bit poorly, too."

The poor man. I knew how tender he was about his wife and children. "I'm so sorry to hear this. Thee is using cold compresses and plentiful fluids for the fever, I trust."

"We are. Which is why I didn't sleep last night. If anything happens to my boy, Miss Rose, why . . ." He gazed at the floor and then turned away to wipe a tear from the corner of his eye. When he faced me again his shoulders were straight but his eyes were rimmed in red. "I'm thinking you want to have a discussion with me about the murder."

"Yes. But only if thee is able."

"Bosh." He swatted away the idea. "Of course I am. Come along back, then."

I followed him to his office. On the way he stopped and asked a young officer if he'd bring us each a cup of coffee. The station had a small kitchen in the back.

"There won't be enough coffee in the known world to keep me going through this day, but I have to start somewhere," Kevin said once we'd arrived in his office.

"I felt the same way yesterday, myself. I am often up all night long with a laboring woman."

"Yes, I suppose you are. Please have a seat."

I removed a stack of papers from the chair in front of his desk and set them on the floor while he sank with a groan into his own chair.

"I've learned several things I thought thee would want to know," I said, clasping my hands on my lap. "My niece's friend works with a man named Leroy Dunnsmore at the Parry Carriage Factory." I relayed what Zeb had said. "And last night I was with a group of women and two of them also knew of this man's feelings. I suspect he might be a good person to look at for Rowena's death."

Kevin jotted down the name with a pencil. "I dare say quite a few gentlemen share your opinion about women and the vote."

"Perhaps. But this Leroy is apparently a particularly vocal one. Thee should look into his alibi. He lives on Whitehall Road.

And also keep an eye on him tomorrow."

He rolled his eyes at the mention of tomorrow but didn't address it. "All right. What else?"

"I saw Guy bring in a man named Hilarius Bauer yesterday."

"And what of it? He has a record of larceny."

"He's done work for David Dodge's father in Newburyport. David said he's quite trustworthy and a good worker. And last night the man did me a generous favor unbidden." I hoped Kevin wouldn't ask what the favor was. Frederick didn't need a reputation as a drunkard family man to become any more widely known than it already was, what with him sitting right there getting himself sloshed in a public place.

"How nice for you." Kevin leaned his chin on his palm. The young officer came in with a tray holding two cups of coffee, spoons, a chipped cream pitcher, and a half-empty sugar bowl. "Thank the blessed Mary. Oh, and you, too, son."

"Yes, sir."

The young man, who didn't look much older than Faith, unloaded the tray and went out. We took a moment to doctor our drinks and Kevin took a long drag from his before heaving a sigh of relief.

I sipped mine and put it down on the desk. I should have known the brew would be thick and bitter. It was police coffee. I'd make more at home if I needed some.

"Where were we?" Kevin asked.

"Talking about Hilarius Bauer. Did thee determine if he has an alibi for the time of the murder? Because when I asked him, he didn't answer and he looked . . . well, uncomfortable. Either fearful or nervous or both."

"So far we haven't been able to locate a witness, no. But I have no evidence to arrest him, either. And I'll tell you, Rose, I expect the chief to come in any minute now. He'll tell me to solve this thing, and soon." He pulled a piece of paper out from a drawer. "Take a look at this."

I read the handwritten note. It asked Rowena to meet in front of her house at ten o'clock p.m. "Goodness." I'd forgotten about the paper Rowena had grasped.

"Indeed."

"So this means the author of the note planned to kill her?" I wrinkled my nose. "If so, why didn't he leave her body on the front steps to continue the ruse of a robbery caught in the act? Why drag her body under the bush?"

"I had the same questions, Miss Rose. Sure looks like the killer wanted the body to be found, in either case. She wasn't exactly hidden from view under that shrub."

I nodded slowly, examining the note. "The handwriting is unusual," I said. "It's unfortunate the missive isn't signed."

"More's the pity. A signature would make our job too easy, now, wouldn't it? Do you think the hand looks like a woman's or a man's?"

I examined it again. "The writing is fairly delicate. I'd guess a woman's, but I suppose a man could have written it, too. And it's just plain paper, with no monogram or color, so we can't tell anything from it." I handed it back to him.

"Exactly. Tell me, have you heard from Dr. Dodge about Dr. Felch being away at a medical meeting?"

"Not yet. And have you learned anything about Zula Goodwin?" I asked. "Last night she said her father wouldn't let her come here to be questioned. That sounds like a flimsy excuse, to me."

"I've learned nothing." Kevin spit out an exasperated sound. "You are correct. She did not comply with our request for an interview. Her father turns out to be good buddies with the chief."

"I'm not surprised. But I forgot to tell you something yesterday. After the Woman Suffrage Association meeting I saw Zula and Rowena walking away together. Zula appeared to be arguing with Rowena."

He stared at me. "So she might be the last person to have seen the victim alive. Other than the killer. Unless she's our culprit, herself. Very interesting, Miss Rose."

"I should say."

"And since young Miss Goodwin is in the scandalous position of living alone at age twenty-one, there's no one to vouch for her whereabouts after your meeting let out Saturday night." He leaned closer over the desk. "How am I supposed to solve a crime when I can't even question one of the suspects?"

TEN

The rosy-cheeked woman reclining on my chaise for her antenatal exam had a slightly higher pulse than I would have liked. It was still within the normal range, though, but at the top end.

"Thy heart is beating a bit higher than usual, Emily, but I think it's fine. Let's check the baby now."

"Whatever you say, Rose." This was Emily Hersey's third baby, and Zula's sister knew the routine. She bent her knees and lifted her skirts and chemise above her nearly at-term belly, then pulled down her silk knickers.

I palpated her stretched-smooth skin with both hands to ascertain the position of the baby. "It's nicely head down and already in a good position for birth. Has thee been having any practice pains?" Women often experienced a semblance of contractions in the weeks leading up to the birth, but they were irregular in timing and weaker than those of true labor.

"Oh, yes." She waved off the idea. "But after bearing two girls, I know what the pains are by now. It's nothing to stop me from going about my life. I still have my piano students coming to the house for lessons."

"And your prior labors were easy, I believe thee said?" She'd told me she'd been attended by a midwife across the river in Newburyport, where she'd been living, for her earlier births. Now that she and her husband had moved back to Amesbury, she'd elected to hire me for her midwifery care. Her and Zula's family was quite wealthy, so it had surprised me when Emily told me she taught piano, but said she loved it and it made her feel useful.

"The first labor was longer, maybe twelve hours. My second popped out in about an hour, though. That was nearly two years ago now." She smiled. "I'm not sure little Zadie's ready to be supplanted by a newborn, but she'll learn."

This pleasant maternal woman was quite the contrast to her single suffragist sister. I pressed the Pinard horn gently against Emily's womb and listened. "Baby's heartbeat is strong and healthy. I'm going to feel for the opening, if thee is ready."

"I'm ready."

"Remember to breathe down into my hand if it feels at all uncomfortable." I pushed up first my glasses and then my sleeve, and slid my hand into her opening.

The end of the womb, the cervix, which in a nonpregnant woman is a tight little knob not much bigger than a plump cherry, begins a process in the last month or so of thinning and readying itself to open a whole fist's worth, or more, at the time of the birth. It's an efficient and miraculous process when things go smoothly, with the womb pulling up and away as the baby's head presses down and prepares to emerge.

"Thy cervix is completely effaced and" — I felt more carefully — "beginning to dilate." I slid my hand out and wiped it clean. Glancing at her face I spied a look of confusion. I sometimes forgot and used the medical terms with clients who didn't know those words and didn't care to learn. "I apologize. By that I only mean that thy labor could start at any time. Thy body is ready."

"You don't say." She frowned.

I stood. "Thee can restore thy garments."

She pulled up her drawers and lowered her skirts. "But I thought my due date wasn't for two more weeks."

I checked the paperwork on my desk. "That's correct. But this is thy third child, and the baby is plenty big enough to thrive out in the world by now. I wouldn't worry. I would ensure that everything is in place for the birth itself, though, because thy baby could be wanting to make its appearance soon. Thee has someone to care for the older children during thy labor?"

"Yes, we have a nursemaid. And my older sister will come to assist in the birth and with the baby. Zula, though, is far too occupied with her suffrage work, even though she loves her little nieces." She shook her head, but it was with a fond smile playing about her lips, not a disapproving look.

"She's quite active in the organization. I saw her several times recently."

"Oh?" Emily cocked her head. "Are you a suffragist, too?"

"I suppose I am. I haven't lifted a finger for the cause as yet, but I plan to attend the protest at the polls tomorrow."

"Yellow sash and all?"

"Yellow sash and all." I marked Emily's status in my file and turned back to her. "Does thee have any concerns about thy labor or how thee is feeling?"

She thought for a moment. "No, in that regard I am well and content. I know other ladies have problems bearing their babies, but my body seems built for it. I am a well-oiled baby machine. I'm concerned about my younger sister, however. She's quite torn up about the death of her friend."

"Rowena," I murmured. I chose not to mention that I had found her body. Well-oiled baby machine or not, a woman this close to term didn't need to have an image of a violent death linger in her mind.

"Yes. They were very close." She smoothed her pale plum-colored dress, of a fine wool weave, over her belly.

When she paused her hand I saw a bump move under it, a healthy baby's kick. "Is that why she won't also be attending thee in thy labor?"

This made Emily snort. "Zula? She's my polar opposite, not interested at all in raising a family of her own. Why, as a child she would stage battles with our dolls instead of dressing and playing with them like a normal girl, and she's always been something of a rebel. But I don't mind, and she's quite good with Zadie and her big sister Hattie, who adore their Auntie Zu. Besides, not everyone should be the same in this world, don't you think?"

After my last client left at eleven o'clock,

the morning post brought a note from David. I stared at it for a minute, then opened it with a trembling hand.

My dearest Rose,

I want to thank you for the splendid dinner yesterday. I always enjoy time with your family — and you, most importantly. I hope Mr. Bailey returned and made his peace with the family before too long. I could see he still suffers greatly from the loss of his wife, your sister.

I sat back, gazing at the linen paper in my hand. David really was extraordinary, to see that Frederick's rage came out of grief, of hurt, which of course it did. I read on.

I was able to discover a portion of the information you sought. My colleague here at the hospital has told me that, indeed, Oscar Felch has been attending a medical convention in New York City. But it ends today, so he should be back in Amesbury tonight or tomorrow. I have written separately to Detective Donovan of Mr. Felch's whereabouts.

So the husband's absence was explained, and the convention very likely gave him an alibi for the murder.

I saw how much my words hurt you yesterday, Rosie, and I can't adequately express my chagrin at having said them. I only wish I could withdraw the moment from your memory. I truly want to marry you, create a family with you, grow old with you. Nothing will make me happier. Please believe me. We shall face your Quaker women together and endure whatever may come with hands joined, if it is your wish.

I shall take my leave of you now, as I have patients awaiting my services.

I remain ever

Your adoring servant,
David

I caressed the paper once before folding it and stowing it in the carved box where I kept all his correspondence. He was trying to make amends with me, certainly. I had trusted him with my feelings from the beginning of our relationship, or nearly so. Now, with these words of his echoing in my brain and with a bit of distance between yesterday and today, my doubts began to shrink again. I hoped they would never have occasion to revive themselves, although I did wonder why I didn't feel more secure in his love. I didn't wonder long. I knew it was based in the long-ago horror from my teenage years, when I'd been abused and abandoned by my first love. I'd thought with my engagement that I had put that nightmare firmly behind me. Apparently not. But I resolved for the rest of today, and going forward, that I would. I would take one day at time in my healing.

I sat and thought. I could spend the next hour wandering off into reveries about my intended husband or into whatever grim scenario the Women's Business Meeting might present me, but what I really needed to do was learn more about who might have had cause to kill Rowena. Bertie had said Rowena was a lawyer. If I knew where she practiced, I could visit the firm. I snapped my fingers. I had a home visit with Lyda Osgood scheduled for today. And her husband practiced law.

Twenty minutes later a young maid led me up the stairs at the Osgood home, which sat on a hill heading north on Market Street. Lyda, cradling her eight-month-pregnant belly under a floral-print fabric that strained at her full bosom, opened the door to her airy and spacious bedroom and invited me in.

"Will this do, Rose?" Lyda asked, waving her arm to encompass the space. A four-poster bedstead draped with creamy brocade curtains held position of honor. Two upholstered armchairs nestled near the east-facing window and a marble-faced fireplace was tucked into the opposite wall. She smoothed chestnut-colored hair off her brow with a faint whiff of violet. The color was high in her creamy skin, as befit her late stage, and her breaths were slightly shallow, also normal for her condition. A woman's lungs could become quite compressed by a full womb pushing up on them.

"It will do quite nicely, Lyda." I made home visits to every client, whether the wife of a mill owner or the young mill worker, herself. I thought it passing odd Lyda had even asked if it would do, since she'd given birth here twice before, although my teacher Orpha Perkins had attended her.

"My maid will bring you whatever you need during the labor and birth," Lyda said with a calm smile. "And Mr. Osgood says we should summon the carriage should we need a doctor in attendance."

I'd assisted at her prior births as an apprentice, but I was confident to be the lead midwife this time around. "I doubt we'll need a physician. Thy previous births were quite easy, as I recall."

Her brows knit together. "Mr. Osgood is very much in favor of having a male doctor attend me. But I don't agree, and I've put my foot down. The birthing chamber is the realm of women, is it not?"

I smiled. "I believe it is. And I will take good care of thee." It was an honest answer. But how was I going to raise the issue of what Elbridge Osgood, her husband, might know about Rowena? As it happened, I didn't need to.

"Rose." Lyda lowered her voice. "I heard Mrs. Felch was killed. And that you found her body yesterday morning. Is it true?" Her eyebrows drew up.

"Why don't you lie down and I'll assess thy progress." I led her to the bed and fetched my satchel. Talk of murder wasn't exactly the calming topic one would wish for a near-term mother-to-be, even though it was the one absorbing my thoughts. After she reclined, I went on. "I did find her, sadly. I was returning at dawn from a birth."

"Mr. Osgood said she was bashed in the back of the head. What a terrible death." She brought her hands to cover her mouth.

"Any violent death is a terrible one. Rowena was a lawyer, like thy husband. Was he acquainted with her?"

Lyda's nostrils flared. "Acquainted? Why, she stole his job!" Lyda suddenly looked neither surprised nor saddened about Rowena's death.

Oh? Stealing a position was quite the accusation. I took a moment to listen to the baby's heart, which sounded good. "How so?" I kept my expression even, despite my keen interest to learn more about this story. I took her wrist and counted her own beats, watching the clock on the mantel.

"They're both employed by Bixby & Batchelder, or were. When my Elbridge was up for promotion, they chose that woman, instead." She nearly spat the word *woman.* "And sacked Mr. Osgood." The anger slid off her face and sorrow crept into her voice. "Just like what happened to my papa when I was a girl. He was a wrecked man after being fired."

"I'm so sorry, Lyda. I trust Elbridge will find a new position soon. I'm going to check inside you now."

She drew up her dress and shift. She wore the older fashion of split drawers, so she didn't need to remove them. "Maybe, if people about town stop laughing behind his back." She rubbed at a spot on the back of her hand. "Not only did Mrs. Felch rob my husband of his livelihood, then she makes plans to up and leave her own husband high and dry. There's just no decency in this world, Rose. What have we come to?"

ELEVEN

I cycled past the police station after I left Lyda and penned a note for Kevin to look into Elbridge Osgood. If Elbridge harbored a grudge against Rowena, he should be investigated. For that matter, Lyda should too. I hated the thought of a woman with murderous intents carrying an unborn child, but I'd seen it earlier this year.

A stiff wind had commenced, and I watched clouds scud by as I remounted my bicycle. Fall was already giving way to winter. The business with Frederick and the tavern weighed heavy on my mind. I checked my pocket watch. It was one o'clock, a good time to pay John Whittier a visit. The elderly Friend had helped me with weighty matters in the past, mostly by being a good listener, and he'd always welcomed my visits.

A few minutes later I sat in his study. Warmth radiated from the coal stove and a poem in progress lay on John's small desk. His bookcase was full of his own works as well as those of his good friends: Long-fellow, Emerson, Celia Thaxter, Lucy Larcom, William Lloyd Garrison, Oliver Wendell Holmes, and others.

"I see something troubles thee, Rose," he said, tenting his fingers. "Is it in connection with the recent murder in our fair town?"

"The murder is truly troublesome," I said. "But this is more personal. A disturbing thing happened yesterday." I explained the conversation with Frederick after our First Day dinner and how he stormed out. "He was gone the rest of the afternoon and early evening. Betsy was upset at his absence and Faith told me he'd been frequenting the tavern."

John blinked several times under his snowy white eyebrows. "Friend Frederick has been indulging in alcoholic spirits?"

"Apparently so. I went down to Hoyt's to find him, where he was in his cups. A friendly fellow helped me get him home. Thee knows, perhaps, that Frederick is a difficult man."

He nodded slowly.

"His manner has worsened since my sister's death. I have to share a house with him, and I'm worried about the children.

125

Now, with intoxication in the mix, I don't quite know what to do." I paused, thinking. "The bartender, a kindly woman, as it turned out, mentioned she thinks Frederick is lonely. Does thee know of any widows in need of a grumpy man with five children?"

"Let us pray together on this matter, Rose, for a short time."

I closed my eyes and tried to clear my mind of thoughts. It was my nature to want answers and want to act on finding them. Friends' practice of waiting until way opens, until one discerns what God wants one to do, was difficult for me.

After John cleared his throat, I opened my eyes, having neither heard nor felt a message of any kind.

"I have been wondering about Friend Frederick," John said. "Perhaps it's time for him to be eldered in the matter of his drinking. His first responsibility is to his family, and he cannot care for them well under the influence of spirits."

I wrinkled my nose. "Oh, dear. I didn't mean for him to get into trouble with the Meeting. I was looking more for counsel for myself."

"Worry not, my dear. I'll speak with another Friend who has a good way with people. The eldering will be gentle, I prom-

126

ise. He need not know we spoke of this. And I shall also consider whether I know of a kindly lady who might be willing to take him on as husband. Along with the children, of course."

"I thank thee. Speaking of eldering, I received a dose myself yesterday."

"Hmm." He stroked his beard as if he already knew what I was about to say.

"Ruby Bracken warned me marrying out will certainly result in my being read out of Meeting."

"And how does thee feel about this prospect?"

"I feel I have discerned the path God wants me to take, and it is to marry a fine and gentle man who loves me and supports my wish to continue my midwifery practice. So I will accept the consequences. It won't be easy and I won't be happy having to stay away from Friends. But I'll do it." The lapse of a day had somewhat softened the sharp edge of yesterday's news. David's note had confirmed I would have him at my side during my time as an expelled Friend, and his support would make the process easier to endure.

"And I shall do my own gentle prodding to make sure thee is reinstated after the prescribed time," he said. "I believe the stricture against marrying out is an outmoded custom, dating from the time when Friends were persecuted for our faith and we needed to keep our numbers strong. However, this danger is no longer the case and I think it's time for a change. I am not sectarian, and I have good fellowship with people of all denominations. I think more highly of practical piety than of mindless adherence to doctrine."

I smiled. What a good and generous soul he was.

"But as thee knows well, it's not the purview of the men at Amesbury Friends Meeting to make these decisions." He tapped his knee.

"I do know. And I thank thee for thy support."

"Now, is thee ready for tomorrow?" he asked, his dark eyes now twinkling.

"Does thee mean the demonstration? How does thee know —"

"Elizabeth Stanton paid me a brief visit yesterday afternoon. I was happy to see her again."

Of course he would know her. Two great champions of different versions of human rights.

"She's very inspiring," I said. "I was at a gathering with her last evening. So I suppose I'm ready. I have my sash, at any rate. And my mother is coming to town tonight to join us."

"Splendid. I shall stand with the group for a time after I vote." He smiled.

"I hope there isn't any trouble. I find it worrisome that Rowena Felch, a prominent suffragist, was the murder victim. I'm afraid her killing is tied up in the movement, or in someone's angry reaction to it."

"I trust thee is helping the detective again?"

"I'm trying to. But the case is confounding. Nothing is clear."

"Thee will discern the path with sufficient prayer. And now it's time for my afternoon rest, Rose."

After I arrived home, had a bite to eat, and set the bread to bake, I busied myself with paperwork at my desk. I liked to keep my records up to date: my various clients' due dates and health concerns, who needed a home visit, and who owed me money. After a birth I made sure to jot down notes about the date and length of the labor, the vigor of the baby and its name, and if the newborn had any health problems.

I pushed back my chair once I was caught up. I'd never gotten around to writing down my thoughts about the murder case because I'd been summoned to the tea party, so I pulled out a fresh piece of paper and listed everyone I could think of who had a connection with Rowena's death. Sometimes matters clarified themselves to me by the simple act of writing.

I started with Elbridge Osgood. Knowing about him losing his job was a new piece of information. Where had Lyda said he'd worked? Yes, Bixby & Batchelder. Perhaps I could pay them a visit soon if Kevin didn't have time. Next I entered Zula Goodwin's name and what I knew about her. Maybe I should pay her a visit, too. I added Hilarius Bauer, Leroy Dunnsmore, and Oscar Felch. Then I crossed out Oscar. He'd been at the medical convention, David said. But . . . what if Oscar had hired someone to kill his wife? He would still have the convention as an alibi. I scribbled his name again.

It was only two o'clock. I had time to head downtown and act the sleuth. I could stop by the post office on my way. Bertie would know where Zula lived. But what could I hope to find out from her? And what would be my reason for the visit? I supposed paying a social call would not be remiss — but on a Second Day afternoon? I shook my head. I'd think of something. I always did.

I'd just stood when I heard knocking at the door. I opened it to see Annie standing on the stoop, her hand securing her velvet hat from flying away with the wind.

"Annie, come in. What a nice surprise." I led her into my parlor. "Please sit down."

"Thank you, Rose. I wanted to talk with you about my apprenticeship." Annie sat and removed her gloves. She tucked her curly red hair back up under the floppy hat. "Attending the birth on Saturday with you confirmed my desire to become a midwife. Mrs. Roune is very nice, but I don't want to be a companion to a rich old lady in a mansion on Elm Street the rest of my life."

"I'm glad thee has started, and that the birth observation affirmed thy sense of being called to the profession."

"It truly did, Rose."

"Last night I thought I was being summoned to a second birth, and I was still exhausted from the first one. Once thee acquires more experience, thee could at least sit with the woman during the first part of her labor if I needed to catch a few hours of sleep."

"I'm so pleased." She clapped her hands in delight. "I've started reading the midwifery book you gave me — the one by Dr. Leishman."

"*A System of Midwifery.* It's quite the tome, isn't it? But he covers so many of the complications and disorders we see, as well as the normal process of pregnancy and birth. And as it was published only nine years ago, the information is still quite current."

"It's rather slow going for me." Despite being seventeen, Annie had learned to read only earlier this year, with Faith and Betsy tutoring her with enthusiasm.

"Keep at it as thee can. Jot down words thee doesn't know and I can help." I made a mental note to buy her a small dictionary to assist with her studies. "What is thy work schedule with thy elderly employer? And what is her Christian name, by the way? In case the next birth takes place on a weekday and I need to contact thee."

"Mabel. Mabel Roune. I am usually with her at her home on Elm Street every weekday. It's on the right just past Washington Street. But this afternoon, for example, she was having a morning session and she let me go early."

"Well, next time I'm called to a birth I'll let thee know. If Mabel doesn't need thy company, thee can come to the labor again and help me. Thee will need to observe a goodly number of births to learn the necessary techniques and see all the different birthing positions."

Her entire face lit up. "Thank you, dear Rose."

I cocked my head. "What did thee mean, a morning session? How can she have that in the afternoon, and what is it?"

Annie laughed. "Mourning. As in sadness. Don't you know? Mrs. Roune was Rowena Felch's grandmother."

My goodness. "No, I didn't. How interesting."

"Mrs. Roune is Mrs. Felch's mother. Mrs. Roune said her granddaughter was named for their family name, that Roune is just a different form of Rowen."

"Is Mabel grieving terribly? It must be awful to lose a granddaughter."

"I believe she's quite sad. But she's the kind of lady who tries to hide her feelings, which I think is rather silly. I mean, if you're sad, why conceal it? I can tell, though. She's very distressed." Annie narrowed her eyes as if she was thinking. "You might want to know this, Rose. Mrs. Roune mentioned something about Rowena's husband. She said he was given to fits of jealousy and had a rather violent temper. She said she wouldn't be surprised if he'd killed her himself."

I filed this bit of information in my brain.

"Are you working with Detective Donovan on this case?" Annie asked.

"Not working with him, exactly. But yes, I am seeking the facts of the murder, in order to share with him."

"I thought you would be."

"Had Mabel mentioned Rowena was planning on leaving her husband?"

"Oh, yes." Annie nodded.

It was remarkable and unusual that so many in town knew of, and were speaking about, the breakup of this marriage. Rowena must not have had any compunctions about sharing her status

"Mrs. Roune planned to make her a gift of money to make the departure possible," Annie went on. "And she has loads of money."

Mabel's gift would have enabled Rowena to leave her husband. What a tragedy the departure had been one of a very different sort.

TWELVE

I walked into town with Annie after we finished talking, and after the bread had finished baking, as well. We parted ways at busy Market Square. I joined the back of the line at the post office, newly rebuilt since the terrible fire of last Fourth Month. Bertie and the young woman who acted as her assistant were busy selling stamps, fetching packages, and answering questions. Bertie waved at me when she saw me and pointed to a door at the side of the room. I nodded and headed into her small office.

"Eva can handle the counter by herself for a while," she said. "What brings you here, my friend?" Bertie wore a neat striped shirtwaist with a dark skirt today. A jaunty bow in her blond curls picked up the bright blue stripes in the shirt's fabric, and the tailoring of the shirtwaist was in the very latest style, full in the shoulders and close-fitting forearms leading to the wrists. Bertie was an avid follower of the latest fashions.

"First I wanted to thank thee so very much for the party last night."

"It was fun, wasn't it? Sophie and I both thought it was quite the success."

"Exceedingly so. And please thank Sophie for me, too. What a brilliant woman Elizabeth is. And so inspiring."

"You've got that right, Rose. Mrs. Stanton is a national treasure. It's truly an honor she's bestowed on Amesbury, traveling here to support us in the cause."

I nodded. "My errand today is not quite a tea party. I feel moved to call on Zula and see if I can learn more about her and Rowena, and somehow discern if Zula could be our murderer."

Bertie stared at me. "You're serious, aren't you?"

I nodded. "If she felt spurned, perhaps her anger rose up and she hit Rowena on the head. She's tall enough to do it, and she looks strong."

"She is. She's always talking about doing her calisthenic exercises to stay healthy."

I'd heard about this new craze, where women donned loose-fitting garments and ran through a prescribed set of movements to increase their physical well-being. It seemed better suited to the idle upper classes than to working women like Faith and myself. We received plentiful exercise of our muscles and joints by the mere tasks of living: cooking and cleaning, not to mention her work on four textile mills at a time, and mine, cycling here and there and assuming all kinds of awkward positions to catch babies.

"I sensed Zula was in love with Rowena and was crushed when her offer to share living quarters was rebuffed," I said.

Bertie tapped her cheek. "I think you're right."

"Does thee know where she lives?"

"Yes. But if she's a killer, it's crazy to go see her alone." Bertie folded her arms and eyed me. "You don't want to get bashed in the head, too, do you?"

"No," I said slowly. "But —"

She held up her hand. "Come back at five when I close the post office and we'll go together. How's that for a plan?"

"You always come up with the best ideas. That's a very good plan," I said. "My mother is coming in on the train tonight, but not until seven o'clock."

"Then it's firm."

"Thank thee, my friend. I wondered what excuse I'd have to make up to visit Zula.

Now we'll just be two friends paying a call." I stood.

"And we can talk about the plans for tomorrow," Bertie added. "Now I'd better get back to work."

I said good-bye and let myself out. I stood on the street for a moment, my bonnet flapping in the wind, as I determined what my story would be at Bixby & Batchelder. I certainly couldn't pretend to talk about a woman suffrage demonstration with those lawyers. Or . . . maybe I could. Rowena, a leader of the suffrage movement, had worked for the firm, after all. Or I could ask them what their plans for a memorial gift might be, and see if I could learn more about Elbridge Osgood's firing while I was there.

I headed back up Water Street to the square and then made my way along Main Street to the attorneys' offices.

"Yes, miss?" A middle-aged lady at a desk facing the door looked up over her glasses. "How may I help you?"

"My name is Rose Carroll. I'd like to speak with George Batchelder if he has a minute, please."

"Mr. Batchelder is a very busy man, Miss Carroll, I'm afraid." She glanced at an open appointment book and then back at me, removing her spectacles. "You don't have an appointment. What would this be in regard to?"

"It's about Rowena Felch."

The woman's face fell. "Poor Mrs. Felch. What a terrible tragedy."

"It is." I cleared my throat. "I'm afraid I was the one who found her body."

The woman's mouth fell open. She recovered herself and pointed to the chair in front of the desk. "Sit yourself right down there and tell me all about it."

I sat and gave her the barest of details of my discovery.

"Mrs. Felch was a fine, fine attorney, despite being a lady," the woman said. "This firm suffered a great loss with her death. It will be hard to replace her."

"I heard Elbridge Osgood recently left his position here. Can't the lead lawyers convince him to return?"

She snorted. "He didn't leave voluntarily. Mr. Batchelder asked him to go. Mr. Osgood threw such a scene when they promoted Mrs. Felch. Why, it was like a young lad stomping around because someone stole his toy truck. He couldn't believe they'd promoted a lady over him. No, they won't be asking Mr. Osgood back. And he wasn't promoted because, frankly" — she leaned in and lowered her voice — "he's not all that bright. Took forever to write up a brief and he was always making mistakes."

"A pity." Lyda hadn't exactly given me the true story. But why would she? She was married to him.

"Anyway." The woman straightened. "What was it about Mrs. Felch? The reason you came?"

"I've come about a memorial to her, from the Woman Suffrage Association. I thought perhaps her employers here would like to contribute." I cringed inwardly about misleading her, definitely not how a Friend was supposed to act. But I could certainly suggest such a memorial to one of the association leaders at the demonstration tomorrow.

"I think this an excellent proposal. I'll bring it to the attention of the Misters Bixby and Batchelder."

"I thank thee." I stood.

"You're a Quaker, then."

"Yes."

"Good for you. I always did admire you all for living the clean life. There's far too much drinking and gambling in the world today, but not from your sort. And you know, I've been meaning to join the Woman Suffrage Association, myself. Maybe I shall one of these days."

"I hope thee will." I said good-bye and made my way out. Elbridge was definitely still on the list of suspects. How could I find out where he'd been Saturday night?

Zula opened the door to her flat with a look of astonishment. "Miss Winslow, Miss Carroll. Please come in." She backed away and ushered us into a spacious room with large windows and electric wall sconces. The flat was the second floor of a large, elegant house on Highland Street. We'd been let in the front door by a uniformed maid and then made our way up a graceful staircase. This room was furnished with chairs, a settee, and a chaise. A gleaming black grand piano stood in the far corner. A tall plant was positioned in front of a window, and one wall featured built-in bookcases. Considerable resources had paid for this residence.

"Please sit down." She gestured toward the sitting area.

Bertie and I sat in two chairs upholstered in a maroon chintz across from the settee, where Zula perched. Her hair fell in a long braid down her back and she wore a green-and-pink dotted day dress, giving her a softer look than when I'd seen her in public.

"We just thought we'd pay you a call,"

Bertie began, "to express our condolences on Rowena's death." Bertie folded her hands primly in her lap, looking like a proper lady making a proper call.

I had to choke back a giggle, since that was the last thing she was.

Zula regarded her own lap for a moment, letting out a shuddering sigh. Her gaze rose again. "I thank you both, and I appreciate the visit. Let me ring for tea, unless you'd like something stronger. I have some excellent Spanish sherry."

"I don't mind if I do," Bertie said.

Zula went to a cabinet and brought back two small glasses full of an amber liquid and handed one to Bertie. "Miss Carroll?"

"Nothing for me, but I thank thee."

"Rose is a Quaker," Bertie said with a grin. "She never touches the hard stuff."

"So that's why you speak in your odd fashion." Zula sat with the other glass.

I smiled. "That's why, yes."

"We also wanted to ask if there's anything we can help with for the demonstration tomorrow, other than showing up," Bertie went on.

This was the additional ruse we'd come up with for our visit, since Zula was one of the organizers, although there was nothing wrong with a simple condolence call, of course.

Zula blinked a couple of times. "You're very kind." She got up, fetched a piece of paper from a small writing desk in the corner, and brought it back. I glimpsed a list of items jotted down. "No, everything is in order, but thank you. Just be there by eight." She laid the paper on the end table between her seat and mine.

I casually picked it up. "You have quite a list of tasks," I said, but really I was comparing the handwriting with my memory of the one on the note Rowena had held. Zula's writing was also unusual, with upright and almost backward-leaning letters. Was it the same as on the note requesting a rendezvous? I couldn't tell.

"Organizing a large group of people isn't a simple matter," Zula said. "But we have worked diligently on our plans for the demonstration, and I believe it will be a successful gathering. And highly visible to the citizens of the town, which is important."

"Will Mrs. Stanton be joining us at the polls?" Bertie asked.

"She said she would. You were given sashes the other night?" Zula asked.

"Yes," I said. "We both were." I gazed at Zula. "After the meeting on Seventh Day evening, I saw you walking away with Rowena. Were you having an argument?"

She stared at me, and then sighed. "The same old argument. I wanted her to move in. She didn't want to. I couldn't seem to make her change her mind. Look at this place. There's plenty of room for two. She'd have had her own bedroom."

There was indeed far too much space here for only one person. Why had Zula's family set her up here in such a large, independent apartment?

Zula shook her head. "But Rowena refused, said she needed to strike out on her own. And now she never will." She sniffed.

"Did you walk her all the way home?" Bertie asked with an innocent look on her face.

Zula cleared her throat. "Why, no. I continued on Highland when she turned onto her street." She lifted her chin as her eyes filled. "I wish I had. I might have been able to protect her against the brute who killed her."

Was she a good actress or was she telling the truth? If she had left the note, then it was a ruse, because why ask Rowena to meet her if she was already with her? Perhaps we were only adding to her hurt by asking her overly painful questions.

THIRTEEN

I bounced on my heels on the platform at the Water Street train depot as the Boston and Maine steamed in. The scream of its brakes announced the arrival and steam billowed white into the night sky as if in a celestial celebration. I couldn't wait to see Mother. We'd never experienced the mother-daughter conflicts many of my friends had. I'd long admired my unconventional parent for her disregard of the tongues that wagged when she became active in the suffrage movement. She was honest and funny and energetic, and I loved her.

A minute later I spied her climbing down from the third car and I waved, hurrying in her direction. Silver hair peeked out from a rich maroon bonnet matching her cloak, and her eyes shone. Friends were admonished to wear plain dress free of adornment, but she'd always told me the practice didn't mean we had to wear drab colors, too.

"Rosie, darling." She set down her valise and embraced me.

I'd grown a couple of inches taller than Mother in my teen years, and it still seemed odd she was shorter than me. I hugged her, feeling her strong slender back under my hands.

"I'm so glad thee came," I said. "How was the trip?" I pushed up my spectacles and lifted her case.

"Oh, thee knows the route. I had to change four times — in Bradford, Georgetown, and Salisbury — and it seemed to take all day. But I'm here now and that's all that counts."

"The children are beside themselves with excitement. And Faith has decided to come to the demonstration tomorrow, as well."

"Excellent. She's plenty old enough."

"Frederick doesn't think so. Let's go home and thee can see for thyself." As we walked arm in arm, I filled her in on yesterday's argument and my subsequent extraction of my brother-in-law from the saloon.

She made a tsking sound. "I never did understand what Harriet saw in Frederick. But he's part of the family now. I'll have a word with him about the drink."

"Good luck." While Frederick had seemed

146

penitent, I doubted her word would have much effect. On the other hand she could be persuasive. It might work.

"So, my darling, I read in the *Lawrence Sun American* Amesbury's had another murder, and the story said the body was discovered by a local midwife. I suppose such midwife might have been thee?"

"In fact it was. I haven't had time to look at the papers. I wonder if the *Amesbury and Salisbury Villager* or the Newburyport papers said the same." I wrinkled my nose. I didn't mind investigating murders as an amateur, but I didn't want my clients thinking I was somehow tainted by violence, or that they might be at risk from a criminal pursuing me.

"Thee is infamous, dear. Tell me all about it, and what thee has discovered so far."

Mother supported my sleuthing tendencies. I told her my thoughts on the case and about the various people who might have had an urge to do away with Rowena. I ended with Zula.

"Even a suffragist?" Mother asked. "I hope it wasn't her."

"She claims it wasn't, of course. Just a couple of hours ago she told Bertie and me she'd parted ways with Rowena before they reached Rowena's home that evening. But I sensed she was lying. A misleading statement doesn't mean she killed Rowena, of course."

We passed the ornate four-story Merrimack Opera House. Lights blazed and a round of applause broke out from within, drifting out through the open doors. A police officer strolled up and down in front, wearing the white helmet the police switched to in the winter months.

"It's a big Republican rally," I told her. "Gathering votes for Harrison and the other Republican candidates, I suppose. The Democrats held theirs last Thursday."

"What are the president's chances here in Amesbury, does thee think?" she asked.

"I don't know. I have heard more people say they support Harrison than Cleveland. But we won't truly know until after tomorrow."

We turned up the path leading to the Bailey house. "I forgot to tell thee about meeting Elizabeth Stanton. She gave us a stirring call to action at the suffrage meeting on Seventh Day. And my friends Bertie and Sophie hosted Elizabeth at a gathering last night, where she spoke movingly about equality and personal responsibility. She remembered meeting thee."

"What a woman. I look forward to seeing

her. I mean, if she hasn't already gone back to New York."

"No, she's staying for the demonstration."

"Splendid."

"Mother, I have a concern I want to share with thee." I paused at the base of the steps.

"Yes, darling?"

"The clerk of the Women's Business Meeting eldered me yesterday. She made it quite clear I'll be read out of Meeting when I marry David."

The lights in the house pushed out a welcoming greeting into the darkness, but they also illuminated the concern in Mother's eyes.

"I wondered about your prospects for being expelled." She set her hands on her hips. "I might have to have a word with this clerk, too. It seems to me to be the very opposite of rights for women, of Friends' clear position on equality between the sexes, for this stupid old-fashioned custom to be perpetuated. What on earth could possibly be wrong with thee wedding a fine, upstanding man like David, just because he's not a Quaker?" Her voice rose in indignation. "It's an outrage. Why, Lawrence Meeting dropped reading members out for that reason years ago."

I set down her bag and embraced her

quickly. "Thee has already made me feel better. Things will work out, as way opens."

She snorted. " 'As way opens.' As far as I'm concerned, we need to open it *our* way, not that of those old biddies."

FOURTEEN

Faith, Mother, and I hurried around the corner onto Friend Street toward the polling site at eight the next morning. Mother had been given an exuberant greeting by the children last night, and even Frederick had shed his unpleasant manner for the evening to welcome her.

When we'd left the house this morning, Faith had shown us a small notebook and two sharpened pencils. "I'm going to take notes on the demonstration and write an article for the *Amesbury and Salisbury Villager.*" Her cheeks were rosy with excitement at the prospect of being published again in our weekly newspaper. We'd invited Frederick to walk over to the polls with us, but he'd declined. At least he hadn't raised a fuss again about Faith accompanying us. Perhaps the calming presence of my mother had something to do with it.

Voting was taking place at the Armory, a

recently completed town building, and the polls had already been open for an hour. I wore my bright yellow sash slung diagonally across my torso, and Mother wore one from a previous event, since the color was a symbol of the movement. She'd told me using the color of sunflowers was chosen because the flower always turns its face to the light and follows the course of the sun, as if worshiping the archetype of righteousness. She'd brought a sash for Faith, too. We received a couple of rude comments from men we passed on our way here, one glare from an older matron, and several admiring glances from women in shops we walked by.

Now I gasped. In front of a three-story brick home on the other side of the street from the Armory a hundred women in matching yellow sashes lined the sidewalk. The women stood mostly in silence, watching men file in and out of the polling place. One demonstrator held a placard reading WOMEN BRING ALL VOTERS INTO THE WORLD. LET WOMEN VOTE, and it showed a drawing of a mother cradling a baby. I wished I'd thought to create a poster like hers. Other signs read BALLOTS FOR BOTH OR EQUAL SUFFRAGE, and a number of others simply had VOTES FOR WOMEN printed in large block letters. Many were decorated with a yellow matching our sashes.

Elizabeth Stanton stood in the middle of the line next to a woman holding an American flag on a pole, and I spotted Zula at the far end handing out sashes to newcomers who needed them.

Faith's eyes went big. "Granny Dot, this is stunning. Has thee ever seen a demonstration so big?"

"I have, but today's numbers are quite impressive for a town this size."

The dark-haired teenage girl I'd seen at the suffrage meeting waved to us. She wore her own yellow sash. "Faith, over here."

"She's my friend Jasmine." Faith waved back. "I'm going to stand with her, all right?"

"What a curious appellation." Mother said.

"She told me her mother read a translated Persian poem called 'Rubaiyat.' " Faith smiled. "Jasmine is some fragrant tropical flower the author mentions."

"It's a lovely name. Go be with thy chuckaboo," I murmured, using the term for "pal" Faith herself loved to say. I wasn't surprised Faith had a friend with similar views and a similar courage to express them.

Mother and I joined the group and stood next to Ruby and Frannie. After my eldering on First Day, I wasn't particularly happy to see Ruby, and she gave me a somewhat stern glance as I introduced her and Frannie to Mother. I stood a pace away as they chatted in quiet voices.

Two tall and wide arched windows flanked the arched door in the middle of the red brick building opposite, which was draped with red-white-and-blue bunting. Representatives from both the Democratic and Republican parties handed colored ballots to the men entering, the Republicans wearing tall white hats with black bands, the Democrats the same hat but with a pearl-colored band. A half dozen men held posters mounted on sticks. Several featured the president's and A.G. Thurman's images, and others had the faces of Benjamin Harrison and his running mate, Levi Morton. An older police officer stood with his hands behind his back, his eyes roaming constantly.

A thickset man in a bowler and overcoat approached the polls. When he saw us, he lifted his fist and shook it, an angry look on his face. The flag holder raised her standard and waved it at him in return. It was our flag, too, after all. He turned and stomped up the steps into the building.

A sashed Bertie hurried up, breathless, and squeezed my hand. She held a placard, which read WHAT WILL YOU DO FOR WOMEN'S SUFFRAGE?

"No Sophie?" I asked.

"She had a case to try, more's the pity. And I'm late because I had to open the post office and get my assistant settled."

I looked around for Mother to introduce her to Bertie, but she was striding toward Elizabeth.

"Isn't this a fine turnout?" I asked.

"Splendid. Just splendid." She gazed across the street. "I guess the men haven't wised up and brought their own anti-suffrage signs." She grinned.

It was true. The only signs men held were for the candidates. "And we couldn't have gotten better weather." The newly risen sun shone down on us and the air was mild, as if God himself approved of our actions. My cloak would be too warm later on this fine autumn day.

The women near us quieted and looked to my left. I followed suit to see John Whittier strolling toward us, swinging his silver-tipped cane.

"Good morning, Rose," he said. "May I stand with the ladies for a bit?"

155

"John, thee is most welcome. And we thank thee for thy support."

"It is a worthy cause. Might I borrow thy placard?" he asked Bertie.

She grinned and handed him the sign. "Be my guest, Mr. Whittier."

He held the sign in front of him. He didn't smile, but I caught the characteristic gleam in his eye. This was a man accustomed to acting contrary to society's expectations.

"If I might say so, sir, your poem 'The Lakeside' has always been one of my favorites." Bertie clasped her hands in front of her.

Along the sky, in wavy lines,
O'er isle and reach and bay,
Green-belted with eternal pines,
The mountains stretch away.
Below the maple masses sleep
Where shore with water blends,
While midway on the tranquil deep
The evening light descends.

"I love the mountains," she said, "and those words transport me there." She let out a happy sigh.

John smiled at her. "I wonder why thee burdens thy memory with all that rhyme. It is not well to have too much of it. Better get rid of it as soon as possible. Why, I can't remember any of my scribblings."

I glanced at him. Surely he was teasing.

"I once went to hear a wonderful orator and he wound up his speech with a poetical quotation," John went on. "I clapped with all my might. Someone touched me on the shoulder and said, 'Do you know who wrote that?' I said, 'No, I don't, but it's good.' It seems I had written it myself."

"Truly, sir?" Bertie put her hand to her mouth to keep from laughing too loudly.

I had to do the same.

He nodded gravely. "The fault is, I have written far too much. I wish half of it was in the Red Sea."

I saw Elizabeth peering our way, Mother now standing at her side. Elizabeth waved at John. After he nodded his head at her in return, she resumed chatting with my mother. Faith saw John standing with us and grinned, scribbling madly in her notebook. Across the street Kevin approached the Armory. He stopped, faced our line, and put his hands on his hips, then dropped them and shrugged. When his gaze fell on me, he tipped his hat before turning in to vote.

He didn't have to worry. What we were doing was peaceful and perfectly legal. We weren't disrupting the voting process, but every passing runabout and wagon, every workman and maid who walked by, every man going in to vote — they all saw us. They read our messages and understood this issue wasn't going away.

An hour later, a crow scratched out a call from a lamppost as more and more women joined the line, including Georgia Clarke, the affluent wife of one of the most successful carriage factory owners. Zula walked the line and counted, and reported at our end that one hundred and sixty-two women had turned out. Ruby had made her way to the other side of the group, to my relief.

John had gone in to vote after half an hour of standing in solidarity with us. A woman in an apron stood with the Cleveland-Thurman ballot distributors. She'd set up a small table with a large flat cake on it, and offered squares of the sweet as an enticement to vote the Democratic ticket. John had selected that ballot but declined the cake.

"I wonder how many of those taking Democratic ballots are Mugwumps," Bertie said.

"I hope a lot of them are," I said. "What a funny word for someone who switches parties, though. Where did it come from?"

"It's an Indian word for person of importance," Mother said, who had just returned to stand with us again. "Charles Dana of the *New York Sun* decided to use it in a derogatory way in the last election for the Republicans who voted for Grover Cleveland."

"Why did they leave their party?" I asked. I knew the word *Mugwump* and its general meaning but I'd never learned the details behind it.

"They were mostly well-off New Yorkers who thought the Republican candidate, Blaine, was corrupt," Bertie chimed in. "I say good for them. And for our country." She giggled. "But I love the image I saw in a cartoon, with one of them astraddle a fence. The caption was something like 'He has his mug on one side and his wump on the other.'"

When John came out of the Armory, he spoke with Elizabeth for a moment, then passed by where I stood. "This is a good thing you all are doing," he said, leaning on his cane with both hands. "I'm afraid I am too old and infirm to stand here all day, but I wish you strength."

All in earshot thanked him. Someone farther down began singing the "Daughters of Freedom" anthem we'd sung at the meeting. Every voice was raised, including

159

John's, with several women harmonizing in lower and higher versions of the tune. The beautiful sound resonated as we finished the last repetition of the chorus, *"Sunder the fetters custom hath made! Come from the valley, hill and glade!"* Faith wiped away a tear.

We had come today from the valley, the hill, the glade, from the mansions, the tenements, and modest homes like mine. I was blessed to be playing a small part in this unifying effort. I watched John leave, and turned back toward the polling place. Guy Gilbert, the young police officer I knew, arrived and exchanged a salute with the officer guarding the door. Guy waved to me before he went in to cast his vote.

Bertie nudged me. "Let's make up a new song. How about, *'Mine eyes have seen the glory of the coming of the vote, we have . . .'* What's next?" She sang it to the tune of "Battle Hymn of the Republic."

"I love it. Let's see. *'We have marched and demonstrated, we have held onto our hope.'* "

She chimed in with, " *'With Stanton, Mott, and Anthony we know we will prevail, women's vote is coming soon.'* "

I joined her in, " *'Glory, glory, hallelujah. Glory, glory, hallelujah. Glory, glory, hallelujah. The vote is coming soon.'* "

"Sing it again," Frannie demanded with a big smile, so we did, until our half of the line had picked up the words and sang along.

We'd just finished a few rounds when I saw Zeb walk toward the polls. The Parry factory must have let the men take time off to vote. He stood facing us and began to clap with a big smile on his face. Faith clapped back, too, and set off a chain reaction until all who didn't hold signs were clapping, too. Zeb laughed and called out, "Votes for women!"

Elizabeth answered, "Votes for women!" The call echoed off the buildings as the women took it up until we were chanting in unison.

A man with a card reading PRESS stuck in the brim of his hat walked up to our end of the line, pencil and notebook at the ready. "Tom Kennedy, reporter for the *Boston Evening Transcript,* miss. What can you tell me about what's going on here?" He shouted to be heard over the chant.

"It's a demonstration for equal suffrage." Couldn't the man read?

"Organized by the Amesbury Woman Suffrage Association," Bertie chimed in.

"Anybody famous here?" he asked, his eager eyes reminding me of a puppy's. "I'd

161

heard Mrs. Stanton might be in the area."

Bertie pointed to Elizabeth. "There, in the middle. With the lace collar."

"Thank you."

"And John Greenleaf Whittier stood in solidarity with us this morning for more than half an hour on his way to vote," I added.

"*The* Whittier?" The fellow didn't look like he believed me.

"Of course. He lives just up the street, in case thee didn't know. He and I are both members of the Religious Society of Friends, which is well known for fostering and supporting equality, including between men and women."

He jotted quick notes on his pad. "Your names, please?"

I shook my head. Did I really want my name in a Boston newspaper? Bad enough I was more well-known locally than I'd like. If this was a story about my caring professional midwifery skills, that would be different. But I did want to make sure news of John made it into the article.

"Rose Carroll, midwife." I caught Faith's eye and beckoned her over.

"Got it. You, miss?" he said to Bertie.

"Bertie Winslow, Postmistress of Amesbury. It's a crime women can't vote, and you can quote me." She flashed him her brilliant smile.

"I appreciate that, Miss Winslow."

At Faith's arrival, I said, "Tom, this is my niece, Faith Bailey. She's also a reporter."

His eyebrows went up, but he extended his hand with a rakish grin. "Nice to make your acquaintance, Miss Bailey. You seem a bit young for the business, but I guess you have to start sometime."

Faith blushed but shook his hand. "Thee is correct. Our local paper has printed my stories before. I hope to make journalism my career."

"I wish you all the best in it, then. I'll be looking for your byline." He jotted down Faith's name in his book.

"I thank thee," Faith said, standing a little taller.

The reporter bade us farewell and strolled in Elizabeth's direction. Faith had told me once a cardinal rule of journalism was, Names make news. This reporter must have had the same lesson. Before he reached Elizabeth, though, the bowler-topped man who'd shaken his fist earlier emerged from the Armory. Had it taken him an hour to vote? I hadn't seen him leave. Maybe he'd been conversing inside.

"Never!" he shouted, his face an alarming

shade of red. He stomped toward Elizabeth. Four other men walked up and flanked him. "You'll never get the vote."

"Never," his companions taunted, sounding like a rude Greek chorus.

The reporter stopped and watched. He began scribbling furiously. So did Faith.

"You ladies should go home to your husbands and your babies. This is shameful and disgusting," one yelled, glowering.

"Who's that tabby in the middle?" another man in the group taunted, using the insulting term for an old lady. "Stirring up trouble."

Our chanting faded away. Zeb stood watching. The reporter observed with rapt attention. A woman in a house next to the Armory shook a rug out of a second-story window with a whacking noise, then set her forearms on the windowsill to see what was happening. A carriage driver pulled his horse to a halt.

"You aren't capable of making rational decisions," one of the men said in a growl. "Our democracy would crumble if you could cast votes."

"Yeah," another chimed in. "Next thing you know we'll be taking care of the babies and you'll be out at the saloon." He shook his head in disgust.

Bowler man nodded. "Women's suffrage will only lead to men suffering. And worse," he said in a dire tone, mouth set, nostrils flaring.

Elizabeth linked arms with Mother on her right and the woman on her left. "We *will* be enfranchised," she called in a clear, unwavering voice. "You cannot stop us. Whether we get the vote next year or in thirty years, it will happen. Women are your mental equals, whether you like it or not, and we have every much a right as you do to decide who our lawmakers will be." She stood as tall as her short stout figure was able.

The arm linking spread down both sides of the line until it reached us.

"Not if we have anything to do with it," Bowler man spat out, and then spat on the ground.

"This could get ugly," Bertie whispered.

The line of men, which looked ridiculously short compared to ours, took a couple of menacing steps forward. The one who had spoken of democracy clenched his fists. To a one, these bullies looked both mean and mad.

I checked on Faith and Jasmine, who stood frowning, their arms tightly linked. What Jasmine had worried about earlier seemed to be coming true. Across the street, the officer on duty took several steps toward the men. I wished he was moving faster.

Bowler man reached into his overcoat pocket and pulled out a gun. He pointed it at Elizabeth.

"Look out!" I shouted to her.

In a blur of movement and a burst of speed, Zeb rushed the attacker. He took him down in a flying tackle. With a sharp crack, the gun discharged and Elizabeth fell backwards.

FIFTEEN

"Zeb!" Faith cried out.

I gasped, as did those around me. Had Elizabeth survived the attack?

Zeb, at least, was fine. He wrested the gun out of the man's hand as he lay face down. Zeb put his knee on the older man's back, but the fellow had a lot of bulk to him and he struggled mightily. Where had that blasted police officer gone?

"Come on," Bertie said. We ran to Zeb, with Faith following. Zula must have had the same idea because she arrived at the same time. Bertie stomped on one of the attacker's hands and he cried out. She planted her foot on his wrist. I stepped forward onto his calf, kneeling and leaning my forearms onto my knee.

Zula knelt on the man's other arm, which was good, because Bertie was such a peanut I doubted her weight was much of a deterrent. Frannie ran up and anchored the fellow's other leg. Faith looked unsure as to what to do. She watched, her brow knit, with her arms by her sides, pencil and paper grasped in one hand.

"Men, help me here," the attacker called out, his voice half muffled by the cheek resting on the cobblestones.

"You let go there, miss." One of the would-be assassin's companions reached for my arm.

Guy Gilbert rushed up. "Hands off the lady, mister," he ordered. "You," he addressed the four men. "Sit down on the ground over there. Right now." He brandished a billy club as his fellow officer finally strolled up. "Guard them, officer."

The bullies frowned and muttered but did as he asked. "We didn't do nothing," one snarled.

"I saw the whole thing. It sure looked like you were about to," Guy replied. "Ladies, you can stand down now." He tried and failed to keep a grin off his face at the sight of his four new lady assistants.

Bertie looked relieved. I knew the man could have grabbed her ankle and flipped her onto the ground if he'd had better leverage. A crowd had gathered out of nowhere.

But what had happened to Elizabeth? Was she hurt, or even alive? I glanced over, but a cluster of women bent over where she'd stood and I couldn't see our leader. My heart was a lead weight pounding against my ribs. A call hadn't gone out for help, medical or otherwise. I prayed the man's shot had gone wild. Zula and Bertie had headed for Elizabeth. Before they got there, the group parted and Elizabeth herself emerged, supported by Mother on one side and Ruby on the other. A roar of clapping and women's cheers arose.

"Thank you, Mr. Weed. I'll take it from here." Guy pulled out a set of handcuffs and, after Zeb stood, clicked them onto the man's hands behind his back where he lay.

Zeb stood and dusted off his hands. He winced at skin scraped raw along the side of his right hand.

"Officer, this man's name is Leroy Dunnsmore," he said.

The man Zeb had talked about at dinner on First Day. His virulent views explained his actions today. But had he also killed Rowena? I saw the reporter jot down the name.

"He works with me at the Parry Carriage Factory," Zeb went on. "He's well known for being anti-suffrage."

"I expect he's going to be anti-jail soon enough, because the clink is where he's going." Guy hoisted Leroy to his feet and laid his hand on his shoulder. "Leroy Dunnsmore, you are under arrest for attempted assassination of a public figure."

Several other police officers jogged over. At Guy's direction, one hustled Leroy away, and two others ordered his cohort to stand and come with them. The election-duty officer ambled back to his post. A lot of help he was.

"And no funny business, either," Guy warned the ruffians.

"Guy," I beckoned. "Make sure Kevin knows about Leroy Dunnsmore."

"I will, Miss Rose."

Faith took Zeb's left hand.

"Ladies," Elizabeth called out. "That misguided man missed me, thanks to this courageous young fellow." She held out her hand to Zeb, who stepped forward and shook it. "He deserves all our thanks."

Whoops and cheers went up, and Zeb blushed.

When the noise subsided, Elizabeth went on, her voice strong. "However, I stepped back in alarm when I saw the gun, and I turned my ankle badly. I'm not a young woman and must retire to rest it. Thank you, every one of you women, for braving these brutes and for supporting our cause.

You must continue your presence here throughout the day if you are able." She raised her right fist. "Votes for women!"

We all answered her with "Votes for women!" as Mother and Ruby helped her hobble away.

Georgia Clarke approached them. "My driver and carriage are waiting just around the corner. Please come with me."

Elizabeth thanked her. Mother caught my eye.

"I'll return soon."

I nodded my agreement. The crowd of bystanders dissipated, back to work or play or voting or whatever they'd been doing before the men accosted us.

"I had no idea today would in fact turn into such a dangerous scene," I said to Bertie as we returned to our place in the line.

"Told you it was going to get ugly." She tucked a few escaped curls back under her hat.

"I guess you did," I said. "What a blessing Elizabeth was not seriously hurt."

"I wonder if she should be going out in public like this if she's at risk of being killed," Bertie said, picking up her placard where she'd dropped it. "It would be awful to lose her."

"She's brave. I imagine she's been threatened plenty of times before. Zeb had said on First Day this Leroy Dunnsmore was always speaking negatively at work about women and the vote. I've already told Kevin about him in connection with Rowena's death."

"But if he owns a gun, why wasn't Rowena shot, too?" she asked.

"Thee poses a good question. That was a very foolish thing he did today, and I think he wanted to be noticed. But one employs a quiet weapon if one wishes to murder someone without being noticed."

"Like whacking them on the head," she muttered.

"Like whacking them on the head."

Sixteen

By half past eleven my feet started to ache from standing. Faith and Jasmine had left to go to work, Faith having asked me to take note if anything else newsworthy happened. Several of the other women had trickled away, too. We'd passed the last couple of hours talking among ourselves, singing, and sometimes answering questions from passersby. Mother had returned from making sure Elizabeth had her ankle elevated with cold compresses on it, and stood with Bertie, me, and Frannie.

Two well-dressed matrons walked by. One lifted her head and didn't make eye contact with any of us, while the other glared at Bertie's placard and pursed her lips in disdain. Bertie just smiled at her. They trailed a cloud of lavender scent after them, which jiggled loose a memory of the faint scent I'd detected near Rowena's body.

Bertie snorted. "That perfume was rather

overapplied, I'd say."

Frannie gave a low, sad laugh. "Rowena would have been sneezing her head off at the smell. She had the worse reaction to scents."

"Many people do." So the scent I'd smelled wouldn't have been Rowena's own. Interesting. I gazed at my mother's dress. "Mother, I just noticed how short thy skirts are." In fact, I could see the top of her lace-up shoes. It was the same hemline Rowena had sported.

"It's the new thing," she said, sticking out a foot and twirling her ankle. "They say the longer skirts sweep tuberculosis germs into houses. So I hemmed mine up a few inches."

"It makes sense, I suppose," I said. "I should probably do the same. The last thing I want to do is introduce germs into the birthing chambers I visit."

A tall, thin man with stooped shoulders and a long beard approached the polling place across the way. He swept the line of us with his gaze but stopped at Zula and stared. She stared back, chin in the air, lips compressed into a thin line. He shook his head slowly and trudged into the polling place like he was walking in thick mud.

I made my way down to Zula. "Who was staring at thee just now?" I asked.

"Oscar Felch." Her nostrils flared.

"So he's back."

She cocked her head. "Where had he been? Rowena had said he would be traveling, but not the location."

"At a medical convention in New York City." David had said the convention ended yesterday. Such a schedule would give the attendees a day to travel home and cast their votes today.

"How do you know where he was?" She frowned, looking confused.

"My beau is a doctor. He asked around. The police detective wanted to know why Rowena's husband wasn't home."

"You're kind of cozy with the police, aren't you? Why didn't they find Oscar themselves?"

I shrugged. "I had a connection with several other murders in town earlier this year. As I am a midwife, the detective has grown to appreciate I can go places and hear things he can't." I saw Oscar emerge from the building. "Excuse me," I said to her. "I need to pay my respects to him."

She snorted but didn't say anything.

I walked briskly across the street. "Pardon me, sir. I believe thee is Oscar Felch?"

"I am."

"My name is Rose Carroll. I wanted to

express my sympathies on the death of thy wife."

His eyes, which already carried a haunted look, looked at me with deep sorrow. "Miss Carroll. You're the lady who found her, my dear Mrs. Felch."

"Yes, I did. I'm so sorry."

"Do you think she suffered?" His voice was gravelly.

The same question Zula had asked. "I can't say, but it's possible she passed out immediately after being attacked. Has thee been in contact with Kevin Donovan, the police detective on the case?"

His expression turned stony. "I certainly have. The man was most unpleasant to me. He implied I might have contracted a killer to do away with my wife. My own sweet wife! I never would. I adored her, and was heartbroken at her . . ." His voice trailed off.

"Her plans to leave thee."

"Yes, how did you know?" His gaze drifted over to Zula, whose back was to us now. "Oh. That despicable unnatural woman told you."

I nodded.

"She put all kinds of rotten ideas into Mrs. Felch's pretty head. Like she didn't have to have children if she didn't want

176

them. What lady doesn't want to bear her husband's babies?" He shook his head in disbelief.

I suspected Rowena had had her own ideas on the matter, but I kept my thoughts to myself. And his feelings were perfectly understandable. His expectations for a happy personal life had been dashed.

"It's all I ever wanted beyond my profession, to have a wife and a family. And now I won't have either, at least not with Rowena." He tipped his hat. "Good day, miss. Now I've done my civic duty, I have affairs to attend to. Which include planning a funeral."

Frannie had left the demonstration about the same time as Faith. Now, as the clock on the Armory read noon and my stomach grumbled accordingly, she returned pulling a wheeled cart. She went down the line handing out individual meat pies and ladling lemonade from a large pot into cups. I'd brought my own telescoping cup, which I opened and shared with Bertie and my mother when our turn came.

"Thee is an angel, Frannie." I said. "Did thee just bake these pies?"

"No, my daughter and I made them yesterday. I'm glad I baked extras. I suspected we'd get a big crowd today."

"I'm glad, too," Bertie mumbled around a mouthful of the savory pastry.

"We all thank thee," Mother said.

I spotted Hilarius Bauer sauntering around the corner. I swallowed my last bite and headed in his direction. "Hilarius," I called.

He looked around and stopped. "How's that brother-in-law of yours, miss? I didn't see him at the tavern last evening."

Good. Of course, Frederick had been home with all of us, greeting Mother. "He's well, as far as I know. I wanted to thank thee again for thy assistance in getting him home. I couldn't have done it alone."

"You're welcome, miss. I like to help people out."

"Is thee here to vote?"

"Correct. It's our obligation and our privilege as citizens." He glanced at the still-long line of women. "I don't see no rhyme nor reason why you ladies can't vote, too. I hope they change the law one of these days so you all can cast a ballot."

"Thank thee. We hope so, too. I appreciate thy support." I wanted to ask him more about the night of Rowena's murder, but I couldn't figure out a plausible way to approach it, so I kept my silence.

"Off I go, then." He lifted his cap at me,

accepted an orange ballot at the door, and disappeared inside.

Mother tucked her arm through mine when I returned to our spot. "So Rosie, dear, tell me all about what's new with David. I so enjoyed meeting him in the summer, as did thy father."

"What's there to tell? He loves me and I love him. He's kind and funny and handsome." I smiled. "And he makes me laugh."

"And does thee like his parents, as well?"

I wrinkled my nose. "I quite like his father, Herbert. But Clarinda doesn't seem to care much for me. She wanted him to marry a distant cousin, a society girl. She doesn't approve of him consorting with me — not only a Quaker but also a happily employed woman."

"So thee has obstacles coming from all sides." She raised her eyebrows. "And how does he propose to persuade this Clarinda thee is his choice?"

"I'm not sure. I just hope he can."

"Will thee continue with thy midwifery business after thee and he are wed?"

"I'd like to. And he's said he supports my doing so. We both want to have a family, too, so I suppose I'll take time away from midwifery for a few years. I'm starting to train Annie Beaumont as an assistant. She's a friend of Faith's and wants to be a mid-wife, too."

"A wise idea." She frowned. "I think perhaps I should pay a call on Clarinda Dodge. Maybe I can find common ground with her as a mother and convince her you are a good match for her boy."

"I don't know, Mother. She's not easy to become close to. Or at least hasn't been for me."

"But I'm of a similar age as she. And we've both raised children. Let me try."

"I think it sounds like a good idea," offered Bertie, who had been listening. "It can't hurt, right?"

"I suppose not." I had a thought that such a visit might hurt my chances, but Mother was a cheerful and persuasive sort. If anyone could worm her way into Clarinda's good graces, it would be Dorothy Henderson Carroll. "I have another obstacle closer to home." I told Bertie about being eldered. "It's not going to be easy, being expelled."

Mother gazed at me. "I'll give this problem some thought, too."

A black runabout with gold striping pulled up across the street. A man handed the reins to his companion, jumped down, and strode to the ballot distributors, selecting a red one. I peered at the vehicle. A woman in an advanced stage of pregnancy sat looking over as us. I waved at Lyda Osgood and crossed the street.

"Good afternoon, Lyda. Was that thy husband gone in to vote?" I hadn't met him yet.

"Yes, that was Mr. Osgood. I'd heard of this ladies' demonstration and I wanted to see for myself." She sniffed.

"We have many supporters." I gestured to the line behind me.

"I don't think it's right. Elbridge and I share the same views, and he votes. It's all a lady needs."

I hadn't encountered many women with her opinion, but she was clearly one. "Many of us feel differently. We'd like to change the system as it stands, and soon. Think about it." I smiled to cushion my words. "If thee could vote and didn't care to, thee wouldn't have to. But those who want to exercise their right to vote would be able to do so."

"I doubt ladies' suffrage is going to come about any time soon." She rubbed her belly.

"How is thee feeling today?"

"My back aches a little, but it's not too bad."

"Thy labor could start at any time, now thee is in the final month. Be sure to send

181

for me as soon as the pains begin. The length of a woman's labor with second and subsequent babies often gets shorter and shorter."

"I will. There's Mr. Osgood now. Let me introduce you," she said. "Elbridge, this is Rose Carroll, my midwife. Rose, Mr. Osgood."

I shook his hand. "I'm pleased to meet thee, Elbridge."

He tucked his chin in surprise and Lyda laughed.

"Quakers always use Christian names, Mr. Osgood," she said. "You'll get used to it."

He tipped his bowler. "Good to meet you, too, Miss Carroll." He had a wide brow with a high receding hairline, and his trim red beard was sprinkled with gray.

"Please call me Rose." Although, no matter how many times I'd said those words to Kevin and Guy, they still insisted on compromising by addressing me as Miss Rose.

"I shall address you as Miss Carroll as is only right and proper." He glanced at my sash. "So you're one of those woman suffragettes, are you?"

"As thee can see. It's a worthy cause and I believe in it."

"I told her we didn't support such nonsense," Lyda added.

He shot her a quick glance both tender and grateful.

"Thy wife told me of the loss of thy position in the law firm," I said in what I hoped was a sympathetic tone. "I hope a new opportunity presents itself soon."

"Mrs. Osgood!" His voice was sharp. "What are you doing airing our dirty linen to a stranger?"

"She's not a stranger. She's my midwife." Lyda lifted her chin. "I've been seeing her for months. And it's public knowledge, after all. Don't be so fussy."

I watched their interaction. Lyda seemed to be a faithful and obedient wife to her husband in one moment and to assert herself in the next. Even though she didn't care to support the choice of other women to vote their opinions, I was pleased to see she wasn't completely under Elbridge's thumb.

He cleared his throat. "In fact, it's true. I was asked to leave the firm. But it was one of these types who took my job." He gestured to the line of women as he spoke, uttering the word *types* as if it was an obscenity.

"Rowena Felch," I said softly.

"Yes." He set his fists on his hips, glowering. "I'm glad she's dead. I wish I'd thought to kill her myself."

"Mr. Osgood, don't say such a thing!" Lyda's mouth pulled down in horror.

"Well, I do." He climbed into the runabout, grabbing the reins from Lyda's hands.

"I guess we're off." Lyda hesitantly said good-bye. Elbridge didn't utter a word nor even look at me.

Uh-oh. I hoped the birth would go smoothly. It was always best if I was on good terms with the new father, and this exchange had not been an auspicious one.

A maid in a crisp uniform hurried up to me. "Miss Rose Carroll?" she asked.

"Yes?"

She gave a brief curtsy. "Mrs. Hersey says to tell you she's laboring and could you please come right away?"

I knit my brows, thinking of our visit yesterday. True, the opening to her womb had been completely effaced, and I'd told her the birth could happen at any time. I hadn't expected it today, though.

"Please, miss?" The maid clasped her hands in front of her. "She said she thinks the babe is coming right along. We have the family's carriage waiting just there." She gestured to the side street.

I'd better go with all due dispatch, since

184

Emily's last baby had arrived in the space of an hour. "I'm just coming. Give me one minute to tell my mother where I'm bound." Of course I had to leave the demonstration. In my life, laboring mothers always took priority.

SEVENTEEN

I'd rejoined the demonstrators by half past four. Emily's baby had indeed been well on its way when I arrived, after a brief stop at my house to pick up my birthing satchel. Emily's older sister was in attendance, too. She seemed to provide just the right amount of care to the laboring mother without the nervous hovering I sometimes saw from kin. I'd had only enough time to wash my hands and lay out my kit when Emily began to groan. Four pushes later and I held a healthy baby boy in my hands, the family's first son. Such was often — but not always — the case with second and subsequent babies. As the experienced Emily had had no issues with feeding her son, nor had he taking the breast, I'd cleaned up, and left, telling her I'd be back in two days' time to see how they were doing. I gratefully accepted a ride retracing my steps to the demonstration. Would that all births were so easy and happy.

A steady stream of men entered and left the Armory. Frederick had shown up, voted, and left with only a brief hello for us. Two young fellows in tweed caps strolled in front of the Armory, one taller and heavier, the other shorter and slight. The latter carried a silver flask, and they both sported flushed faces. They crossed the street toward the other end of our line and walked along its length, raking each woman up and down with their gaze. The officer guarding the polling place watched the men but didn't intervene, just as he hadn't earlier with Dunnsmore. I thought I might have a word with Kevin about him if I got the chance.

When the men approached where I stood, I could hear rude commentary.

"Here's a pretty one," the taller of the two said as he passed me, fumes of alcohol tainting the air.

"Oh, yes. Hey, missy, you free tonight?" the other asked, then sniggered.

I just watched them go. Engaging with such an insult could only make things worse, and I was glad Faith and Jasmine weren't there. Being pretty and young, they surely would have been subjected to worse words and would be less well-equipped to handle them. Bertie folded her arms and stepped in front of the scoundrels.

"Not so fast, boys," she said. "You apologize to Miss Carroll and do it now. Did your mother teach you to be rude to ladies in public?"

The one with the flask unscrewed it and took a drag. "You're all putting yourselves on display like ladies of the night. We're just treating you like we do them."

I saw Kevin coming up behind them and I smiled.

"I said apologize, and I meant it," Bertie demanded.

Kevin grabbed the collar of each young man. "These scoundrels giving you trouble, ladies?"

"Hey," the shorter one said, trying to twist away.

"They certainly are, Detective," Bertie said.

"Detective?" the taller one screeched.

"You bet," Kevin said.

"They've said something rude to every one of us, including Rose, and they're well liquored, too."

"You're both going to be sobering up in jail tonight." Kevin blew his whistle and the officer across the street ran over. "Take these idiots out of here, will you?"

"Yes, sir." He marched the two suddenly

subdued rascals away.

"Thank thee, Kevin," I said.

"Anybody else been bothering you ladies?"

"Not since this morning," I said. "You heard about the attack, I trust?"

"The stupid act of one Leroy Dunnsmore? Indeed I did. I've already had a little conversation with him in his jail cell."

I introduced Kevin to my mother.

"You raised one smart and brave daughter," he told her.

"I thank thee," she replied. "It's really of her own doing, though." She regarded me with pride etched into her face.

Kevin glanced at Bertie and back at Mother. "Will you excuse us for a moment?" He took my elbow and we walked around the corner onto Pond Street where it was quiet. I gladly perched on a stone wall in the shade of a tall maple.

"How are thy wife and son, Kevin?"

"Both blessedly on the mend. Thank you for asking. But what I wanted to tell you is Dunnsmore claims he had nothing to do with Mrs. Felch's death, that he didn't even know her." Kevin removed his hat and rubbed his hair. "Regardless, he's still in big trouble from the attempted shooting."

"Thee could check his statement with Zebulon Weed. Leroy might have spoken of

189

Rowena at work."

"Good idea. That Weed boy did a brave thing this morning. I'll see to it he gets a glowing commendation from the department."

"Thee will run a good risk of embarrassing him, but I think giving Zeb recognition is an excellent idea."

"Dunnsmore also claims he was with his wife all night Saturday, but as we know, marital attestation isn't a particularly reliable alibi," Kevin said. "Husbands and wives will go to great lengths to keep each other out of trouble."

"If a gun is his weapon of choice, though, wouldn't he have shot Rowena, too?" I asked.

"Hard to know."

"I think I told thee about Elbridge Osgood. I had a little conversation with him and his wife, Lyda, today when he came to vote. Apparently neither of them believes a woman should have the same right. He also seemed quite bitter about Rowena taking his job."

"Thank you. He's on my list to talk to."

"In fact, he said he wished he'd killed her himself."

Kevin's eyes widened. "You don't say."

"I do. I heard him with my own ears. His

wife scolded him for saying it, but the words were already out."

He made a tsking sound and shook his head. "Some men are just idiots."

Did he mean stupid but not homicidal? I couldn't tell. "Bertie told me Sophie Ribeiro said Elbridge isn't regarded as particularly smart."

"Who's this Ribeiro lady?" Kevin frowned.

"She's Bertie's, um, friend, and she's a lawyer, too. She and Bertie live together. The name is Portuguese."

"Unusual."

"Anyway, I wanted to tell thee I stopped into the law firm of Bixby & Batchelder yesterday. It turns out they let Elbridge go. Lyda had told me it was because Rowena was promoted. But the secretary at the firm said it was because he wasn't a very good lawyer, and that at the time he was furious at their action."

"You've been busy, Miss Rose."

"I'm just trying to help. I also spoke with Oscar Felch this morning when he came to vote. He seems quite bereft at Rowena's death but had no understanding of her desire not to become a mother. He seemed to blame Zula entirely for Rowena's plans to leave him."

"I had a rather unproductive conversation

191

with him, myself."

"He told me he felt you suspect him." I watched a work horse plod by hauling an open wagon piled high with coal.

"Well, I have to, don't I? Here's my thinking: He's angry she's spoiled his plans for a family, he doesn't want to continue to support her if she's off lawyering, and he wants to find a new young wife who doesn't have so many independent thoughts. It makes sense to me."

"I suppose, although he has cause to feel abandoned and sad at the loss of his dream. Most spurned men do not become killers, do they?"

"Of course not."

"But if you're correct, then you'd have to find the person he hired to do the deed." Like Hilarius, maybe. I didn't voice my thought. I liked the man and didn't want him to be a killer, but I did wonder if there was underlying history of his I wasn't aware of. I expected being a hired killer might bring in a tidy sum of money that he was desperate for. David had said Hilarius supported an ill mother as well as his own family. Perhaps her medicines were quite dear. I'd ask David. He would know. How awful if he killed a woman to save a woman, though. "Is there any other news on the case?"

"I am exceedingly sorry to say there is not. My chief is even sorrier, I'll tell you." He let out a deep sigh. "Solving a case requires a detective be three things. Can you think what they might be?"

"Thee must be persistent, I'd say."

"Yes, dogged is one. Imaginative is another, exploring ideas which on the face of them might not appear possible."

I nodded. "And lucky must be the third?"

"Precisely. Very good, Miss Rose. Sometimes luck is kind enough to lend us her fair hand. But we must have all three to be successful. Being dogged and lucky without creativity doesn't bring the answers, neither does luck plus imagination without being stubborn enough to follow up leads."

"Nor would being dogged and creative without serendipity." It hadn't been particularly creative to round up the petty thieves in town earlier, though. Kevin didn't always practice what he preached. I kept that thought to myself. "And speaking of luck, I did happen to see Zula's handwriting yesterday. I thought it bore a similarity to the scribing on the note Rowena held."

"Oh?" His fair eyebrows went up.

"Yes, it also featured upright kinds of letters. But they leaned almost backward. Have you asked her for a sample of her writing?"

"Not yet, but I will. Good sleuthing, Miss Rose."

From around the corner came the strains of the women singing our invented "Battle Hymn of the Vote." I hummed along.

Kevin rolled his eyes but smiled. "I rather like your ditty."

"Bertie and I made it up this morning."

"The more I consider it, the more I think you ladies are right. You should be as equal citizens with men. And I should thank you all for maintaining such a peaceful demonstration today. Maybe if we had more ladies in our government, we'd have less war, and fewer quarrels and disturbances people like me have to handle."

"I'm glad thee has seen our side of the argument." That would be the day, when women could not only vote but also run for office. And win. Maybe we'd even have a female president one day.

EIGHTEEN

Tired and with sore feet, but satisfied with having made a public statement about suffrage, the women started to drift away home when the polls closed at five o'clock. A half dozen of us gathered in a small knot to review the day. Georgia had returned from taking Elizabeth to her rooms earlier and reported she was resting comfortably. The sun vanished beyond the tall brick edifice of Saint Joseph's Church around the corner as we talked, all of us looking a bit worse for the wear.

"We had a number of women interested in joining the Association," Zula said. Hair which had escaped its pins curled around her forehead, which bore a smudge of ink from one of the placards.

"New blood," Frannie replied with a grin, her brown eyes still bright.

"Except for the shooting and the rude young men, I thought most of the men were remarkably well behaved," I said.

"We got our share of glares and fists, but they kept it across the street," Bertie added.

"But we also had men who approved of our action, like Zeb this morning." I took off my glasses and rubbed my eyes.

"This was wonderful, but shall we be off?" Mother asked. "I'm eager to see my grandchildren." She looked wearier than the rest of us. She was older by a decade than Frannie, who was nearing fifty.

"May I entice you all to my flat for a bite of Election Cake and a cup of tea, or something stronger?" Zula asked. "My cook insisted on preparing the sweet and it's far too large for me to consume alone. She said her mother used to be hired by the government to make an enormous cake for all the voters, and she simply can't abandon the custom."

"And now others use the cake as a bribe for votes," Frannie said. "Although I noticed more than one of the gentlemen accepted a slice this morning from the Cleveland camp and then chose a Harrison ballot."

"Zula, doesn't thee want to visit thy sister and new nephew?" I asked. I'd told her about the birth after I returned to the polling place.

She batted away the suggestion. "They're

in good hands. I'll go tomorrow."

Bertie said, "I'm game for cake."

"I think I'll go back to the house, Rosie, if thee doesn't mind." My mother cocked her head at me. "I want to see the children and keep an eye on someone else, if thee understands me."

I nodded. Of course she wanted to make sure Frederick didn't head straight for the tavern as soon as she arrived home. "Does thee care if I go to Zula's?" I still wanted to learn more about Zula, about her motivations.

"Of course not. I'll see thee later on." Mother had always encouraged my independence.

"Can thee find the way home?" I asked.

Mother laughed. "I was visiting Harriet in Amesbury before thee moved here, darling. Of course I know the way." She said goodbye to the others and walked off.

"Cake and a drink sounds like fun," Frannie said. "I told Mr. Eisenman not to expect me until late."

"I need to decline," Georgia said. "My nursling will be hungry."

I'd delivered her most recent baby in the summer. I'd noticed she'd left the line several times today to go home and feed her daughter. She was fortunate enough to have a prosperous husband who provided a driver and carriage to transport her. Her husband had been the first to rebuild his carriage factory after the disastrous fire last spring, and he was a loving and forward-looking man who clearly supported his wife in her interest in the suffrage movement.

"Then we're off." Zula began gathering up the various placards and posters.

"I can take those home in the carriage," Georgia offered.

We accepted with relief so we didn't have to carry them.

Across the way, groups of men lingered outside the polling place. I hadn't really followed previous elections, as I'd been too busy with my apprenticeship. How soon would they have the results for Amesbury? A couple of men staggered by, brandishing large Harrison-Morton posters on wooden sticks and looking like they'd spent the afternoon enjoying liquid refreshment.

I spied Hilarius in a clutch of men holding Cleveland-Thurman signs. Then I spotted Kevin and Guy striding toward the group. *Uh-oh.* Hilarius saw them, too. He turned away from the group and hurried in the other direction, toward us women.

Kevin blew his whistle. "Halt, Hilarius Bauer," he shouted.

Guy broke into a run, but he didn't need to. Hilarius stopped. He was close enough I could see the sweat again on his forehead and his tense, fearful expression. Guy took his arm as Kevin arrived.

Kevin laid his hand on Hilarius's shoulder, a move I'd learned was required by the police at the time of an arrest. "Hilarius Bauer, you are under arrest for the murder of Mrs. Rowena Felch."

Oh, no. I prayed he was wrong, that Hilarius was not the killer.

Hilarius shook his head mutely. He glanced over at me. "I didn't do it, Miss Carroll. I swear I didn't do it."

"A neighbor of the Felches has come forward placing you in front of their house that very evening," Kevin said.

"But I didn't *kill* the lady," Hilarius protested. "I . . ." His voice trailed off and he clamped his mouth shut.

Guy clicked the cuffs onto his hands behind his back and marched him away. Kevin started to follow, but I hurried after him and tugged on his sleeve.

"Has thee any evidence?" I asked in a low voice. "Has thee found the murder weapon, or blood on Hilarius's clothing?"

"No, but we will." He lifted his chin.

I stared at him. "Kevin, thee has arrested

199

the wrong man for a crime before." I gazed over my spectacles. "Isn't it too early to bring in Hilarius with only hearsay as proof?"

He sighed. "Miss Rose, you have to let me do my job as I see fit — and my chief is seeing fit to demote me if I don't solve the case and soon. Mr. Felch is a prominent doctor in town and he's putting a lot of pressure on the boss. The chief as good as told me to arrest Bauer."

I lifted a shoulder and let it drop. "I'm only concerned for thy reputation." And Hilarius's, too. The poor man. Unless he was a liar, in which case justice had been done.

We sat around a low table thirty minutes later in Zula's apartment. We'd each taken a turn in the lavatory to freshen up. I'd enjoyed the running water from the shiny brass tap, the flushing toilet, and the look of the marble porcelain fixtures and gleaming marble floor. Zula's family certainly had money.

Zula had driven her Bailey runabout home, saying she needed to alert her maid to prepare things. The rest of us walked, but it wasn't far. I found it more refreshing to walk briskly, even on tired feet, than to stand in one place for hours on end. As we walked, I kept thinking of Hilarius. He'd been about to say something and then had stopped himself. Could Kevin get it out of him? Maybe, if he was more interested in the truth than in making an arrest because of pressure from his superior officer.

Now I gratefully accepted a cup of tea, even though all the others chose sherry. Zula used her left hand to cut slices of the large cake. I took a bite of the golden brown cake, the top of which was studded with raisins and currants. I savored the spices: cinnamon, allspice, and perhaps coriander, too. The taste was rich and the texture moist. The maid had turned on all the lights before we'd arrived and the room glowed. It must be nice to have sufficient funds to live in this kind of comfort, and with a maid and a cook, too, I thought idly. I didn't aspire to such a life myself, though.

"Careful, Miss Carroll, since you don't imbibe," Zula said. "Cook puts a quart of brandy in the cake." She smiled at me.

Bertie threw back her head and chortled.

I sniffed the cake. "I am going to assume the alcohol cooks off and the brandy merely adds to the richness."

"And what if it doesn't?" Bertie asked. "A touch of spirits will do you good. We won't tell those Quaker elders of yours."

I didn't want to spoil the evening by thinking about any elders, particularly not Quaker ones. "Well, I'm too hungry not to eat it." I smiled back. "And, Zula, please call me Rose. I don't support the use of titles."

"Very well, Rose." Zula seemed relaxed, perhaps from fatigue. Or maybe it was from seeing Rowena's possible killer behind bars.

Bertie tasted her own piece. "Mmm, delicious. Must be nice to have a cook. Does she make delicacies like this every day?"

"No, she and the maid both go home from Saturday afternoon to Monday morning. Everyone needs time away from work, and I dine with my parents on the Sabbath."

Bertie had been up to something with her question. Now we knew Zula was alone Saturday night.

"Was thee glad to see the detective make an arrest in Rowena's murder?" I asked her.

"Right in front of our eyes, too," Bertie said.

Zula sat up straight, her face sobering. "Of course I'm glad. I don't believe a word that man said about not killing Rowena. Of course he did. Now we can all walk peacefully again."

I wondered about that. Maybe we could, or maybe not.

"Who do you think won the election?" Frannie asked the group. "I would have voted for Mr. Harrison if I'd been able to."

"Cleveland would have gotten my vote," I said.

"But the polls won't close in the western states until a few hours from now," Bertie chimed in. "California and Oregon are at the other end of the continent. We'll be lucky to hear the winner in tomorrow's papers."

"I suppose," I said. The railroads had instituted four time zones in the nation a few years ago, which had greatly improved the on-time running of the trains. I'd read every little town all the way to the west had previously kept a different clock, using high noon as their standard. But high noon was not the same here as it was in Ohio, which differed from the time in Texas, which was yet again not the same as California's.

"I'll bet the telegraph wires are humming tonight." Frannie looked excited at the prospect.

We ate and sipped and chatted for some minutes. I set down my cup and saucer. "Zula, how did thee become interested in women's suffrage?"

She considered for a moment. "I was always a tomboy. I hated turning thirteen and having to let down my skirts and put up my hair. And it just didn't seem fair men could vote and we couldn't. I met Rowena at my first Association meeting . . ." Her voice trailed off as her eyes turned misty.

"Poor Rowena," Frannie said. "She was an inspiration to every one of us."

"Is there any idea about making a memorial to her?" I asked. I'd forgotten to raise the issue during the demonstration earlier. "I think the law firm she worked for would like to contribute."

Zula wrinkled her nose. "How would you know such a thing?"

I thought fast. "I had occasion to stop in there yesterday on another matter, and the woman at the front desk spoke of Rowena."

Zula looked like she didn't quite believe me, but she shook it off. "We're talking about how to remember her, yes."

"Tell me more about Rowena," I said. "I didn't know her at all, having met her only once before the meeting." I looked from Zula to Frannie and back.

"She was a brilliant lawyer," Zula said. "She graduated from Union College of Law in Chicago, and she had aspirations to be the Attorney General of the Commonwealth."

"Could she hold the attorney general's office?" Bertie asked, scrunching up her face. "If they don't even let us vote, would they allow a woman into such a position of power?"

"She was determined to make it so," Zula said with pride in her voice. "She was always citing the congressional legislation from nine years ago. It determined if a woman is licensed to practice law, she must be allowed into the highest court in the land."

"The Supreme Court?" I asked.

"The Supreme Court."

"And Rowena was a gifted leader of our movement," Frannie added. "She knew how to lead without ordering us around, and she lit a spark in everyone with her vision and her commitment. She could have been the next Elizabeth Cady Stanton."

"She was all of that and so much more." Zula gazed at a likeness of Rowena in a frame on the end table where she sat. "She could make you laugh. And she was brilliant." She coughed and blinked, appearing to cover up a rush of emotion.

"Didn't she have any flaws?" Bertie raised one eyebrow. "You make her sound like a saint."

Zula half glared at Bertie. "She didn't suffer fools lightly, true."

So maybe she had other enemies out there

I wasn't even aware of. "I'm still not sure the detective has the right man for her murder," I said.

"Why did he arrest that fellow, anyway?" Frannie asked, cocking her head.

I sighed. "Hilairus Bauer has been in trouble with the law before, for petty thievery. But I know someone who vouches for his character."

Bertie nudged me. "That someone happens to be Rose's intended, David. Look at the pretty ring he gave her."

I blushed but held out my hand to display the simple ring of engagement featuring a love knot done in gold. David had given it to me in the summer. Zula glanced at the ring without interest, but Frannie complimented me on it.

"Anyway, Kevin said a witness placed Hilarius at the scene of the crime," I went on. "But I have an uneasy feeling about the statement. I just don't think he was the villain, so to speak." I gazed at Zula. "Is there anyone else who might have wanted to do away with Rowena?"

"How about Mr. Felch?" Zula curled her lip. "He was most certainly not happy about her deserting him, as he put it."

"He was away Saturday night, though, in New York." I pursed my lips. "Does thee

206

know of an Elbridge Osgood?"

Zula's thick dark eyebrows went up. "The one Rowena was promoted over. She talked about him."

"Do you think he killed her, Rose?" Frannie leaned forward, her hands on her knees.

"I really don't know. I'm just thinking about who might have thought they had cause to commit murder."

"What about the anti-suffrage hothead with the gun today?" Bertie asked.

"Leroy Dunnsmore. Yes, he's on the list. And the detective has him in jail. But if Kevin thought Leroy murdered Rowena, he wouldn't have arrested Hilarius." I sighed. My head spun with possibilities. And of course another possible suspect sat across from me, not that I was going to add her name to the discussion.

Zula regarded me. "You're quite the detective, Rose. How does such an interest comport with being a midwife?"

I laughed lightly. "Midwifery is my profession. But it turns out I have another calling, to be an unofficial assistant to Kevin Donovan in cases where I have an interest."

"Is this so? And he welcomes your advice?" Zula asked with narrowed eyes.

"It's not advice. I just pass on information

I learn."

"Were you angry with Rowena because she wouldn't move in with you?" Bertie asked Zula, a calm innocent expression on her face.

I shot Bertie a quick glance. Another not-so-innocent question, but not a very kind one to someone grieving as Zula must be.

Zula blinked. She picked up her glass and took a sip. "I was frustrated in love, do you hear me? I'll be honest with you. I wanted her. But she didn't want me back, not in the same way." She stared at Bertie. "And in case you're wondering? No, I didn't kill her."

NINETEEN

By eight the next morning Frederick and the children had all gone off to work and school, and the kitchen girl was busy scrubbing pots. Mother and I took our coffee into the sitting room. She'd been busy reading to Betsy, Mark, and Matthew last night when I arrived home, so we hadn't had a chance to talk. Today had dawned blustery and cold, in sharp contrast to yesterday, and the coal stove warmed the room nicely. Winter was once again on its way.

"How was the gathering at Zula's?" Mother asked.

"It was pleasant, and the Election Cake delicious."

"Thee said this Zula might be a suspect in the murder. Was it safe going to her house?"

"I'm here, aren't I?" I smiled. "I was with two others, remember. Nothing at all happened. And Bertie managed to weasel a couple of bits of information out of her."

"I like Bertie. Thee and she are good friends, it seems."

"We are." I nodded.

"Tell me what information she elicited from Zula."

"We found out she was alone in her apartment the night Rowena was killed."

Mother raised her eyebrows. "No one to vouch for her."

"Right. Zula employs a cook, a maid, and a stable boy, and they go home from Saturday afternoon to Monday morning."

"Interesting. Did thee learn anything else?"

"Yes, in a way. Zula had romantic feelings for Rowena that weren't reciprocated. Bertie asked her if she was angry about Rowena's rejection. Zula got the drift of the question and ended by saying she didn't kill Rowena."

"She knows thee works with the police now and then, I suppose."

"Yes, we talked about my assisting Kevin last evening."

"I think thee needs to be very careful, Rose." She took my hand and squeezed it. "Whoever killed could kill again, and if he or she knows thee is asking questions around town, thee could be a target." Her voice broke as she gazed around the room, which still bore little touches of Harriet everywhere. "I've lost one daughter. I can't lose thee, too."

I realized with a start how painful it must be for her to be staying here in Harriet's home and be reminded of her at every turn. "You won't lose me, Mother. Don't worry, I am careful." I squeezed back. "I have no intention of putting myself in harm's way. At least no more than we did yesterday." I smiled at her. "Did Frederick behave himself last evening?"

She sniffed and wiped away a tear. "Indeed. He was here reading to the younger children and helping Luke with his homework all evening. Just as he should be." She nodded once in a satisfied way. "Yesterday was a heartening demonstration, wasn't it? Complete with Elizabeth Cady Stanton herself."

"I was so pleased to be able to meet her. For her to stand with us made the day extra special."

Mother nodded. "She's like that. She's such a luminary, and yet she makes herself available to everyone."

"I hope her ankle will heal well." I sipped the last of my coffee.

"I'm sure it will. She said she's returning

home to Seneca Falls today, so she can have her own physician look at it."

I watched out the window as a small cloud of leaves blew down the path. "I wonder which way the presidential election went."

"Frederick will bring home the newspaper, won't he?"

"Yes. But I'm going out soon. I'll pick one up in town."

"I'm eager to see it." Mother drained her coffee cup and set it on the end table. "I wanted to tell thee I spoke with Ruby Bracken about thy situation during our long hours at the demonstration yesterday."

"Oh?" I raised my eyebrows so high my glasses slipped down the bridge of my nose. I pushed them back up. "And?"

She shrugged. "She did not seem willing to budge in her position."

I slumped in my chair, and Mother reached over to pat my hand. "Thee is not to despair, Rosie. We'll figure out something."

I wasn't so sure we would, but I didn't want to wallow in that particular problem right now.

"Now tell me, the couple who came to vote in their runabout yesterday," she began. "What was their last name again?"

"They are Elbridge and Lyda Osgood.

He's a lawyer — or was until he was let go. And she's one of my clients, due to deliver her third child within the month."

"I thought Osgood was the name thee had mentioned. The name is familiar to me."

"It's a large family and they own a good deal of land here in town," I said. "One Osgood is the proprietor of a carriage factory, but I'm not sure if he's directly related to Elbridge."

"No, this was at home in Lawrence. I met a Delilah Osgood who spoke of a relative with an unusual name. As I recall it was Elbridge or something like it."

"What did she say about him?"

"Her words are what I can't quite remember. I'll think hard on it. Or maybe I can send a note to thy father and ask him. His memory is always better than mine and I'm sure I spoke to him on the matter."

TWENTY

I left Mother baking at home and cycled over to Greenwood Street at about nine. I had prenatal visits scheduled but not until later this morning, and I wanted to find the neighbor who had reported seeing Hilarius. Had this neighbor actually seen him beat Rowena to death? I wasn't sure I could trust Kevin right now to follow up on every detail about Hilarius. I thought perhaps the strain of his wife and son being sick — as well as pressure from his boss — was temporarily affecting his usually sound judgment.

I coasted down Main Street into Patten Hollow, passing the pond on my right. The wind chilled me and I was glad I'd worn the thick woolen scarf Harriet had knitted for me. After I turned right on Greenwood, I dismounted and wheeled the cycle up the hill, one of many slopes in Amesbury. The road was steep and its paving planks slick with dew this morning.

My friend Catherine lived in this neighborhood, but I hadn't been to her home in four years and couldn't quite remember which house it was, or if it was even in this block of Greenwood. That hadn't even occurred to me the morning I found Rowena's body, likely because of the early hour, the shock, and my lack of sleep.

The Felch home was in the middle of the block. Where to start? I leaned my bike against a tree. The modest cottage across the street might be the best bet, but when I used the knocker, no one came to the door. At the larger house to its right, a young maid answered the door.

"Good morning. I'm helping the police with an investigation." Which was really only a slight deviation from the truth.

At the word *police* her mouth formed the letter O.

"I was wondering if you or anyone in the household might have seen a crime committed across the street last Saturday night." Dispensing for the moment with Quaker terminology for the days of the week, I pointed to the Felch house.

"No, I didn't see nothing." She wrung her hands in her apron. "I won't have to talk to no coppers, will I?"

"I'm sure thee won't." I used my most

215

soothing voice. "Is anyone else at home this morning?"

She shook her head.

I thanked her and moved on, although I caught a flicker of a curtain moving after she closed the door. She acted like she was afraid of something. But what? Maybe it was as simple as her being an uneducated girl brought in from the country to work for a family and not being familiar with officers of the law.

Smoke curled up from the chimney at the next house, and when I knocked I heard the thud of small running feet within. A round-faced woman opened the door. Catherine Toomey held a young girl on one hip while another lass the same size peeked out from behind her skirts.

"If it isn't Rose Carroll!" Catherine exclaimed.

So she did live in this block. I knew her from the Mercantile where she sold dry goods, and I'd assisted my teacher with the birth of Catherine's twin daughters, these very girls, a scant four years ago. Last summer I'd had spent even more time with the congenial Irishwoman when she'd been helping at her daughter-in-law's labor and birth. "Catherine, I thought thee lived somewhere around here."

"What brings you to the neighborhood?" Catherine set down the twin in her arms. "Come in for a cup of tea, will you?"

"I'd be happy to, thank thee. Hello, girls," I added, bending over to ruffle each of their heads. When I straightened I noticed Catherine's dress was turned, the measure of a frugal woman: picking apart the seams of a piece of faded clothing, turning them inside out, and restitching to reveal fresh fabric.

The little ones ran off giggling. Catherine gestured me to follow her to a warm roomy kitchen at the back of the house. "You children go play, now." She pointed to a box of toys in the corner of the kitchen.

A minute later we sat at the table, steaming cups of tea in front of us. I picked up the small milk pitcher in the shape of a cow. "How is thy grandson, Charlie?" He'd been born in July, but unfortunately his mother had suffered from the clap and had passed it to her baby in the birth canal. The disease had damaged Charlie's eyes, a common cause of blindness in children.

"He can't seem to see a thing. But he's happy and healthy, and we've all vowed to help him navigate his world as best we can." She made a tsking sound. "But it won't be easy."

"Indeed, it won't. I heard that Marie's

spirit was released to God a month after the birth." The baby's other grandmother had been gravely ill with cancer in July.

"Yes, may God bless her sainted soul." Catherine crossed herself. "Now, Rose, tell me why you're here today. You don't seem the type to pay purely social calls."

"It's true." I gave a little laugh. "Did thee happen to hear about the murder of thy neighbor, Rowena Felch?"

"Been hearing nothing since. It was quite the shock, it was."

"Mama, what's murder?" one of the girls piped up with a lisp.

I grimaced. Little pitchers definitely had big ears.

"I'll tell you later, my wee sweet."

"I'm sorry, I wasn't thinking." I lowered my voice. "I've heard from the police a neighbor reported seeing a man near the Felch house on Seventh Day night." I knew Catherine was familiar with my ways of speaking so I didn't have resort to calling a day after a Roman god.

"It was I who told them, in fact. I felt a bit queer when he told me why he was after asking, but I said my piece."

"What a relief I don't have to knock on every door on the street. They've arrested this man but I don't think he did it. Can thee tell me exactly what thee saw?"

"So you're involved in solving another case, are you?" Her eyes were bright. She had also been involved, in a way, with the July murder of a mill girl.

"A bit."

"As I told the young officer, I'd heard a noise and was curious about what it was."

"Thee didn't talk to the detective himself? Kevin Donovan?"

"No. They had a pack of men out here asking questions, they did. So like I told the copper, I looked out the side window of the parlor and saw a skinny sort of gent standing looking at the Felch's lilac bush. The moon was well full and bright that night, it was."

"But thee didn't see him" — I glanced at the children — "assault Rowena." *Assault* was unlikely to be in their vocabularies yet, but they might know words like *beat* and *kill.*

"I didn't see her at all and I told the officer as much."

One of the girls, moving behind Catherine's back, fetched a small square box off the work table next to the stove and returned to her sister.

"What time did thee hear the noise?" I asked before sipping the welcome warmth of my tea.

"Mummy!" one of the girls cried out.

"Now what can the matter be?" Catherine twisted in her chair. "Can't two ladies have a nice cuppa and a spot of talk, then?"

The one who had yelled cowered with her hands over her head. " 'Top it, Thithy," she lisped.

"I'm just a-salting her, Mummy," the other said in an innocent voice even as she plucked a pinch of grains out of the salt cellar and sprinkled it on her twin's head.

"Oh, fer Mary, Jesus, and Joseph. You stop plaguing your sister and wasting my good spice, now, my girl. Go put the cellar back where it rightly belongs."

It was my fault again, using the word *assault,* but I could barely keep a giggle inside.

Catherine turned back to me, her shoulders hunched with suppressed laughter. She covered her mouth and shook her head, the amusement in her eyes unmistakable.

"Now then," she said, once she mastered her laugh. "What in blazes were we talking about?"

"Thee was about to tell me what time thee heard the conveyance in the street."

"Yes, of course. Well, it was a little before ten. Mr. Toomey had just gone up to bed and I was turning off the lamps and such.

220

So you're not after thinking the skinny one did the dreadful deed, after all?"

"He's down on his luck, but I've heard he's a decent sort. So, no, I'm inclined to look elsewhere for the culprit. Did thee see anyone else, hear anything else?"

Catherine sipped her tea and gazed at the table as if she was thinking. She looked up. "I'd just turned away when I heard some kind of conveyance go by. Our street isn't paved yet and the wheels thump something fierce on the planks."

"Was it going away from the Felch home or toward it?"

"I'm not sure."

"And did thee see a conveyance parked at the house when thee spied the man?" I asked.

"No, nary a one."

I finished my tea. "I thank thee, Catherine. For the tea and for the information. One more question. Did thee tell Kevin Donovan about the conveyance?"

"No, I didn't think to. And he didn't ask. You girls be good now," she directed her daughters. "Mama will be right back."

As she showed me to the front door, we passed the parlor. "I was looking out that window there, do yeh see?" She pointed.

"May I?" I asked.

When she nodded, I peered out the window. There was the Felch's home across the street and down one house. I could see the lilac, but a large rhododendron in front of Catherine's window blocked the view of the rest of the house. I thanked her and made my way out. I stood at my bicycle for a moment, thinking. She'd heard a vehicle. I doubted Hilarius had the means to own one. Perhaps he'd borrowed a conveyance. Of course, it could belong to any citizen of Amesbury simply driving home after a visit with relatives or a dinner out. Or maybe it belonged to the murderer.

I walked my cycle past the Felch house and spied a phaeton with its top up harnessed to a dappled horse. It looked like Mr. Felch was getting ready to go out, or someone could be paying a condolence call. Either way, I had an urge to speak with him. I approached the front door. Boards were nailed over where the broken glass had been. I rapped the knocker, remembering again how odd it was the door had been locked the morning I'd found Rowena.

He pulled open the door. "Yes?" he began. He took a closer look at me. "You're Miss Carroll."

"Yes. I was in the neighborhood and

wondered . . ." Wondered what? I hadn't thought this through.

"If you could pay your respects?"

He'd solved my problem for me. "Yes."

"Certainly. Do come in." He stepped back and waved his hand toward a parlor off the hall.

The room was positioned in the same place in the house as Catherine's, but was twice the size. It was genteelly decorated with brocade-upholstered chairs, a fine rug, delicate tables, and oil paintings in gilt frames on the walls. Heavy green draperies were pulled to the sides of the tall windows.

"Please sit."

I took a seat on one of the smaller chairs, while he perched opposite in a big winged armchair. No one else was in the room, so it must have been his horse and carriage.

"I suppose I was short with you at the polls yesterday," he began. "This has all been such a shock. But I'd wanted to speak to you at more length, and here you are." He stroked his luxurious beard. His expression was much less grief-stricken than the day before.

"How is the funeral planning coming along?" I asked.

"It will be Friday. There are still many details to attend to."

"Does thee have family who is helping? Or did Rowena?"

"I myself am without family, sadly. I was my parents' only child and they are both deceased. It's one reason I wanted to be father to a big family." He pondered his long-fingered hands for a moment, and then gave his head a little shake, looking at me again. "Mrs. Felch's parents spend the colder months in the Caribbean islands, but Mrs. Roune, her grandmother, is here in Amesbury. She and I have rather different views on the matter of the funeral, I'm afraid."

Annie had said Mrs. Roune didn't like Oscar much, and was helping Rowena financially so she could leave him. I'd say they might have very different views, indeed.

"I'm sure it will be worked out to thy satisfaction."

"I hope so. She's not an easy woman, Mrs. Roune." He leaned his forearms on his knees and clasped his hands, fixing his gaze on me. "Will you please tell me every detail of when you found Rowena, Miss Carroll? I never expected, when I left for New York, I'd never see her again."

Was he asking out of sadness or for another reason? If he'd hired Hilarius to kill Rowena, perhaps he was concerned whether the murder had proceeded according to plan or not. If he hadn't, my heart went out to a grieving husband. In either case, I couldn't give him the whole story. Kevin had taught me the importance of keeping crime scene details private, in case a killer revealed information he shouldn't have known. I took a deep breath and let it out.

"I was cycling past this house early in the morning. I'm a midwife, and I was on my way home from a birth. I spied thy wife's red shoe under the lilac. I'd seen her only the night before at the women's suffrage meeting."

His eyes filled. "She loved those shoes." He extracted a handkerchief from a pocket and dabbed at his eyes. "Forgive me."

"Please don't apologize, Oscar. There is nothing to forgive. Thee is entitled to thy grief." I felt a pang of chagrin, since my questions might intrude on that grief, but I went on. "After I found her, I hailed a passing man and asked him to fetch the police. Then I saw the glass in the door was broken."

He frowned. "Indeed. The scoundrel had ransacked the dining room. But I couldn't find a thing missing. The silver all seems to be in place."

"Only the dining room?"

"Yes. Which is odd, because Rowena kept expensive jewelry in her room, and there are other valuables in the house."

Odd, certainly. "I believe thee might be acquainted with my betrothed, David Dodge of Newburyport."

"Yes, of course." Oscar pursed his lips. "A fine physician. Young yet, but he'll go far, mark my words."

"He said thee was away at a medical convention recently."

He narrowed his eyes. "He did, did he? I was, of course. But what business is it of yours where I was?"

"We only were curious about why thee wasn't at home when thy wife was murdered." I watched as he cringed at the word *murdered*.

He recovered and stared at me. "Who is *we*? You and Dodge?"

"No, Detective Donovan and me."

His nostrils flared. "What, you work for the cops?"

"Not at all. But you understand I needed to summon the police after I found your wife's body."

"Yes, of course." He gazed at the floor, then at me. "But now you're speculating on my whereabouts not only with the detective but with your beau? Isn't talking about a murder investigation a little unseemly, Miss Carroll? Not the type of thing ladies normally get themselves involved in, now, is it?"

No, it certainly wasn't. But, then, I wasn't exactly a society lady, either. "Had thee known Rowena would be going to the suffrage meeting that evening?"

"I did not." His eyes glinted like new steel. He clapped his hands on his knees. "You must excuse me. I'm expected elsewhere." He stood.

I followed suit. "Let me again express my condolences on the death of thy wife."

He strode to the door and opened it. "That's all very nice. But it won't bring my wife back, will it?"

TWENTY-ONE

I cycled slowly toward home, thinking. Someone was lying. Was it Oscar? His dining room — and only his dining room — was ransacked with nothing missing. Combined with the locked door, things just didn't add up. And he didn't seem happy with anyone investigating him, me least of all.

Was Hilarius lying about his innocence? Zula had said Rowena didn't suffer fools lightly. Had she wronged Hilarius in the past in connection with her employment as a lawyer? Maybe I should go back to Bixby & Batchelder and ask the voluble receptionist if Rowena had ever been involved in a case involving Hilarius.

And what about Elbridge? He'd said he wished he'd killed her himself. Maybe he said so to cover up that he had, in fact, killed her.

Zula could be lying. She'd clearly been

angry the night of the suffrage meeting, and no one had seen what time she'd arrived home, or in what state. Maybe I could find a time soon to talk all this over with David. His calm, intelligent brain might be able to help me make sense of the matter. But I didn't want to lay it all out in a letter. What if the missive went astray and landed in the hands of one of the suspects? Such a mishap would be most unfortunate — and likely dangerous for me.

As I rode, I sniffed. Beyond the ever-present scent of horse manure, I detected again the sharp smell of impending snow, a smell matching the slate-colored sky. What a blessing yesterday had been fair. We demonstrators might not have lasted the day standing outside in a snowstorm. Or we would have all gone home wet and cold and then contracted the grippe or worse.

A detour to the police station wouldn't take long. I wanted to tell Kevin about Catherine's report of a conveyance outside Rowena's home. Unfortunately, once I arrived I learned Kevin was out. My small piece of news seemed too complicated to leave a note about, so I merely asked the officer at the front desk to tell the detective I'd been in.

I was eager to get home to Mother, whose

visits were rare, so I steered my steed toward home. When I spied John Whittier strolling toward me I halted, reaching one foot to the ground for balance. Perhaps I could ask his counsel on these matters of the murder. We exchanged greetings when he approached.

"I'm off to a meeting with the trustees of the library. They're planning to construct a new building for the library and wanted my ideas on the matter." John had been one of the founders of the public library twenty-two years earlier, buying most of the books for the collection, and had been a trustee ever since.

"What an excellent project."

"It is indeed. I fear I might not prevail with my views on simplicity in this effort as well as I did with our Meetinghouse." He shrugged. "Regardless, I'm late and those fellows don't like to be kept waiting." He said good-bye and walked on.

"I'll stop by to see thee soon," I called after him. I wheeled away, too, chilled from the damp, cold air. But when I arrived home after buying the *Newburyport Daily Herald,* it was to the welcome sight of four round loaves of bread lined up on a cooling rack, the peaks and craters of their toasty brown crusts still letting steam wind upward.

Mother was just sliding a pan of a dozen fat turnovers into the hot oven, with tops glistening from an egg wash. I inhaled deeply of the warm, yeasty air as I removed my cloak and gloves. My day was looking up.

"Mother, thee has outdone thyself."

She turned and smiled. A white smudge of flour decorated her nose and her apron was stained with egg, ash, and something golden. "I like to take care of my lovies, thee included, while I'm here. I know how much the children miss Harriet."

"It's true. They are coping, but sometimes a memory rises up and one or another of the children dissolves into tears. Even Faith."

"Even me." She nodded. "Food always soothes the spirit. And I think I might stay an extra week or two, if Frederick will have me. I was to have gone from here to Washington City to attend a national suffrage meeting, but it's been postponed until the spring." She frowned. "A rift continues between the factions. The National Woman Suffrage Association, which I support, is often at odds with the American Woman Suffrage Association, and the differences sap the energy of both sides."

"Why are the two groups at odds?"

She sighed. "NWSA wants progress in more areas than the vote. We want it to be easier for women to obtain a divorce, for example, and are pushing for equality in employment and pay."

"This group has ambitious plans," I said.

"Yes, but those are part of our rights. Or should be. The AWSA promotes only the vote. It's hard to maintain momentum with the women's rights movement split." She shook her head.

"Does thee think the sides will come together in time?"

"I pray so."

I sniffed the alluring air. "What's in the pies?" I pointed to the oven.

"A curried chicken filling."

Curry explained the gold-colored stains on her apron. My stomach gurgled audibly despite it being not yet noon.

Mother laughed. "Have a bite of bread with me and tell me about thy morning." She brought a loaf and the butter crock to the table while I fetched small plates, the cutting knife, and a couple of table knives.

"What did thee learn?" she asked while cutting two thick slabs.

After I finished my first mouthful of the chewy, crusty, slightly sour bread, I pointed to the paper I'd dropped on the table. "Harrison has it."

"Oh?" Her eyebrows went up as she spread the paper open. "So he does. 'Harrison Will Go to the White House. Republicanism Triumphant,' " she read.

"Even though Cleveland received a larger popular vote, Harrison won the electoral college. The discrepancy between the popular and the electoral vote never seems quite fair to me," I said.

"It's our election system." Mother shrugged. "Now, what did thee learn in thy investigation?"

"It was interesting. I heard from a neighbor of the Felches about a conveyance which passed by the night of Rowena's murder." Christabel strolled over and purred as she rubbed against my skirts. I picked her up, set her on my lap, and stroked her with my left hand as I ate with my right.

"Surely carriages must pass along all the streets with regularity. Did the neighbor think the vehicle belonged to the man thy detective arrested?"

"She had no opinion on that. Of course it could have been an innocent passerby. I think it was the timing she remarked on. I doubt Hilarius owns any kind of vehicle. He's quite hard up financially."

"If the murderer came in a conveyance, maybe the police have the wrong man. Had she told the authorities?" Mother asked.

"No. I stopped by the station on my way home to let Kevin know, but he wasn't there. The neighbor, Catherine, is an acquaintance of mine. I hadn't known exactly where she lived." I chewed and swallowed another bite of the enticing bread. "After I left Catherine's, I paid a visit to Oscar Felch." I told Mother what he'd said about nothing going missing in the apparent burglary. "He was exceedingly curious about the details of when I found her, but I kept my tale vague."

"Thee is becoming quite the detective." She cocked her head, studying me with a smile playing about her lips.

I shrugged. "It's something I learned from Kevin. If a criminal reveals during questioning a detail about the crime scene which hasn't been made public, it can help the authorities to convict him."

"I see." She cleared her throat. "I want to let thee know I've decided to call on Clarinda Dodge this afternoon. I think it might further thy cause with her."

I wrinkled my nose. "Is thee sure?"

"Yes. Does thee want to accompany me?"

"No, I most definitely don't. Does thee

mind?" I asked.

"On the contrary, I think the conversation might go more smoothly in thy absence. However, I felt obligated to ask."

"I'm relieved. I think it might snow soon, though."

"It's no matter. I've arranged for a hack to pick me up." She finished her piece of bread.

I smiled at my ever-resourceful parent and didn't even ask her how she'd managed to arrange for a ride.

"Oh! The turnovers." She jumped up and grabbed a cloth to take the fast-cooking treats out. Their tops now shone golden with the egg wash and the edges were a toasty brown.

I stood. "Thank thee for the bread. I'm off to do some quick paperwork before my client comes at eleven thirty." I wished I had time to update my scribblings about the murder, too.

I tried not to frown at my last client of the day as she reclined on my chaise, but I couldn't help it. Charity Skells, a fellow Quaker, had put on very little weight for a woman six months along. I finished listening to her heart, which at least sounded strong and normal. She lay with her eyes closed as if grabbing a few minutes' rest was a rare commodity. She'd pulled back her walnut-colored hair, already shot through with silver, into a braid coiled at her nape, and her dark blue dress resembled mine, except the threads were worn thin. I expected she'd already turned it once.

I sat back and gently laid my hand atop hers. "Charity, is thee eating enough?"

Her eyes flew open. "I'm sorry, Rose. I'm just so fatigued this time around. What did thee say?"

"I asked if thee had been eating well." She was a normally lean woman, anyway, all angles and planes. And she stood as tall as I. But I remembered her previous pregnancy, since the baby had been born only a year prior. That time she'd gained a healthy amount. The newborn had been of an adequate weight, too, around seven pounds, as I recalled. Not the chubby nine-pound infants some of my mothers birthed, but certainly big enough to survive and do well in the world. "Thee is a bit thinner than I would like to see at this stage."

She grimaced, then pulled her mouth to the side, chewing on her inner lip. She regarded me for a moment with a face too lined for her thirty-five years, as if deciding how much to share. "Between Howard's scanty employment of late and six children under the age of ten, I don't eat enough, not nearly. We don't have food to go around, and that's a fact. And, you know, the children come first."

I suspected what they did have to eat was potatoes and watery soup, too, not exactly the meat- and milk-rich diet I preferred to see my clients consuming. I had urged Charity to practice family spacing but had so far been unsuccessful.

"Remind me of Howard's job." I pulled the tape measure out of my bag and measured the mound of her uterus from the fundus at the top to the pubic bone at the bottom. Because the womb expands with the baby, the measurement is an indication of fetal size. This number also wasn't quite what I would expect for a woman twenty-four weeks gravid.

"He's a chandler, like his pap and his grandpap before him. But now, what with all the gas and electric lights, why, nobody wants candles anymore. He's been trying to become known as an odd-jobsman. He's handy with a hammer and whatnot, and the man can fix anything. But the work just isn't coming in."

"I dare say thee could bring this matter to the Women's Business Meeting, Charity." I jotted down the measurement and her heart rate in her chart before turning back to her. "They might be willing to organize temporary assistance, and perhaps spread the word of thy husband's ready skills." My grandmother's clock on the mantel chimed once, a clear bell I'd been hearing for my entire life. I was fortunate never to have gone hungry, unlike many. And I was sure we had odd jobs around this very house we could offer Howard, if I could persuade Frederick to pay for the work.

Her shoulders sank and she shook her head. "Despite my name, I never wanted to ask for help. I'd rather give it, but I'm not in a position to do so. Because of my little ones, I did, anyway. I went to the women and appealed my case." She worked her thin, worn fingers in her lap, staring at them. She glanced back up at me. "Does thee know what they said?"

I shook my head, waiting.

"They did offer food assistance, which I reluctantly accepted. Donations of milk and bread began to arrive this week. But." She swallowed. "They also advised me to seek the care of a different midwife. They said they disapprove of thy stepping out with a gentleman who is not a Friend."

So it had begun. Oddly, learning of the

elders admonishing Charity did not throw me into the panic I would have expected. My heart did not pound and my hands did not sweat. I felt the inner calm of a smooth sea free of storm or turbulence. "If thee believes thee must see a different midwife, I will not stop thee," I said gently.

"No! I don't care whom thee loves, Rose. I trust thee, and Orpha before." She sat up straight, the first energetic move she'd made since she arrived. "I'll not leave thy care, and I'll tell anyone who asks why I'm staying. Thee is an expert in thy called profession, but even more important, thee is a gentle and caring presence."

"I thank thee, Charity." I smiled. "Thee is indeed in a position to give. Thy faith in me, and thy willingness to give testimony about my skills, are a greater gift than any material good."

TWENTY-TWO

The afternoon post clacked through the mail slot in the door early, at a few minutes before two o'clock. Mother had just ridden off in the hack to Newburyport, and I hoped her mission to Clarinda was a successful one. I flipped through the letters, sorting out Frederick's, then slit open one addressed to me but missing any return address.

I sucked in a quick breath as I read the message, written in blocky capital letters.

STOP SNOOPING WHERE YOU DON'T BELONG OR YOU WILL DIE NEXT. YOU ARE BEING WATCHED.

I let the plain white paper fall to my desk, my hands suddenly icy. The murderer was threatening me. I glanced out the window. The snow had started to fall. Was he watching me right now? My heart thudded against

240

my ribs. Had I locked the door after Mother left? I shivered, feeling bolted to my chair, my feet leaden.

I swallowed hard. I would not let this immobilize me. I'd been threatened before, although not in writing. Not this directly. Still, I'd survived then and I would survive now. I couldn't let fear govern my life. I clenched my hands into fists and then shook them out, trying to release the tension. Closing my eyes, I held myself in God's grace, trying to calm down and trust He would protect me and reveal my way forward. But my agitation persisted.

I stood and hurried to the back door. I turned the key, and checked the front door, too. I paced in my room, too restless to do anything. I kept checking the front windows for someone lurking out there. I needed to take the note to Kevin, but thought it wiser to wait until a family member could accompany me at the end of the day, or until the snow ended. I wished once again for a telephone, and vowed to find a way to pay to have one installed.

As I paced my mind raced. Which of the suspects could have sent the letter? I sat at my desk and pulled out the paper where I'd written down what I knew about the case. Certainly neither Hilarius nor Leroy could have sent such a message from jail. I'd asked questions of all three of the rest: Zula, Elbridge, and Oscar. Of course, Rowena's murderer might be someone else entirely.

A movement outside caught my eye. A man trudged along the path which served as our road. But he was in plain view, not trying to hide. This couldn't be the letter's author. He was both taller than Oscar and slighter than Elbridge. To my surprise he turned up the walk to our house and a moment later rapped on the door. This had all the signs of me being called to a birth. In the snow.

I opened the door. The fellow was barely older than Luke, although he was taller than I. His nose was covered with the unfortunate acne pimples of the teen years, and straight light hair poked out from his cap.

"Miss Rose Carroll, the midwife?" he asked.

"Yes."

He handed me an envelope. "Gent paid me to bring it to you, miss."

"Who was it?"

"Dunno, miss." He tugged at his hat and ran down the steps.

"I thank thee," I called after him and shut the door.

In my parlor, I puzzled over the note.

Please come attend my wife. She's laboring with our first child and we have no family in the area. We're in an apartment in the carriage house. — James Smith

I examined the note in a moment of fear, but the writing did not resemble the threatening note, and my heart slowed. This looked to be an authentic request for midwifery assistance. The man had added an address far up the steep hill on Powow Street. Interesting that they were in the carriage house. Perhaps the husband was the stable man, or a driver for the family who lived in the big house perched on the side of Powow Hill.

I didn't have any clients currently with a surname of Smith, so his wife hadn't received antenatal care from me. Had anyone else watched over her pregnancy? And I certainly hadn't done my usual home visit. Maybe they'd recently moved to town. I groaned. I had no choice but to go. This was my calling, to help women birth their babies. Like the postal service. I could not allow bad weather to get in my way.

At least I'd had a nice lunch of beef stew and more bread and butter with my mother not too long ago, so if it turned into an extended labor, I would be fine for some hours. I'd wanted Annie to accompany me to the next birth I attended, but I had no way of contacting her at her workplace, and this weather didn't permit me going to fetch her in the opposite direction from the laboring woman. One more reason to obtain a telephone.

I checked my birthing satchel and left the family a message on the table about my mission. I pushed the threatening note to the back of my mind for now, donning bonnet, gloves, scarf, and cloak. I exited the house and, with my hood up, clutched my cloak close around me and made my way a block away to Powow to begin my climb. The wind picked up, blowing the white weather sideways in front of me. When I was younger I'd once ascended Mount Wachusett, the state's highest mountain, with my father. He'd said, "Be as a camel. One foot in front of the other." His advice came in handy this afternoon.

As I trudged, I thought again about the name. Now that I pondered it, one of my clients had mentioned a pregnant friend with a last name of Smith. Had it been Emily? Or Lyda? I couldn't recall. But there were Smiths aplenty in every town, and this must be a recommendation from a client of mine. Otherwise how would James know to send for me?

I finally arrived at my destination. The last neighboring home I'd passed was much farther down the hill, and had been a beacon of lamplight and chimney smoke. Here the house stood dark, unpeopled. The family must be away.

I headed around the right to the carriage house. It was one of the larger ones, to match the scale of its master house. Its architecture also matched that of the main residence, and it was certainly large enough to include a few rooms for a caretaker. I slid open the wide door and stepped in. A Bailey carriage was parked within, but I didn't see any horses in the stalls. A set of stairs hugged the wall to the left, so the apartment must be above, partitioned off from the hayloft.

"Hello," I called. "It's the midwife."

No answer. The door to the apartment must be closed since I couldn't hear the woman's labor cries and groans. I was about to slide the door shut and head up the stairs when I froze, hearing a small still voice inside my brain.

Danger, it whispered. *Danger.*

I had no time to heed it. A blow crashed

onto the back of my head with a mighty force. I cried out and fell forward.

TWENTY-THREE

A scrabbling noise awoke me. My head pounded and my hands were icy. *What?* I opened my eyes but my glasses were askew. Why was I sprawled on the floor of a . . . *a carriage house*? I pushed up to sitting, straightening my spectacles. A gray mouse scurried past me and darted under the carriage. A carriage house . . . *Oh.*

I'd come for a labor. Someone had attacked the back of my head. The note had been a ruse to lure me up the hill. I now knew without even looking that there was no apartment upstairs, no woman in travail, no baby on its way.

I pushed up to standing, dusting off my still-gloved hands, wincing at the pain the movement brought to my head. I reeled with a moment of dizziness. I heeded it, standing still until the vertigo passed. I needed to get out of here. I grasped the door's handle but it didn't budge. My knuckles on the handle tightened, and I swallowed down a sudden lump in my throat. Someone had not only attacked me but had locked me in.

I stared at the door. I tried to slide it again, putting all my weight into the effort. It wouldn't move. I shivered from the cold, and even more from fear. If I didn't come home after dark, the Bailey family wouldn't worry. They were accustomed to me going off to births and staying up to several days. My heart beat so hard I could barely breathe. Whoever attacked me hoped to have left me for dead. Just like Rowena. I removed a glove, lowered my bonnet, and touched the back of my head. My hand came away damp with blood, but not a lot. I must have been unconscious for some time for the blood to be already coagulated. Scalp wounds were heavy bleeders.

I was about to dissolve into tears, but crying would help nothing. "Be strong, Rose," I scolded myself out loud. "Thee must think."

I looked around and decided to make a circuit of the carriage house interior. I didn't see any other egress, and the only windows were shut tight, the light filtering through them dim from the storm. I couldn't tell how late it was except night hadn't yet fallen. I passed a water trough and ran my hand inside it, but it was dry.

I turned to look at the stairs. I was sure there was no apartment but I lifted my skirts and trudged up, anyway, to be certain. Sure enough, all I saw were bales of hay. No bed, no lamp, no laboring woman crying out for my help.

As I sank onto one of the steps halfway down, my heart sank, too. I was alone and cold in a snowstorm with no way to get out. This had to be the doing of the murderer, who wanted to assure that my questioning self was well out of the way, possibly permanently. I was an idiot. My brain had deserted me, letting a note delivered by a boy persuade me to come to a birth of a woman I'd never met, especially after receiving the anonymous threat. The whole thing was a trick. There was no James Smith, nor a pregnant Mrs. Smith. I should have paid attention to the small, elusive voice I'd heard in my head after I'd entered. But it was too late now.

My throat was thick with fear and worry, and my full eyes threatened to overflow. I had to find a way out before despair overwhelmed me. I might survive here for a few days, but without water, I wouldn't last much longer than that. I didn't have any hope of the property owners returning before spring. The only person who might open the door would be the one who lured me here in the first place. Next time he might have a gun to finish me off with.

Or was it a she? If Zula were the guilty party, she could have done the luring, hitting, and locking. Although the boy had said a man gave him the note.

I shook my head and sniffed back my self-pitying tears. Right now it didn't matter who the villain was or how scared I was. What mattered was getting out. My exit was going to involve going out a window. I went to each fenestration in turn and tried with both hands and all my strength to raise the sash. None would budge. They must have been painted or even nailed shut. At least they were the newer style of window where the glass was in two pieces broken up by only one vertical wooden muntin. I prowled the carriage house, searching for a tool I could use to pry open one of the windows, but I came up empty handed.

Was I going to have to break the glass? I spied my birthing satchel near the door where I'd dropped it. I rummaged through the bag, but the only sharp object I had was my scissors, and I expected they would break if I tried to use them as a pry bar. I made the rounds of the windows again and my heart sank even further. While the front of the carriage house was at the level of the road, it was, of course, built on the hill. The bottom of the side windows stood a good eight feet from the ground outside, and the one in back was even higher. I was going to have to jump out.

I hurried around the space, searching for something with which to break a window until I located a metal bucket with a handle near the trough. I had to get out of here before the storm got any worse, or before my attacker returned. Widening my stance, I braced myself and turned my head away, not wanting to risk shards of glass flying into my eyes. I swung the bucket fast at the glass. My aim was poor though, and my improvised hammer bounced off the wooden window frame.

"Haste makes waste," I scolded myself out loud. I took a good look at where the pail needed to go, braced my legs into a strong stance, turned my head, and swung again.

With a crack, the glass shattered and made a tinkling sound as it fell on itself. I glanced down to see an icicle-shaped piece embedded in my woolen cloak and I carefully extracted it. I drew a cloth out of my satchel and wrapped it around my hand, making something like the padded boxing glove I'd seen in a newspaper article about the violent sport. With great care I punched out the flimsy muntin and the jagged shards all around the frame. The cold air rushed in along with the driven snow. My teeth began to chatter but I kept moving. I found a dusty lap rug in the carriage and spread it, thickly folded, on the bottom of the sash's frame, since I couldn't get all the points of glass out.

The window's sill was three feet off the ground inside. Grateful for my long legs, I hoisted myself up and swung one leg over the sill. *No!* I'd forgotten my satchel. I climbed back down and grabbed it, then repeated my moves until I sat with both legs out the window. The snow now covered the ground and it swirled in the air such that I couldn't tell if any obstacle lay under the white covering. I had to take my chances. I took a deep breath and leapt.

TWENTY-FOUR

I lay stunned in the snow. My right hand burned and my knee ached. My head throbbed something fierce. But I was alive and out of my prison. When I put pressure on my hand to sit up, it stung even worse. I held it in front of my face to see a shard of glass poking straight into my gloved palm like I'd been shot with an arrow. No wonder it hurt. I took hold of the shard with the fingers of my other hand and steeled myself as I yanked it out. When I sensed warm blood gushing into my glove, I grabbed a fistful of snow and squeezed tight on it.

I pushed up to standing. Retrieving my satchel from where it had fallen a few feet away, I trudged toward the road. At least my spectacles hadn't gone flying. Snow crept into my shoes, stung my face, clouded my glasses. Setting the satchel down for a moment, I removed the spectacles and stashed them in the pocket of my cloak. I could see no worse without them than with them coated in snow. Then I had a terrifying thought. What if my attacker was still lurking, making sure I didn't get away? My heart started thudding all over again.

What else could I do but face the unknown? I crept toward the road. And let out a cry of relief when the front of the carriage house was deserted. I couldn't see any vehicle, no horse, and not a human soul. Of course, I hadn't seen any signs of life when I'd approached the building, either. Whoever hit me and locked me in must have been hiding as I approached. He'd likely left his transportation farther up the hill.

I hurried down Powow Street as fast as I could. No one was about and the storm was worsening. "I am never going on a call like this one again," I shouted to the road, to the storm, to the world — but mostly to myself. "I'll just tell them they have to go to the hospital." Although of course I wouldn't want to send them elsewhere. It was quite harsh to refuse to assist a woman in her travails. My foot slipped on a hidden patch of ice and I cried out, flailing my arms, but I remained on my feet, just.

When I reached the occupied house I'd passed on the way up, with its lights signaling warm signs of life, my spirits lifted. I considered knocking and asking for help. I was halfway home by now, and pushed on instead. I passed Lake Street a few minutes later and was almost to Central Street, where I would turn to reach the path leading to my own warm home.

A wagon pulled by two horses roared toward me on Powow from the direction of town. Last summer a murderer had tried to run me down only a few blocks from here. Was it happening all over again? I took a quick step to the side of the road, but I tripped on a snow-covered rock and fell, sprawling on my elbows. Flooded with fear, I tried to boost myself up and cried out from the pain in both my hand and my head. The horses were almost upon me. My throat constricted and blood pounded in my ears.

"Whoa," a man's voice called out. The horses came to a halt two yards away. A tall figure in an overcoat and white police hat jumped down and took two long strides toward me. "Miss Rose, what are you doing here?" Guy Gilbert knelt next to me.

I stared. "Guy? I could ask thee the same."

The officer extended his hand and stood, helping me up. "Get in the wagon and I'll tell you." He handed me up into the passenger side and hurried around to climb into the driver's seat.

While the back of the police wagon was enclosed for carrying prisoners, the front had only a roof overhanging our seats and open sides. Snow blew in everywhere. Still, it was better than walking. The comforting smell of warm animals wafted back and filled my nostrils. Gratitude flooded through me at being rescued by friend rather than run over by foe.

"We got a telephone call at the station from a house halfway up Powow, saying a woman was walking alone in the snow," Guy said. "They knew the residents of the house farther up were away for the winter. The unoccupied one is the last house on the hill, and after the news of the break-in at the Felch home, they worried this person was on her way back from robbing it."

"It was me, so thee doesn't need to search any longer." A nervous giggle escaped me. "Did they think I was going to fill my empty satchel with valuables and then just walk home with it?"

"It did sound a bit far-fetched, but we told them we'd go see what was up. And I'm glad I did. What were you doing out in the storm, then?" He directed the horses, who turned the van around.

"I was summoned to a birth in the carriage house of the empty residence. But it was a ruse. There was no laboring woman. Someone hit me on the head, pushed me, and locked me in." I shivered again.

Guy twisted in his seat to stare at me, concern written all over his face. "Are you hurt, Miss Rose? Shall I take you to a doctor, or to the hospital?"

"No, but I thank thee. My head does ache, and I managed to cut my hand. But it's nothing needing urgent care." At least, I hoped not.

"If you're sure. But who would do such a dastardly thing to you? Did you see who it was?"

"I don't know who did it, and I didn't see anyone. I walked in and experienced a powerful blow to my head. The next thing I knew I woke up on the floor, with the only door locked from the outside."

"How'd you get out, then?"

I told him about my battle with the window. "But I escaped, and here I am. I've been asking a few questions around town to assist Kevin in the murder investigation, and I think it must have been the killer trying to shut me away."

"I guess you're lucky to be alive, then."

"I certainly am."

"You know what Donovan's going to say

to you, I expect," he said as we swung onto Central.

"To stop looking into Rowena's death?" I asked.

"Precisely."

"To be honest, I'll be glad to cease my activities in that regard, and thee can tell him as much. Guy, does thee know what time it is?"

He pulled the horses to a stop in front of my house. "It was about three thirty when I left the station."

While I'd had a life-threatening experience, I hadn't been unconscious for too long. The house was dark. Mother must still be visiting Clarinda, the children were at school, Faith and Frederick were working. I gasped and brought my hand to my mouth.

"What is it, Miss Rose?"

"What if my attacker is inside? I received a threatening letter this afternoon before I went out."

"You did?" Guy's voice rose.

"Yes, an anonymous one." I told him what had been written. "Would thee mind terribly coming in with me?" I asked. "Just to be sure I'm safe in there, since the family isn't home yet."

"Of course I will." He jumped out and secured the horses to the post, then helped me down.

"And I can give thee the letter to take to Kevin," I said.

"Let me take the note summoning you to the birth, as well."

"Good idea."

Five minutes later we'd checked every room in the house, not finding any lurking criminal, and Guy had left with the letter and the note safely stowed inside his overcoat. With lamps lit, the door locked, and the kitchen stove stoked, my only tasks were the domestic ones of dressing my cut and pondering what to cook for dinner. I felt safe. For the moment, anyway.

Half an hour later I sat near the wood cook stove with my hands wrapped around a mug of hot chocolate. I'd bandaged my left hand and wiped my spectacles clean, restoring them to my face. I wasn't sure how to treat my head wound without help, so I simply left my hair in a long braid.

I couldn't seem to grow warm despite having stoked the stove. I knew it was the shock wearing off which left me feeling drained like this, but I didn't know how to fix it other than with a warm, nourishing drink. The steam from the rich milky chocolate curled up and floated away. I'd have thought

Mother would be back from her visit by now. The snow must have delayed her. I glanced out the window to see the sky growing lighter as the storm passed through. It was snowing only sparsely now.

A stomping on the side stairs startled me, followed by a rapping on the door. Kevin's voice rang out before I had time to grow afraid.

"Miss Rose?"

I stood too fast and my head spun. Grabbing the back of the chair, I waited until my vision cleared before unlocking the door. I greeted him and stood back so he could enter.

He stomped the snow off his feet and peered at me. "Miss Rose, you're as pale as a shroud. Sit yourself down again." His brows knit in concern.

"Yes, I'm still suffering a bit from my afternoon." I gratefully took my seat again.

"May I look at your head?"

When I carefully ducked my chin down, he inspected my wound without touching it, then sat across the table from me. "It doesn't look too bad. The monster who delivered the blow either held back or missed in his aim. Now, I want to hear every detail. If you're up to it, that is."

"Guy gave thee the threatening letter?"

"He certainly did. I don't suppose the writing looked at all familiar to you?"

"No. It's hard to tell with those block letters, isn't it?"

"Yes, although I suspect it was written by a female hand." Kevin drew out the letter and smoothed it out on the table. "See? The writing was formed rather carefully and the letters aren't overly thick."

"Oh, dear. Does thee mean . . ."

"Zula Goodwin? You have to admit it's a possibility. Or it could also have been a lady companion doing a man's bidding."

"True."

"Officer Gilbert told me only you were summoned to attend a lady in labor. What was the nature of the summons?"

I told him about the boy, who'd said a gent had paid him to bring the note.

"Did you know the boy?"

"No. I'd never seen him before. He wasn't much older than Luke, though. Fourteen, maybe. Tall and skinny, with blond hair and a face reddened by acne."

"You're a sharp observer, Miss Rose. I'll keep an eye out for the lad."

"Did thee see the note I sent along, too?"

"I have it here, as well." He produced the note and lined it up with the letter. "The ink looks similar. We have a fellow in the department who specializes in analyzing this kind of thing."

"Good. I didn't recognize the name James Smith, and I knew I didn't already have a pregnant client at such an address. But it's hard for me to turn down a woman in need. So off I went."

"You have a big heart that way."

I shrugged. "It's my calling. When I arrived, the house was empty and cold, but he'd said an apartment in the carriage house, so I slid open the door. I'd only stood there a moment when I felt the blow to my head. I fell, and when I awoke a while later the door was locked."

"Did you have any clue at all to the identity of your attacker? Hear anything, smell anything?"

I thought for a moment. "I can't say I did. It all happened so fast. But maybe a memory will come to me later. I do know I didn't see any conveyance outside. The carriage house held a Bailey phaeton but no horses."

"I'll tell you, Miss Rose, I'm going to be of a mind to row that fellow up Salt River when I find him." He clenched his fists like he was ready to start the beating right then and there. "Attacking a fine person like yourself. It's just not right."

"I thank thee, Kevin. But I'm sure letting

262

our justice system deliver the punishment will be the better choice."

"Of course. I just hate to see you hurt. Anyway, Gilbert said after you woke up you broke a window and jumped out?" He gazed at my hand. "And cut yourself, by the looks of it."

"I did. A shard pierced my glove. But it's not too bad." I sipped my drink. "And when I saw Guy's wagon charging me on Powow Street, I thought I was being attacked all over again." I shuddered. "I'd never been so glad to see the driver was Guy Gilbert. I could have kissed him."

Kevin laughed. "Let's not get carried away, Miss Rose. He's a happily married man, Gilbert is."

"Thee knows I was kidding. Is Nell faring better now, does thee know?" Guy's wife had suffered terribly from postpartum melancholia in the spring, and the herbs I'd given her to treat the condition had been slow to take effect. I scolded myself for not paying her a visit in too long.

"He says she is, thank the blessed Virgin. It was a rough spell, it was."

"I'm glad to hear it. And how does thy boy fare, and thy wife?"

"Another blessing. They are both much improved, and thank you for asking." He

263

cleared his throat. "Now, Miss Rose. I know we have collaborated before in investigations, and I know you're talented in that regard. But I must ask you to refrain from asking any more questions around town. We can't be having you attacked. And I hope you'll take great cautions when you go out, especially at night, until the murderer is behind bars."

"I will, believe me. And I won't be going to attend the labor of anyone I don't already know, either. But speaking of bars — doesn't this mean Hilarius can't be the killer? He's still in jail, isn't he?"

Kevin shook his head slowly. "He was released this morning. Magistrate said we didn't have enough evidence to keep him, more's the pity."

I tapped the table. "But why did thee arrest him in the first place?"

"A neighbor saw him at the house. We thought we'd find the club that struck the blow at Bauer's house when we turned it out, but alas, we didn't. I also hoped he'd crack under interrogation, but we had no such luck." He held up a hand. "I know, I know, you predicted this. I never should have let the chief pressure me into making the arrest." He exhaled a heavy sigh. "So Bauer is back out at large. I'm not sure he's educated enough to have written either of these messages, though." He stared at the papers.

After a sudden clatter of footsteps, the door burst open to three rosy-cheeked children and a rush of cold air. Matthew and Mark's eyes lit up. They were always excited by a visit from a police officer.

"Detective Kevin!" Mark burst out.

"Can I wear thy hat again?" Matthew asked eagerly.

"Hello there, boys." Kevin beamed. "Good afternoon, Miss Betsy." He handed his hat to Matthew, shook Mark's small hand, and ruffled Betsy's hair. "And what did you learn in school today?"

All talk of attacks and murder suspects ceased, but our conversation had left me with new thoughts to consider. I filed them for later and concentrated on the blessed joy of children for the moment.

TWENTY-FIVE

I was beginning to worry a bit by five o'clock when Mother still had not returned. The children had eaten a snack and were playing. The snow had stopped, so where was she? And for that matter, where was Faith? She was usually home by now, too. But worry would get me nowhere. And I was exhausted and in pain. "Children, I'm going to rest a bit."

Mark barely looked up from the game of jacks he was playing on the kitchen floor with Matthew, but Betsy jumped up from tucking her doll into a small cradle.

"Auntie Rose, how is thy head feeling?" Betsy asked. They'd all noticed the matted blood on my head after Kevin had left.

"It aches a bit, my sweet, which is why I'm going to lie down. Let me know when thy granny returns, please."

She stroked my arm with her small hand. "I'll stand watch."

I had to smile at her earnest expression. "I thank thee."

In my room I unplaited my hair and reclined, half sitting, supported by pillows. It seemed I had only just closed my eyes when I felt a hand stroking my brow. I opened my eyes to see David bending over me, worry writ large on his face.

"David, what is thee doing here?" I struggled to sit up, but felt a sharp pain for my efforts, so I lowered my head again.

"Detective Donovan telephoned me. He told me what happened. He was worried about your injury and wanted me to make sure you were well."

Mother appeared in the doorway to my parlor. "This young man kindly gave me a ride home. Clarinda called and asked him to."

"I was happy to bring you home, Mrs. Carroll," David said.

"None of this *Missus* stuff, now," Mother said with a mock frown. "Thee shall address me as Dorothy and that's that."

"Yes, ma'am." He smiled.

"Mother, I was worried about thee." I peered at her.

"I wanted to wait out the storm. And Clarinda and I were having such a good visit, the time flew by. I knew it would."

I glanced at David, who winked at me, and back at my mother. Would wonders never cease? I'd never had what I would call a "good visit" with Clarinda. I held out my hand to David.

"Help me sit up, please."

With the help of his arm around my shoulders, I sat slowly enough not to bring back the pain in my head. Mother bustled all the way into the room and lit both lamps. Faith popped her head in, too.

"Rose, thee was attacked?" she asked in a low voice.

"Did the children tell thee?" I'd told them only that I'd had a small accident so as not to concern them.

"No, but David and Granny Dot gave me a ride home from just outside the mill." Faith's place of employment was a short distance down the hill in town. "David told me about the attack on thee."

"Good," I said. I looked from face to face. "But I don't want to relive the details right now. Is that all right?"

"Of course, dear," Mother said. "Faith, let's get supper on, shall we? David, will thee join us?"

"Thank you, but I'm afraid I can't. I promised my father I'd attend a meeting with him. He's been quite successful establishing a health clinic for his workers at the shoe factory, but we have business to attend to."

"Be sure to check out Rosie's wound before thee goes." She and Faith left the room.

David perched on the bed next to me. "Tuck your chin down for a moment."

I obliged, spying his black doctor's bag on the floor. His hands were gentle, probing my scalp, but I jumped when he touched the wound itself.

"I'm sorry, my sweet. Now look directly at me." He held a finger in front of my eyes. "Keep your eyes on my finger." He passed it back and forth.

I tracked the movement without difficulty. He held up three fingers.

"How many?" he asked.

"Three." I kept answering as he varied the numbers of fingers he held up.

He brought the small table lamp close, then pulled it to the side at arm's length, then brought it back in front of my face.

"Good," he declared.

"It looks like thee is testing me for a concussion."

"Exactly. I guess I'm not surprised you know about shock to the brain."

I smiled wanly. "Did I pass the exam?"

"I suppose. You cried out when you first sat up, though. Are you having headaches?"

I acknowledged I was.

"You're going to need to rest and not do anything taxing for a few days to let yourself recover. I'd like to admit you to Anna Jaques for complete rest. The hospital nurses can monitor your status."

I wrinkled my nose. "I'm not going to the hospital, David. Surely a trip there isn't necessary? Mother is here, she'll take care of me." The hospital, only a few years old, was named for its primary benefactress. Anna Jaques, a wealthy unmarried woman with no heirs, died the year after the first patient was admitted, but she lived to see her dream of helping her community realized.

"Are you certain?" He waited a second, then went on. "It would keep you safe, too. I hate the thought of a murderer coming after you, Rosie. If anything were to happen to you, my life would be over, too," he murmured.

How could I ever have doubted him? "I don't want to go to the hospital." I patted his hand. "But nothing's going to happen to me. I already promised Kevin I wouldn't go out alone at night, and that I'd cease my

270

investigation. This afternoon frightened me badly."

"All right," he said, but his frown remained.

"David, yesterday Kevin arrested Hilarius Bauer."

"No! For the murder?"

"Yes. But when Kevin stopped by today, he said Hilarius was released."

"What a blessing. I truly don't see him being a killer."

"I don't either," I said.

"Now, my darling, I am going to have to dress your wound. And I'm afraid it's going to hurt."

I hunched my shoulders but agreed. He drew scissors out of his bag and trimmed my hair around the area. I gritted my teeth, wincing when he daubed gauze on the injured spot.

"I know it stings, but the carbolic acid in the gauze will keep it from becoming infected. Lister made quite the discovery with this technique."

"Didn't he cut his surgical team's mortality rate almost in half by cleaning wounds thoroughly?"

"Precisely so." David patted my head with dry gauze before kissing my forehead. "You should wear a clean sleeping cap to bed each night for several days. When you are up tomorrow, I'd remove the cap so the wound can get air on it, but put on a fresh cap if you lie down to rest."

"Yes, sir, Doctor Dodge," I said playfully. "Thank thee for coming. I'd never seen such a pleasant sight as thy face in front of mine when I awoke."

He kissed me again, this time on the lips, then stood. "I wish you would have a telephone installed. I would feel more secure in your safety if you did."

"The thought has crossed my mind, I admit. But aren't they quite dear?"

"Yes. I can pay for it, though. I'd be happy to."

"Don't be silly, David. My business has been thriving. I can pay for my own telephone. It would be a great help in my work." *If I'm still able to work.* What if I was called to a genuine birth in the next few days? What if the headaches persisted and I wasn't able to help the women who relied on me to give their precious babies safe passage into our world?

TWENTY-SIX

After our supper of chicken pies and roasted squash, I retired to my room. Frederick had been curious about my incident, but I didn't want to speak of it in front of the young ones. And I needed quiet away from the bustle of the family. I tried to read. Instead the words decided to go for a swim on the page, frolicking up and down as if floating on the waves at Salisbury Beach. I closed the book with a sigh.

It was only eight o'clock, but I changed into my nightdress and donned the promised clean cap, selecting the oldest, softest one I had. I plumped up the pillows and reclined half sitting in bed as I had earlier, pulling my knees to my chest. Kevin had asked me to think if I'd had any clue as to my attacker's identity. In my mind I moved through the sequence of events again.

Arriving at the property. Seeing the big house dark, unoccupied. Making my way to the carriage house. Had I seen any movement, any footprints in the snow? I didn't think so. Sliding open the wide door. Surveying the inside, the horse stalls, the stairs, the graceful phaeton with its tall narrow wheels and gleaming metalwork. I paused there for a moment in my memory. Had I caught a faint whiff of a scent? But what had the scent been? I continued in my memory to feeling the blow. Falling forward. Passing out, although I couldn't remember the last part.

The only clue might be in the scent. What with the wind blowing the snow and my preoccupation with the impending birth, I hadn't heard a step, hadn't sensed anyone behind me.

The door to my parlor cracked open. "May I?" Mother asked, holding a cup and saucer. "I brought thee some feverfew tea. It should help any pain in thy head."

"Of course." I patted the edge of the bed and accepted the tea. I sipped the hot herbal concoction, which she'd sweetened with a bit of honey. "This is perfect. I thank thee, Mother."

She held up a tiny brown bottle. "Thee can also rub peppermint oil into thy temples, forehead, and jaw. It soothes and helps healing."

I gazed at her with a heart full of gratitude. "Thee is the best mother ever. But speaking of mothers, I wanted to ask thee more about thy visit with Clarinda."

She laughed as she sat. "She was wary at first. Far too polite, as ladies in her position tend to be, hiding behind the façade of etiquette. But when we fell to talking about David's childhood, and thy own, we became simply two older mothers. We had more in common than she expected and the visit wasn't a bit dismal." She squeezed three drops of the oil onto her fingertips and began to massage it into my forehead.

I closed my eyes and inhaled the candy-like scent, but it didn't take my mind off our conversation. "Did thee happen to broach the topic of our engagement?"

"No, I decided to leave thy marriage for the next time. And I now know there will be one." She stroked the oil onto my temples on each side. "Don't worry, Rose. Thee and thy sweetheart will marry as way opens."

I rolled my eyes just a little. Patience was not my strong suit and I'd struggled with waiting for God to open the way forward my whole life. "Yes, Mother."

"Is thee willing to share thy experience of this afternoon?" She sat back, her ministering done for the moment.

I took a deep breath and let it out, then told her what had transpired. "I was quite alarmed to wake up on the cold floor of the carriage house. At first I didn't remember how I landed there. And to find the door locked was a test of my fortitude."

"Of which thee has always had in great measure. At a young age thee would go hiking with Allan and when the two of you returned, even from ascending Mount Wachusett, he would report thee uttered not a word of complaint."

"Those were happy times, just Daddy and me," I said softly.

"And when thee resolved to move here and apprentice to old Orpha, it took quite a measure of courage to begin thy life's work far from home."

"At least Harriet and the children were nearby," I said with a touch of wistfulness. "I'm glad I had those few years growing closer to her again." My sister had been ten years older than I, and had married Frederick and started a family when she was only eighteen. Her sudden death a year and a half ago had been a blow much worse than the one I'd received today, to all of us.

"I'm glad too, even though I missed thee terribly. But back to thy story."

I glanced up at a little knock on the door.

Faith popped her head in. "Come in, niece," I said.

Faith perched on the edge of my desk chair. "Was thee terribly afraid in that barn?"

"Yes, of course. But I was determined not to freeze to death in there. And the drop from the window wasn't too very great."

"A blessing," Mother said. "Does thee have any clue about the villain who attacked thee?"

"Sadly, no. I have been giving it careful thought, as the detective asked me to, but I just don't know. The person was wily enough to hide nearby and move without a sound before striking me." I began to shake my head but thought the better of it. "I hope Kevin will take a man or two up there in the morning and look for signs."

"Shouldn't he also interview the neighbors?" Faith asked.

"Alas, there aren't any close by. But a resident of the house farther down the hill was the person who let the police know they thought I was a suspicious traveler, so perhaps they also spied my attacker. I'm sure Kevin will speak to them."

"Rose, I want to write a short article for the paper about thy attack," Faith said. "May I?"

"I'll look the fool, going to an unknown house in a snowstorm." I pressed my lips together.

"No, thee will look like a committed and brave midwife," Faith said. "And thy escape will only confirm it. It's news the town will want to know about."

"I suppose it's all right, then." How could I turn her down, this bright niece of mine, so determined to get out of the mill and into a career as a writer?

"It will be only a paragraph or two. I won't bother thee. I'll use what David told me. And I'll try to get over to talk to Kevin on my dinner break tomorrow." Faith stood, planted a light kiss on my forehead, and hurried out.

"She recognizes what is news and what will affect our community," I said as I gazed at the doorway through which she'd disappeared. "She really wants to make a go of being a journalist."

"And well she might. She needs to extricate herself from the mill. The work is too hard, the hours too long, and she's liable to go deaf as a post from the din of those infernal machines." Mother shook herself and rose. "I hope thee sleeps well, daughter. I'll be just upstairs, so do call if thee needs me."

"I will, Mother. It's a great comfort to have thee here at this fraught time."

She stroked my forehead before slipping out of the room. It hadn't occurred to me until now to consider that the house halfway up Powow might have seen a buggy, a carriage, a wagon, whatever conveyance carried the evil person who hit me up the hill. My spirits rose at the thought. I extinguished the lamp and carefully laid my head down, sliding into sleep.

I awoke in the dark of the night with my head pounding so hard it made me nauseated. I swallowed, feeling close to vomiting. Gingerly easing up to sitting, I took slow deep breaths until my stomach settled and the pounding eased off to a less painful sense of pressure. I touched the wound but it wasn't bleeding.

How long was this going to last? I'd never had a head injury before and didn't have experience with any of my clients having one, either. I knew how to deal with injuries to the birth canal. How to stanch bleeding from tears. Which herb poultices aided healing. How deeply to massage a womb to encourage its contraction back to normal after the birth. And more. But this was a different kind of wound.

What if I was unable to attend the next birth I was called to? Annie wasn't anywhere near experienced enough to deliver a baby on her own. My teacher, Orpha, had retired and handed over her practice to me nearly two years ago precisely because she was too old and frail to continue. She was no longer able to traipse off to a birth in the middle of the night, kneel to examine a woman on a bed, or stay awake for more than a day, as a midwife was often required to do. I wouldn't be able to call on her.

There was a doctor in town who delivered babies, but John Douglass had been rather hostile to me the one time I'd solicited his advice on a difficult pregnancy. I wouldn't be asking him for help. I didn't know where to turn, what to do. I'd worked so hard to build up my practice, to establish trust with my clients, I couldn't just abandon them. But if my current state of health continued, it would be impossible to do my job.

And what if the killer came after me again? A shudder rippled through me. Even when I became well enough to go out, would it be safe? Would I be followed, trapped, threatened? Would I have to look over my shoulder at every turn? Until the police arrested Rowena's murderer, my own life would be at risk. I'd always been a confident, forthright person, but now I couldn't conceive how to go forward without being surrounded by a dark cloud of fear.

I wished I were already married to David. What a comfort it would be to have him beside me in the middle of the night. To be able to reach over and touch him, talk with him about my joys and fears. To know his calm, steadying presence would always be with me. I prayed my mother's meeting with Clarinda would soften her, make her more open to our union.

I scolded myself. For now, of course there was something I could do. I closed my eyes and held my fears in the Light of God as I had done my whole life. Way would open. I would be able to discern how to go out in the world without fear. I simply had to wait for it.

TWENTY-SEVEN

I walked slowly through the soggy streets of town at ten the next morning on a sunny day, with any snow not in shadow quickly melting. The air was cool, of course, given the season, and the sunlight at a weak angle, but the difference between yesterday and today was once again striking. Such was weather in New England. The wags always said, Wait an hour and it'll change.

I'd slept until nearly nine o'clock, which was most unusual for me. I still felt pressure in my head, but the pounding headache had blessedly not returned. My attack of fears in the night had also slid away, and my confidence at going out into the world was restored. If I stayed on public streets and in well-lit and well-populated places, I knew I would be safe.

Guy had dropped by the house as I was having my coffee and said Kevin wanted to speak to me, if I was feeling better. He'd offered me a ride but I'd told him I would walk down after breakfast. I'd left Mother baking a few minutes ago. I told her I was fine and would be back in an hour or so. David had cautioned me not to go out, but I felt so much better I decided it wouldn't hurt me.

Now I trod carefully and in no hurry so as to protect my healing brain, and I took the steps up into the police station with slow deliberate steps. Kevin happened to be in the anteroom. He greeted me and ushered me back to his office.

I lowered myself into a chair keeping my back erect. I'd discovered, while lacing up my shoes at home, that lowering my head brought a wave of pain.

Kevin sat, too, and peered at me. "Are you sure you should have come out, Miss Rose?"

"I'm fine, Kevin. I simply need to keep my head up. What was this matter thee wanted to speak with me about?"

"I'd like you to testify in court about Leroy Dunnsmore and his actions on Election Day. You're a reliable witness and of good character. I want to keep that coot behind bars."

In court? Me? "When would this be?"

"There's a hearing tomorrow at the court-house. What do you say?"

"I am happy to oblige. But I hope thee knows I will not swear an oath." I gazed straight at him.

"And why in blazes not?" He set his hat on the desk and scratched his head, leaving his hair standing on end.

"Friends live with integrity. I will not swear to tell the truth, because I always tell the truth." *Well, mostly.* "Swearing would suggest the rest of the time I might have different standards of truth." I'd never had occasion to exercise this stance in court, but I knew other Quakers who did. "I will affirm to the magistrate that I will be truthful, if he insists."

"That's the craziest thing I ever heard of." Kevin frowned, but it was an indulgent expression. "It isn't enough you all talk funny. What's the difference between swearing and affirming, anyway?"

"It is our practice, Kevin." I smiled at him. "Will thee call on Zebulon Weed to testify, as well?"

"Yes, I plan to."

"Tell me, has thee been able to locate the messenger boy I described?"

"Not yet, but I've alerted all our officers walking their beats to keep an eye out for him. This town isn't so large we won't spot him by and by." He tapped a pencil on the desk. "Were you able to come up with any other memories which might help us find your attacker?"

"Not really. I feel like I smelled a faint scent, but I could be mistaken, and I can't place it, anyway."

"A pity."

"I was thinking thee should interview the residents on Powow Street who reported seeing me. Maybe they also saw my attacker's conveyance driving up or down the road."

Kevin grinned. "Great minds think alike. I'm off for there as soon as we're finished talking."

"Good. I hope they have helpful information." I pushed up to standing. "I will confess I felt quite fearful in the night, thinking I might be attacked again."

"You're going to be very careful and stay in full view of others while you're out, I hope."

"Thee can be certain I will. This fine sunny day has helped to dispel my worries, too."

"Everyone in this department is doing his best to catch the killer before any more damage is done, Miss Rose. You can rest secure with Amesbury's finest."

"Did thee have Zula Goodwin write something down?"

He nodded, fishing in the mess on his desk for something. "Where the dickens is it?" He shook his head. "Yes, I had her come in and write down her statement. She wasn't happy to do it, but I insisted. And you were right, her hand does resemble the writing on the note found with Mrs. Felch's body."

"But it wasn't identical?"

"Can't say. I turned it over to Frenchie, this new fellow over from France we hired recently. Calls himself a graphologist. He'll compare the two samples."

I nodded, but with care. "I thought I had read the science of handwriting analysis was further advanced in Europe than here." I turned toward the door, then halted. I faced him again. "I remember something I meant to tell thee yesterday." Was it just yesterday? It seemed like a week ago I'd been to see Catherine. "I went looking for information in Rowena's neighborhood yesterday, and —"

"Miss Rose! I can't have you snooping about like that." His face reddened. "My team already covered the Greenwood Street area. Talked to every neighbor. It's you asking questions got you hit on the head. Do you understand?"

"Yes. But I have every right to walk the

286

streets in safety, just as men do. No man is going to make me cower at home in fear." I held up my hand. "Hear me out, please. I discovered an acquaintance of mine, Catherine Toomey, lives diagonally across from the Felch home."

"Of course. It was Mrs. Toomey who described Hilarius to a T to one of my men."

"What she didn't tell the officer was she heard a conveyance going by at around the same time. It could have been the murderer's, since Hilarius doesn't own one."

"I can't believe my man didn't ask her that." Kevin shook his head. "He's a young one and still learning. So did she describe what type of vehicle it was?"

"Alas, no. She heard it rather than saw it, because the road is planked."

"Unfortunate." He blinked as if it helped him think. "Maybe I should find out what transport our other suspects own and do a test drive-by with Mrs. Toomey listening."

"I like your idea. The Osgoods came to vote in a black runabout, and Oscar Felch drives a Parry phaeton. Zula has a green Bailey runabout."

"How might you know about all these vehicles now, Miss Rose?" Kevin cocked his head and cast a mock stern look at me.

I pushed my glasses back up my nose.

"After I talked to Catherine I paid a call on Oscar. The phaeton was harnessed to his horse in the drive as if someone was ready to go out or had just returned home. He had no guests visiting him, so it must have been his. And I saw Zula's runabout at the end of Election Day. She invited a few of us to her home for refreshments. That's how I know."

"Fine, then. Let me get those down." He scribbled on a piece of paper, then glanced up. "Did you learn anything from your conversation with Mr. Felch?"

I thought back. "He doesn't get along with Rowena's grandmother, a Mabel Roune. He asked me to tell him all the details of finding the body."

"I hope you didn't oblige."

"I have learned from thee, Kevin." I laughed. "No, of course I didn't."

"What about Miss Goodwin? Are you sure it was safe to be having tea with her?"

"I wasn't alone, so it felt quite safe. And I should also have told thee what I learned Third Day evening. She said Rowena didn't suffer fools lightly. So she might have had other enemies we don't even know about."

Kevin let out a groan like a foghorn.

"And when Bertie asked her if she was angry about Rowena not moving in with her, Zula said she was," I added. "And then told us she didn't kill her."

"We'll see about that, Miss Rose." He stood. "Yes, indeed. We'll see about that."

TWENTY-EIGHT

While I was out, I decided to stop by the Mercantile and see if Catherine was working. Perhaps she had remembered another detail about the night of the murder. I was halfway down Main Street toward the square when a gray horse clopped up next to me and stopped. I glanced up to see Bertie grinning down at me, her fetching navy hat contrasting with her light hair underneath.

"How goes the battle?" She threw her leg over Grover's back and slid off.

"Carefully," I answered. I told her of my head injury and my subsequent escape.

The smile slid off her face as fast as she'd dismounted. "Poor Rosetta. Should you be out and about so soon?"

"I'm all right if I stay vertical and go slowly. And Kevin is on the case. I just came from the station."

"He'd better catch the scoundrel, and soon."

"I agree. What's new with thee, my friend?" I shielded my eyes with my hand, as the sun glinted off a window at George Wendall's barber shop across the road.

"Not much. Think I'm going to have to rename my friend here Benjamin because of the election results?" She patted Grover's withers.

"I wouldn't advise it. I dare say our ousted president might run again in four years." A heavy wagon piled high with hay clattered by.

"I wasn't serious. Grover he was and Grover he'll remain." The horse snuffled and tossed his head as if he agreed. "Is your mother still about?"

"Yes, she's staying on for a bit. I'll admit it was a great comfort to have her nearby yesterday. Even though I'm twenty-six, she's still my mama."

When a shadow passed over Bertie's face, I regretted mentioning Mother. My friend was estranged from her own mother, who lived just across the Merrimack River in nearby West Newbury. I'd never learned the reason for their split.

"And David came by last evening to check on me and clean my wound," I added.

"Ah, the handsome doctor. You caught yourself a good one in that man, Rose."

"I know. I only hope I can keep him."

She scoffed. "You talking about the balderdash the old Quaker fishwife told you?"

"Yes." I sighed. "And she's not a fishwife at all. She's just following the rules."

"Entirely without imagination, too. Listen to Auntie Bert, now. We'll figure something out. Don't you worry."

I smiled at her. "Yes, ma'am, Auntie Bert."

"That's better. I'd best be off. I'd offer you a ride on the back, but I'm not sure trotting on cobblestones would do you any good."

"I agree, but I appreciate the offer."

"You take good care, my friend." She set her foot in the stirrup and hoisted herself into the saddle.

"And thee as well."

A couple of minutes later I pulled open the door to Sawyer's Mercantile, which sold seemingly anything and everything, from fabric to flour, tools to tonics. A few women shopped, and a stooped man in an Irish cap examined a selection of canes. I spotted Catherine at the counter and wove through an aisle crowded with things made of metal: tin cups, pewter pitchers, copper cooking pots, iron pokers. Faith's friend Jasmine, who also worked at the Mercantile, was flicking the items on the top shelf with a feather duster.

I greeted her. "Jasmine, what did thee think of the demonstration?" I asked with a smile.

Her light eyes flashed under a fringe of black curls. "It was splendid, Miss Carroll. Simply splendid. Despite the violence, I took heart at all those older ladies standing up for our rights. I'll be signing up for the next one, you can be sure."

"I'm glad to hear it."

She glanced around and lowered her voice. "I want to be able to vote in the '92 election. We have to change the way the world works!"

"Indeed we do." I made my way to the counter, still smiling at this new young convert to the cause.

"Hello, Rose," Catherine said with a rosy-cheeked smile. She took a second glance at me. "Are you all right? You're looking rather peaked today."

"I had a bit of an accident yesterday."

"I'm sorry to hear it. We've plenty of tonics for sale." She pointed to the glass-fronted cabinet on the wall behind her, which featured glass bottles with names like Dr. Powers' Invigorating Elixir, Mrs. Winslow's Soothing Syrup, Lloyd's Cocaine Toothache Drops, and Hostetter's Celebrated Stomach Bitters.

"I thank thee for the suggestion, but I'll be fine." Most tonics contained high amounts of alcohol or other intoxicating substances. I'd found they had no real effect on health and I always advised my pregnant clients to avoid them.

"Good. Now what can I do for you on this lovely morning?"

"I'm afraid I'm not here to buy anything today." I looked around before lowering my voice. "I wanted to ask if perhaps there was any new detail, no matter how small, you might have remembered from the night" — I spied the twins playing with dolls behind the counter — "about which we spoke."

She nodded slowly. "I did give my memory more thought, and I started listening more carefully as I watched carriages drive by ever since we talked. I'm sure it was a conveyance pulled by only one horse. The planks resound differently with two animals, as you can imagine."

"You've been very helpful. I thank thee, Catherine."

The bell on the door jangled. I turned to see Zula sweep in. She strode toward us bringing a cloud of scent with her.

"Good morning, Mrs. Toomey, Miss Carroll."

We returned her greetings.

"I need to pick up a vial of violet toilet
water, but I also have a notice about the
next Woman Suffrage Association meeting
to be posted on the board." She waved a
piece of paper. "May I?"

"Be my guest." Catherine gestured across
the large space toward the board where the
store let members of the community post
news and personal advertisements. "There
should be tacks to spare already in it."

"Thank you."

"When is the meeting, Zula, and is there
an agenda?" I asked.

"It's tonight, and we will primarily be
remembering Rowena." Her voice faltered
at the end.

"I'll try to be there," I said. If I was up to
it, that is. I gazed at her. Was this my attacker of yesterday? "How did thee pass
yesterday's snowstorm?"

She stared at me and waited just a beat
too long before answering. "What a question. I was indoors, of course. Where anyone
with sense would be. Why, was there another
murder? Will you be suspecting me in every
one of your cases from now on?"

"No, I —"

"Did you think I didn't notice? You and Bertie quizzing me at every opportunity." She leaned in, with pain in her eyes, and lowered her voice to a whisper. "I loved Rowena, Rose. I never would have harmed her. Never." She strode off to hang her notice.

I watched her go, stunned. I was making enemies right and left. And she was grieving just like our family still grieved for Harriet. I'd been too harsh by half in my questioning. And yet I felt I had to do it. Had to get to the truth.

"That's poppycock about everyone with sense being indoors during a storm," Catherine murmured, also watching Zula. "What about postmen and train workers and all the other people who work for a living? Plenty of folks don't have the means to just hide indoors when the weather is inclement. It has nothing to do with sense. That's an overprivileged lady right there."

"I might agree with thee." Or maybe Zula wasn't safe, dry, and warm in her fancy apartment. Perhaps instead she was arranging to deliver a malicious message and then lying in wait to beat me and leave me for dead.

By the time I trudged up the hill toward

home, I knew I'd done too much. My head pounded again and my vision was dim, like I peered through dirty glass. I should have listened to David. After the Mercantile I'd had to pay a postnatal visit to Emily to check on her and her baby. Fortunately for all of us, both mother and newborn thrived, and I'd only stayed for ten minutes.

Now in the house, I greeted Mother before plodding to the easy chair in the sitting room. I sank down, legs splayed in front of me. I prayed I wouldn't get called to a birth any time soon. Because of overextending myself this morning in the cause of sleuthing, I simply wouldn't be able to go. I needed to reorder what was really important to me.

"Let's get thee out of thy wraps," Mother said, following me in. She helped me off with my outer clothing. She took it away to hang, and returned with a steaming cup of tea.

I savored the sweet milky brew. "This is perfect. I thank thee," I said, as the clock chimed eleven times.

"It looks as if thee might have gone a little too far this morning."

"Not in distance, but in effort, yes."

"Shall I look at thy wound?" she asked.

"Please." I removed the cap I'd worn

under my bonnet and inclined my head.

"It's healing over." She pressed gently around it. "I don't feel swelling."

"Good. The shock to my brain presents a bigger problem right now, I think."

"Rest will cure thee, my dear." She handed me a letter. "This came in the morning post. I hope it proves to be restful, as well."

The fancy envelope in a pale blue paper was addressed to me. Intertwined initials pressed into the sealing wax read CCD. I'd venture a guess those letters belonged to Clarinda Chase Dodge. I wasn't sure I wanted to open it, but I did, anyway.

Dear Miss Carroll,

We intend to invite a few friends to dine with us this evening. Will you and Mrs. Carroll do us the favor of forming two of our party? You will meet Mr. Benjamin Lehigh, with whom I believe you are already acquainted, as also several others, to whom I shall feel much pleasure in introducing you. We shall meet at my home at six o'clock; and I feel convinced that, if you have no previous engagement, you will not disappoint me in the pleasure of seeing you and your mother at our simple repast.

> Believe me to remain,
> My dear Miss Carroll,
> Most sincerely yours,
> Mrs. Herbert Dodge

It was as if Queen Victoria herself had commanded my presence. While I'd survived several teas, as well as a fancy dinner dance at the Dodge home over the last six months or so, spending time with David's mother was not my favorite pastime. But if I wanted a life with him, I would need to find ways to enjoy Clarinda's company. And it sounded like Mother had softened her up a bit. Benjamin was a congenial and prosperous Quaker lawyer from Newburyport who had helped with the murder case last July. I knew he was friendly with the Dodge family, and it would be a pleasure to see him again. I hoped David's flighty cousin wasn't one of the invitees. Clarinda had been pushing David to marry Violet instead of me ever since he and I had started courting. Well, I'd simply make the best of it if she was included.

I read it to Mother. "What does thee think? Shall we go?" I asked.

"Does thee wish to?"

"I think I'd better. And it would be a

comfort to have thee with me."

"Rest for the remainder of the day, then, so thee will be able. Now, I'm off to visit with Frannie. I so enjoyed meeting her at the demonstration, and she wants to become more active in the movement."

"Enjoy thyself, and greet her for me. Speaking of the demonstration reminds me that Zula posted a notice in the Mercantile of a Woman Suffrage Association meeting tonight." I set the cup down. "She said it will be largely to remember Rowena. Will thee tell Frannie?"

"Of course. It's a pity we can't go because of the dinner invitation. But I somehow think dining with the Dodges is more important tonight, doesn't thee?"

I nodded very slowly and closed my eyes. All I wanted to do was sleep. From the front of the house came a rapping noise. My eyes flew open and my heart sank. Was it a father or a driver summoning me? Or had I forgotten about a prenatal appointment?

Mother hurried out of the room. She returned with Hilarius following. Good heavens, what was he doing here?

I greeted him. "What can we help thee with?"

He turned his cap in his hat, his shoulders forward. "I need your help. You're like a doctor, ain't you?"

"I'm a midwife, Hilarius. The only medicine I know is in the area of childbirth. Does thee have a wife in labor?"

"No, it's not like that. It's my old ma, see. She's so poorly, and she's worse today. All the worry what with me going to jail just did her in. Could you come to see her?"

Absolutely not. I went off with a suspect in the spring and it ended up being a terribly dangerous situation. I wasn't putting myself in peril again. But how to tell the poor fellow, who was obviously beside himself with worry?

"I'm so sorry thy mother isn't well, but I'm afraid I can't help thee." I spied Mother behind him, shaking her head with vigor. We were of the same opinion.

"But you have to! I think she's dying." His narrow face was drawn down in concern.

"I suffered an injury yesterday, Hilarius. I regret that I'm simply not able to sojourn out at this time. I hope she improves soon and that thee finds the help thee needs."

"I'm going to see a friend, and I believe she owns a telephone," Mother said to him, stepping to his side. "I'll call David Dodge for thee. How does that sound? He's an actual doctor."

"I know he is, and a real gentleman, too." Hilarius said. "But by the time he gets free from his work and makes it here from Newburyport, my mum might already have crossed the dark river."

I'd heard others use the quaint phrase meaning death. "Thee will need to seek out a physician here in Amesbury, then. Perhaps John Douglass is in his offices," I said. "I'm truly not qualified to assist, and I apologize that I can't even come to see thy mother." Hilarius had helped me plenty getting Frederick home from the bar First Day night, and I pitied the man, but I couldn't do anything to help him. "I do hope her lapse in health is a temporary one."

His shoulders slumped even more. "I'll take my leave, then."

"Wait," I said, hoping this wasn't going too far with a man whose mother was so ill. "Might I ask thee a question? It will only take a moment."

"Yes?"

"On the night thee says thee saw Rowena dead, did thee also see a carriage or buggy pass, a conveyance drawn by a single horse?" My words rushed out.

His nostrils flared and his eyes darted every which way but on me.

I waited.

"Yes, I did."

"Did you recognize the driver? Did he stop at the Felch house?" If Hilarius knew who drove the carriage, it could be a critical piece of information.

"No, and no." His voice was low and hoarse as he spit out the words. He turned to go, with Mother ushering him out. Before he left the room he looked back at me. "I didn't kill her, you know."

The afternoon post brought a short note from John. He'd written, in his educated flowing hand, that he was sorry about my plan to visit him, but that he was returning to Oak Knoll by noon. I checked the clock, which read two. I'd not be seeking counsel from this wise Friend until he returned the next time.

I'd penned our acceptance to the dinner before Mother left and gave it to her to post. I'd spent the hours since she departed resting and reading, trying not to think too hard or move too suddenly. Now I gazed around the modest sitting room. The upholstered chairs were a little shabby, and whose wouldn't be with five children in the house? The oval rug was braided, not an exotic Oriental carpet. The bookcase was crowded with books for adults and children alike, as befit a household headed by a teacher. The decor was suitably simple, perfect for a Quaker home. The air still smelled faintly of apple and cinnamon from the pies Mother had baked, and the only sound was the comforting ticking of the long case clock in the corner.

The room couldn't have been more different from the spacious Dodge home on High Street in Newburyport, with its ornate drapery, delicate chairs, plush fabrics, its large rooms and windows. I far preferred the room I sat in now. Would David and I be able to find a comfortable middle ground between the two styles when we set up housekeeping together? And would that day ever come? It seemed like an eon had passed since he'd proposed marriage in July, when it was really only a few short months.

I put my feet up and closed my eyes again. My head pain had eased somewhat. But sleep didn't come. It was crowded out by visions of someone strong swinging a hard object at my head. By Hilarius's odd reaction to my asking about the carriage. By Zula's too-long pause in responding to my question about her whereabouts during the storm. And by knowing my attacker and the murderer — I assumed they were one and the same — still walked free.

Was there any detail I'd missed, any connection I'd failed to make? If I weren't so fragile from my beating, I might go pay a call on Mabel Roune. Annie had reported Mabel said Oscar was given to fits of temper and jealousy. I was interested in knowing the details of those fits. I still suspected he had something to do with Rowena's death, despite his absence from the scene of the crime. And the society matron Mabel might well have refused to share such details with a lowly police officer. But my morning had taught me I wasn't ready to dive back into detecting unless I could do it from where I sat right now.

How could I find out where Zula had been during the snowstorm? Again I rued my injury. If I was able to venture out, I was certain I could find a way to interview one of her servants. Surely on a Fourth Day they would have been at the house and would know if she'd gone out in her runabout or had stayed home. That would at least be one bit of information. The same went for Elbridge's whereabouts. The Osgoods employed at least the one maid and likely a cook and a stable man, too. I wasn't quite sure how I could approach the household staff, though.

It was all moot. I wasn't going anywhere.

I resolved to let Kevin and his crew do their jobs. My task for the moment was to heal, and to get ready for the challenge of dinner with Clarinda.

TWENTY-NINE

A simple repast this was not. I was seated next to David, with his father at the end of the table on my left, in their elegant dining room. Clarinda held place of honor at the other end. Mother was to her right and thin, fair-haired Benjamin Lehigh sat in turn on Mother's right. The other three guests were cordial, but I felt hard pressed to find common ground with them.

David had kindly sent a driver in a Rockaway to pick up Mother and me. I'd donned my best and newest dress, a simple style in a deep red fabric, and I'd done my hair as nicely as I could in honor of the occasion, coiling my braid loosely over my wound and pinning it in place. Mother had worn her best dress, too, and we both sported fresh lace collars. Clarinda, of course, was in a matronly sky blue silk version of the latest style with the narrower sleeves and plentiful embroidery. The other older lady at the table wore a similarly cut gown. The younger one, who sat on the other side of widower Benjamin, was the most fashionably dressed. She wore a gown suitable for her age, which boasted a deep ruffled neckline, ribbed silk bodice, and brocaded satin skirt, all in shades of pinks and blues.

Perhaps Clarinda was trying to act the matchmaker, pairing her up with Benjamin, who had lost his wife some years before and raised his two daughters by himself. Benjamin was around fifty, but he was very much a proponent of healthy, energetic pastimes like swimming, tennis, and hiking. He projected a much younger and more energetic image than what one normally would expect of a man his age. He was dressed tonight in a dark suit with a flashing red cravat. Although a Quaker, he was also a prosperous lawyer and given to bursts of color in his attire.

David had inquired in a low voice about my health when we'd arrived, and I'd told him I was feeling somewhat better, but I refrained from telling him about my overactive morning.

So far we'd already had a delicious oyster soup, crispy fried smelts with *tartare* sauce, and a creamed chicken in puff pastry cups Clarinda referred to as *vol-au-vent*. Now the young uniformed servant was coming around with a platter holding slices of beef roast, offering Polish sauce and grape jelly as accompaniments. I didn't know how he managed to keep his white gloves free of both the bloody beef juice and the purple jelly, but he did.

"Eat up now, Rose," David's father Herbert said, his blue eyes twinkling as always, both the color and the expression echoing David's own. "We need to put meat on those slender bones of yours."

"I'm doing my best, Herbert." I had a slender build, it was true, just like my mother's.

"Mr. Dodge, don't be rude," Clarinda admonished from her position as reigning hostess. She sipped her wine.

David's knee nudged mine and I glanced at him to see a fond smile directed at me. I'd never have gotten through this evening without him. Of course, I wouldn't have needed to without him, either.

"Mr. Lehigh," David said. "Did you win your match?"

"No, more's the pity. Lost to the Amesbury team."

"What type of match would that be, Benjamin?" I asked.

"Cricket. Love the sport. It's all very Brit-
ishy."

I smiled. "Who plays on the Amesbury
team? Perhaps I'm acquainted with some of
the gentlemen, if there are any Friends
among them."

"Mostly lawyers and doctors, including a
man with the unusual given name of Elbridge."

I looked up from my plate. Benjamin
seemed to be sending a message with his
eyes, but I couldn't imagine what it was.

All the guests except Mother and I were
partaking of wine, even Quaker Benjamin,
which surprised me. David had barely
touched his drink, though, and I was happy
with water. Another servant followed the
beef with cauliflower in cream sauce and a
potato soufflé. Goodness, I was going to
burst. I requested small portions of each.

"Rose," Benjamin said in his surprisingly
deep voice. "I hear thee had several unfortunate encounters recently." Being a lawyer,
he'd no doubt had heard about Rowena's
death.

I peeked at Clarinda. She was carefully
cutting her slice of beef and not looking at
either Benjamin or me. Was talking about
murder inappropriate in polite company?
Well, it was her guest who'd brought it up.

"It's true, I'm afraid," I said.

"David told me you're involved in another murder," Herbert said. "Bless my boots, how positively thrilling."

The lady across from me gasped and brought her hand to her mouth. The man seated to Clarinda's left on the same side of the table as me leaned forward to look at me.

"Is this true?" he asked. "You must tell us all about it."

Clarinda's knife clattered on her plate. "Is it entirely necessary to have this kind of conversation at the dinner table?" She glared at Herbert.

"Now, now, dear," Herbert said. "It can't hurt. It's all the talk down at the shop."

It was? In Newburyport? Was I becoming infamous? My head began to pound again.

"Do the police have any good leads?" Benjamin asked. "It's been, what, five days since thee found the body?"

I nodded. "Rowena Felch was killed Seventh Day night. I happened to be passing her home First Day morning and noticed her . . ." I caught myself before saying the word *corpse.* "Lying under a bush," I finished. "As for leads, the detective has identified several suspects but has not uncovered sufficient evidence to convict a

311

suspect, as far as I know."

"David tells me Mr. Bauer, the fellow who did a bit of work here, was arrested recently," Herbert said. "When I employed him, I found him honest and of good character."

"I've met him and he struck me the same way," I said. "He was arrested, but later released for lack of evidence."

"I might have a piece of information for thee," Benjamin said. "I will share it before we part company tonight."

I gazed at him. A piece of information? About the murder, apparently. And one he didn't want to share with the rest of the party. I was dying to know what it was, but I was clearly going to have to wait.

"Rose herself was attacked yesterday," David said. "She figured how to escape to safety entirely without help."

The younger woman across from me stared, blinking. "What a trying situation. And how brave you are." She ran her gaze over me like she was admiring a statue of Joan of Arc.

"You most certainly are a brave soul, Rose," Herbert said, smiling at me.

Clarinda's neck grew red and her eyes flashed. Was she going to admonish me again for being an independent businesswoman? In her world, ladies didn't get themselves into situations like finding bodies and being out alone, which I was sure in her mind only invited the attack. She pressed her lips together in a thin line, apparently thinking the better of scolding me at her own festive supper party.

"Clarinda, I don't think I told thee about our suffrage work on Election Day," my mother said.

If she thought this was a good change of subject, she was in for a surprise. I knew Clarinda did not approve of women pushing for the vote. Was Mother trying to ruin her newfound rapport with David's mother?

The younger woman across looked relieved at not having to hear about murder and attacks. "I heard about the demonstration," she said with interest in her voice. "I wish we had accomplished the same here in Newburyport. You had over a hundred women there, isn't that right?"

Benjamin turned and looked at her with surprise, as if she'd finally gotten his attention by saying something of substance.

"Indeed we did," Mother replied. "The famous suffragist Elizabeth Cady Stanton stood with us. John Whittier lent his support for a time, too, standing in the line for all to see."

"He did?" Clarinda asked, her voice rising.

"Yes, Clarinda," I ventured. "He said it was a worthy cause."

"I hope women gain the vote, and soon." David tapped his glass with his knife, then raised it. "Here's to universal suffrage."

"Hear, hear." Herbert lifted his glass, too.

I raised my glass, as did the others. Clarinda was last, but she finally followed suit. Had the world turned on its end? More likely, her deep admiration for John Whittier had overruled her opposition to the movement.

THIRTY

By eight o'clock I thought I would explode. After the soufflé we'd been served, in succession, rice *croquettes*, larded grouse with bread sauce, potatoes à la Parisienne, and dressed celery. Then came the desserts: Royal Diplomatic Pudding, raspberry sherbet, vanilla ice cream, an orange cake, sliced apples, coffee, crackers, and cheese. The pudding was a work of art, with an outer moulded ring of jellied cherries, an inner mould of the same, and the space in between filled with a rich custard. The cheeses were from France, and one in particular was deliciously soft and creamy, but I was too full to enjoy it.

I was not accustomed to such quantity and such richness of food. How in the world did David keep his trim physique if he ate like this all the time? My energy was flagging from both the surfeit of calories and my injury, and I wished I were already tucked into my bed.

"Shall we go through, gentlemen?" Herbert asked the men. "I've a bottle of excellent port I've been saving." He pushed back his chair and stood. "Mrs. Dodge, that was a fine meal. A very fine meal, indeed." He beamed, patting his stomach.

Clarinda inclined her head in acknowledgment. "Ladies, if you'll come with me." Benjamin hurried around behind her and held her chair as she rose.

Mother glanced at me and stood, as well. "I'm afraid I need to take my daughter home. She suffered a head wound in the attack and needs her rest. Please forgive us for an abrupt departure."

"Of course, of course." Herbert rang for a servant and asked for the driver to bring the carriage around.

I shot Mother a grateful look before addressing our hostess. "I thank thee for the invitation, Clarinda. I very much enjoyed this lovely evening."

"I'm happy you were able to join us, with your busy schedule and all." Clarinda's smile didn't reach her eyes.

I only smiled back at her, ignoring the barb her words delivered. Mother and I both said our good-byes all around and David took my elbow. We'd stepped into the front hall when Benjamin appeared at my side. Of course, the thing he wanted to tell me. What could it be?

"May I have a brief word?" he asked in a low tone.

"Of course. David, Mother, I'll be right out."

David raised his eyebrows but held the door open for my mother. After it closed, I turned to Benjamin. "Thee knows something about Rowena's death?"

He checked the hall, which was empty except for us. The doors to the parlor and the library were closed, too. "I know of the events leading to her promotion at Bixby & Batchelder, and I know thee has done thy share of detective work in the past," he said. "Thee should be careful, Rose. I have had a few dealings with Elbridge Osgood, including on the cricket pitch. I believe he suffers from a kind of illness of the psyche."

"Illness of the psyche. I have made a small study of such things as part of my quest to better treat my pregnant clients. Please go on."

"I've seen Osgood in court. He can be unpredictable in temperament and reason. Sometimes brilliant, but sometimes almost illogical and with a great anger."

Elbridge sounded like Frederick.

317

"I have reason to believe he is being suspected for Rowena's murder." Benjamin continued keeping his voice low. "Does thee know this?"

"In fact I've talked with the detective about him."

David opened the front door. "Rose? The driver is waiting."

"I'm just coming," I told him.

"Be careful is my only message," Benjamin said, locking his gaze on my face. "All right?"

"Of course."

"It was good to see thee and thy mother tonight," he added.

"And to see thee. I know she enjoyed meeting another Friend. I appreciate thy caution about Elbridge, and I shall heed it." I turned toward David, then paused and glanced back. Benjamin's face was etched with concern.

Before David handed me into the covered carriage, he murmured, "I'm going to do what I can to convince my Mother about our union, yours and mine. I'm a grown man and can marry whom I like, of course, but I'd rather have her blessing."

"I doubt my conversation tonight helped thy cause. Talk of attacks, bodies, and murder at the dinner table very much displeased her, I think." The temperature had dropped precipitously since we'd gone into dinner. The moon wasn't yet up, and the glittering star diamonds that littered the black sky did nothing to warm me as I pulled my cloak closer about me.

"Don't worry. I know she'll grow to love you in time."

I very much doubted it. "I'm not so certain." I mentally scolded myself for forgetting to seek out lovely yarn for Clarinda. I could've brought it to her tonight as a kind of hostess gift. Anything to gain her favor.

"It will come to pass, I'm sure of it." David chastely kissed my cheek, since Mother sat just inside the carriage, and we said our good-byes.

As we clattered toward the bridge over the Merrimack, Mother said, "What an astonishing repast. Why, I would be as round as a washtub if I ate such meals all the time."

"I would, too. I doubt it's their everyday fare. At least I hope not. I don't think such rich food is good for the health." I gazed out the window for a moment, feeling dejected about my prospects with both Clarinda and Amesbury Friends. "Mother, does thee think I'll ever marry David?" I heard my voice whine and hated the sound, but whiny was how I felt. Where had my normal strength gone, my usual determination? Had the head injury changed my personality?

She twisted in the seat to face me. "If thee wants to, thee will." She covered my hand with hers.

"But where ever will we hold the ceremony? If I'm to be expelled, Amesbury Friends won't allow the Meeting for Marriage to be held in the Meetinghouse. And I can't imagine being married in David's mother's church, with all its ornate trappings. Organ music and incense, can thee just imagine?"

She laughed softly. "No, I can't. But doesn't David attend other services?"

"Yes, he does, with the Unitarians at the First Religious Society. He brought me to the church once, just to look inside, and it's quite lovely. Not as simple as our Meetinghouse, of course, but still full of light and much less ornate than other churches."

"Maybe his church would be a possibility, then."

"Maybe." I closed my eyes and sank back into the seat to try to ease the returned pounding of my head.

"I have an idea," she said. "Thee knows

our Lawrence Meeting is much less strict than some about certain practices. And it was thy own Meeting for many years. It would make sense to have thy Meeting for Marriage there, if they are willing. Women of many different faiths often return to their homes to be married."

My eyes flew open again and I sat up straight. "Mother, what brilliance. Does thee think they would accept me?"

"It's worth a try. I'll write the clerk of the Women's Meeting a letter tomorrow. Not an official application, just to get a sense of what she thinks."

I leaned against her shoulder, closing my eyes again. "Mother, I love thee."

She laughed again. "Well, that's good, because I plan to be thy mother for a goodly long time yet. I do hope thee will be able to avoid entangling with any more attackers in future."

"I do, too. Kevin will have to apprehend the current one first, though." And I hoped it happened sooner rather than later. Benjamin's words echoed in my mind. Elbridge was *unpredictable in temperament and reason. Sometimes brilliant, but sometimes almost illogical and with a great anger.* And in court, in full view of his peers. What was he like in private?

THIRTY-ONE

I was nearing the end of a prenatal appointment at nine thirty the next morning. My head seemed to be fine for this level of work, which included no physical exertion. "Now that thy baby is growing, it's important for thee to eat nutritious foods." This was the young woman's first pregnancy, now four months along. She'd experienced the normal amount of queasy stomach during her first trimester, but she was past that now. I could talk about foods without needing to have a vomit basin at the ready.

"Like what?"

"Milk, meat, fresh vegetables when thee can find them. Thee is married to a farmer, so perhaps it will be easier for thee to obtain carrots, dark green leafy vegetables, and other brightly colored foods."

"What does the color have to do with it?" She wrinkled her nose.

"They seem to carry a greater quantity of

healthful properties." At least my now-retired teacher Orpha maintained such. And a woman who had delivered hundreds of healthy babies had to be at least partly right.

My client giggled, the gap between her top teeth giving her a childlike look. "So God painted the good vegetables in pretty colors."

"I suppose so."

"My mother-in-law has a big kitchen garden. She'll be happy to dig those things up for me, I'm sure."

I spied a large Rockaway approaching the house. "Excuse me a moment," I said to the woman, who nodded. I opened the front door and called out, "Yes?" I didn't recognize the carriage.

"Are you Miss Carroll, the midwife?" the driver asked from his seat.

"I am."

He hopped down and secured the reins to the post. He climbed the stairs and handed me a folded note. "It's from Mrs. Elbridge Osgood," he said.

The note read, in a flowing educated hand, *Please come quickly. My pains have begun. Lyda Osgood.* So her babe was arriving early. But not dangerously so, at all. It should be well mature enough, at only two weeks short of being full term, to survive the rigors of passing into the world.

"All right. I'll need several minutes."

He tugged at his uniform hat. "I'll wait." He trotted back down the steps.

Five minutes later I'd dispatched my client, donned my outer garments, and given Mother a kiss where she sat reading. "Not sure when I'll be back."

"Is thee sure this is a valid request for thy services?"

"It's a very nice carriage. And it's full daylight. If he doesn't take me to Lyda's home, I'll jump out."

"What about thy head?" She frowned. "Is thee able to do this work again so soon?"

"It's not plaguing me at the moment. But I plan to pass by Annie's place of employment and see if she can get away to assist me."

"Good. I feel better knowing your plan."

I turned toward the door, but paused. "Mother," I said, turning back, "would thee do me a favor?"

"Of course, dear."

"I might have mentioned Elbridge Osgood is one of the people whom Kevin suspects for Rowena's murder. I think it would be prudent to let Kevin know I will be attending a birth at the Osgood home. Could thee walk down to the station and tell him, please? It's not far, and having him know would set my mind at ease."

"And mine as well." She stood. "I'll do it right away."

I thanked her, gave her directions, and we said our good-byes. I made my way out and climbed into the conveyance. "I'll need to make a stop on the way, please," I told the driver.

He didn't look happy about it. "Where?"

"It's on Elm Street, near . . ." Where had Annie said Mabel Roune lived? I came up with it. "On the right just past Washington Street."

"Very well." He drove the horse along High Street, through Market Square, and up the hill Elm Street ascends.

Even though the carriage compartment I rode in had a roof and sides, I shivered from the cold. Today was again sunny, but a brisk breeze drove cold air through the open sides of the box and under my skirts. We passed Carriage Hill on the right, the site of the terrible fire last spring. All the rebuilt factories were now of brick, not wood, and the carriage industry was bustling again. After we passed Washington, the only house likely to be Mabel's was a large square residence with a mansard roof.

I called to the driver in the front, "There."

325

I pointed.

The driver pulled to a halt in front of the house.

"I'll be back out as soon as I can." I climbed out and made my way to the double front doors, each with a tall arched glass insert. After I pulled the bell, a uniformed maid opened it.

"I'd like to speak to Annie Beaumont, please, if I may."

She cocked her head like it was an odd request, but said, "Please wait here, miss."

It was a well-appointed hall, with gleaming woodwork on the staircase and a gilt-edged mirror across from me. I gazed at my reflection. I was still more pale than usual, and I hoped I was recovered enough to undertake a labor of unknown hours and outcome. Annie bustled in from a door farther down the hallway, her red hair pulled back in a stylish do decorated with a green ribbon.

"Rose, what brings you here?" She smiled, took a closer look, and replaced the smile with a frown. "You don't look well. Is everything all right?"

I guessed I truly didn't look well. "I did have a slight accident two days ago. But now I've been called to a birth. Is there any way thee could come away to assist me?"

She stared at me. "Goodness. I want to help you, of course. But Mrs. Roune —"

A door next to us swung open. An imposing woman fully as tall as me, with a battleship bosom in a fine gray wool dress, appeared. Her white hair was done up in a knot on top of her head and she looked at us out of faded green eyes. "I what, Miss Beaumont?"

Annie started. She gave a small curtsy. "Mrs. Roune, this is Miss Rose Carroll, the midwife. Rose, Mrs. Mabel Roune."

"I am pleased to meet thee, Mabel." I extended my hand.

Mabel's lips knit together and her nostrils flared. "Well, I never . . ."

She ignored my outstretched hand, so I dropped it. I didn't know if she was shocked with my uttering her given name or at my use of *thee*.

Her voice trailed away as she peered down her nose at me. "Good heavens. A midwife? And you're called Rose?"

I nodded slowly.

"You're the kind soul who found my Rowie. The policeman told me." She reached for my hand and took it in both of hers as she blinked away suddenly full eyes. "Do come in, Miss Carroll. Do come in." She led me into a large sitting room. Books and newspaper were scattered on a low table and several large floral arrangements filled side tables.

"Thank thee. I will, but for just a moment."

Annie lingered in the hall.

"Come along, too, Miss Beaumont." Mabel beckoned. "Please have a seat, Miss Carroll. I can ring for tea."

"Call me Rose, please." I remained on my feet. I really needed to get to Lyda, although in truth it was rare the call to a birth was of great urgency.

"As you wish. Won't you sit and tell me all about finding Rowena? We are quite devastated at our loss." She frowned. "All except Mr. Felch, that is."

Oh? I needed to move along to the birth, but I wanted to hear more. "I'm so very sorry thee had to lose thy granddaughter, Mabel. Annie has told me thee was very close to her."

"She was my namesake in a way. I cherished her company, her wit, her intelligence." She wrung her hands in her lap.

"I was quite impressed with what I saw of her the last time we met," I said in soft voice. "The night before she died." I hesitated. I needed to leave, to ask if I could have Annie's time, but my need vied with my intense desire to understand Mabel's comment about Oscar. I perched on the chair nearest Mabel. "What did thee mean saying Mr. Felch is not devastated, if I might inquire?"

"That man only pretended to care for her." She tossed her head. "All he cared about was progeny. He didn't love Rowena for herself, for her considerable mental capacity, for her passionate ambition. No, the only thing he wanted was a baby factory and she wasn't having it. I do believe he hired someone to kill her himself."

THIRTY-TWO

Annie nodded. She'd mentioned that when she'd spoken to me of Mabel a few days earlier. Annie glanced at me. "Is it possible, Rose?"

"What would Miss Carroll know of these things?" Mabel asked her, blinking.

"Rose is something of a private detective, Mrs. Roune," Annie said. "She has solved murders in the past."

"You don't say." Mabel examined me with interest. "Are you also looking into my Rowie's death?"

"I'm truly not a private detective at all, Mabel," I protested. "But I have had an involvement, shall we say, with investigating more than one violent death in the past year. And the police detective now welcomes my insights and bits of information, as long as I stay out of trouble." Which I haven't been very successful at just lately, I didn't add.

"Does Mr. Donovan suspect Mr. Felch?" Mabel asked.

"I believe Oscar is under consideration, yes."

"And anyone else?" Mabel's sharp eyes focused so completely on me I felt rather under a microscope.

How much should I reveal? "It's possible her friend Zula Goodwin had reason to wish Rowena harm. She seems both intensely fond of thy granddaughter and angry with her at the same time for rejecting her advances."

"That woman." Mabel curled her lip. "Overeager for Rowie's affections and without scruples. Yes, I wouldn't put murder past her."

Interesting. Both Oscar and Mabel shared a jealousy for Zula as much as a dislike for each other. "And there is a man harboring resentment at losing his job because of Rowena," I went on, speaking quickly to shorten the conversation as much as I could. "Plus a local fellow hard on his luck whom the detective suspects but had to release because he didn't have any real evidence against him."

"You have quite the collection of possibilities. I rather envy you, Miss Carroll. I myself have spent time reading Pinkerton's stories.

The idea of investigation, disguise, sleuthing seems quite attractive. Not that I would do it, alas." Mabel sighed. "One has one's reputation to uphold, of course."

She seemed to make that last remark without a thought for what it might mean to me. I didn't care. My reputation was intact, or would be if I ever got out of here and on to the work at hand.

"But my true profession is as midwife, which I confess is what brought me here today." And why Annie and I had to make our exit as soon as we could. When my left leg started a fast jitter, I pressed my hand on my thigh to quiet it.

"Ah, Miss Beaumont has told me of her interest in this vocation, as well. I think it's a fine line of service. My own children, all six of them, were born upstairs in this very house, with the midwife Mrs. Perkins." Mabel glanced at the ceiling with a fond smile.

I smiled. "Orpha Perkins was my teacher, and a fine one. I still consult with her from time to time, but she has retired from practicing."

"A pity," Mabel said. "But age comes to all of us, and I am certain she trained you well."

A knocking came from the front door. It

had to be the driver impatiently wondering, with good reason, where I was. The maid scurried past in the hall to pull open the front door. Sure enough, a man's voice rang out.

"Sorry to trouble you, miss. I'm looking for a Miss Carroll," he said gruffly.

The maid appeared in the doorway of the sitting room. Mabel looked at me with raised eyebrows.

"Forgive me." I stood, chagrined. I doubted Orpha would approve of me taking so long to arrive at a labor in progress. "I was about to tell thee I've been called to a labor," I told her. "I'm just coming," I said to the driver, who touched his cap and went back outside. I looked at Mabel again. "I wanted to inquire if thee might do the favor of lending me Annie for the day. An important part of her training is to attend births, even at the beginning of her training."

She thought for a moment. "I have nothing pressing to attend to today. I'll let her go with you." She cocked her head. "I knew I wouldn't be able to keep such a smart girl as companion for long." She smiled fondly at Annie.

Annie blushed. "Thank you, Mrs. Roune. I'll get my things." She hurried out.

"I also thank thee, Mabel," I said. "I

enjoyed making thy acquaintance."

She nodded her head. "And I, yours. I hope you'll come to call again when you don't have to rush off to attend a woman in her travails. I don't get much excitement in my life any more. That was one thing Rowena never failed to provide."

"Please accept my condolences on her passing. Are there plans for a funeral service to commemorate her life?" Was it Zula or Oscar who'd said they were in conflict with Rowena's grandmother about the arrangements? I couldn't remember, which worried me. Where had my usually excellent memory fled to?

"It's to be tomorrow. Mr. Felch and I are still in a tussle, though. I insist on having the reception afterward here. He wants to rent a hall. Rent a hall, can you imagine? Can you think of a more unseemly location? No, we'll be having a fine spread of food and drink right there in the next room. I hope you'll join us for both the two o'clock service at Union Church at Point Shore as well as the gathering here."

"I shall be pleased to. I thank thee for the invitation."

Annie appeared. "I'll be here tomorrow morning to help with the preparations, Mrs. Roune."

"Good. Miss Carroll, you've brightened my morning. I look forward to seeing you again."

As the carriage made its way down Elm Street, Annie said, "Mrs. Roune liked you."

"Thee sounds surprised."

"Well, you must admit she is somewhat formidable."

"I think she wishes she'd had a more adventurous life. She saw Rowena starting one, with her law degree and her suffrage work, but her future was cruelly cut short. I suppose my being an amateur detective fills the same bill." I watched as we neared the bottom of the hill before the carriage would head into Market Square. "Let me tell thee about the impending birth."

"Please." She clasped her hands and gave me all her attention.

"It's her third time, so the labor should be fairly easy. A woman's first baby is usually the hardest to produce. The body hasn't done it before and the tissues haven't yet been fully stretched. But there are always exceptions to the rule, as with anything."

"And twins, or a breech presentation can complicate the birth, correct? That's what the book said."

I smiled in approval. "Thee has been

335

studying. Yes, many are the possible complications. But one thing Orpha told me early on in my own apprenticeship has remained with me ever since. A woman's body is designed to birth her baby, and women all over the world do it with barely any assistance at all."

"I'd like to meet your teacher," Annie said.

"I'll bring thee to visit her one day soon. I know she'll like thee, and will approve of my passing along the knowledge I gained from her."

"I hope so."

"She also taught me the best thing we can do is help the laboring woman to remain as calm as possible so the process can go forward."

Annie nodded in thought. "I saw my littlest sister be born at home just last year. Mama didn't have anyone's help but *Mamere*'s."

"Thy grandmother?"

"Yes. It was Mama's seventh baby, so her body had done it quite a few times before. She only labored for two hours, and was up and making supper that very night."

"Is that what made you want to become a midwife?"

Annie smiled. "In part."

The carriage bounced over a deep rut in

the road and I touched my temple, wincing at the throbbing that started up when we landed.

"Rose, are you all right to go to a birth? It looks like your head very much pains you."

"It does hurt some, at that. Thee will be a great help, though. I'll be fine."

"What was the accident you had?"

"I did something foolish on Third Day." I saw her frowning. "What thee calls Tuesday." I described getting the note, being attacked and locked in, and my eventual escape.

She brought her hand to her mouth. "Midwifery is more dangerous than I thought."

I laughed softly. "No, what's dangerous is looking into the lives of criminals. Someone doesn't like me asking questions, and they tricked me. I won't be responding to such a note again. I didn't recognize the name, and I knew I'd never been to the abode, which turned out not to be an abode at all. As I said, it was foolish of me to go and I paid the price. But I'm healing."

Of course, now we were heading to the home of one of the murder suspects. Should I even be taking Annie into a potentially dangerous situation? A mother's life and her baby's were at stake, though. With any luck

Elbridge would be away looking for employment until the end of the day. But I was glad I'd let Kevin know our destination, and of course Mother knew, too.

The driver clucked to the horse to make it up the hill into the square, which was bustling as always. The scent of manure drifted in through the windows and cries of men hawking wares vied with the clop-clop of horses and donkeys hauling all manner of conveyances. From the square we headed north on Market Street on our own assigned employment to assist a tiny new person into this world. This world of work and family was not always safe and warm, but I trusted it would be for this newborn, at least for a few years.

The distraught young maid pulled open the door to the well-appointed Osgood home. "Oh, Miss Carroll, I'm glad you've finally come. She's up there a-screaming."

I cringed inwardly at the *finally*. I might have dallied too long at Mabel's. "Don't worry thyself. It's what women do. I'll attend to her shortly. Are the children about?"

"No." She took our wraps and hung them on hooks near the door. A cylindrical umbrella stand was below, holding several umbrellas as well as a cricket bat. A telephone sat on a low table. "Mrs. Osgood told Nursey to take them to their grandmother's."

"Good. Please bring up fresh boiled water and several basins as soon as possible. Come on, Annie." I lifted my skirts and trudged up the stairs.

"Where have you been, Rose?" Lyda wailed from her bed as soon as I walked in. Her face was flushed and the hair around her forehead curly and damp. The thick curtains were drawn and the only light was from the gas lamp near the window. The air was stifling. "I nearly telephoned for a doctor to come over, instead."

I bustled around opening curtains and cracking a sash open an inch as I said, "We're here now, Lyda." Being well-off financially could normally make people more comfortable, but there was no avoiding the pain of childbirth. I scrubbed my hands at the washstand, knowing how important it was not to bring germs from the outside into the birthing chamber, and particularly not into the woman's body. "When did the pains begin, and how far apart are they?"

"A couple of hours ago. They're getting closer and closer." As a contraction set in, Lyda cried out again.

"Now, now," I said. "Blow out thy breath gently. If thee becomes tense, thy body will have more difficulty letting the baby come out." She should have learned how to give birth after doing it twice before, but perhaps she was afraid of bringing another baby into a family suddenly without a breadwinner. Fear, of whatever origin, could cause a woman's body to try to keep the baby inside as long as possible.

"Annie, please set these things out on a clean cloth on the dresser there." I handed her the bag I kept in my satchel containing the clean scissors and tying cord, a tin of lard, a few herbs, and other supplies necessary at a birth.

Lyda's pain ended and she seemed to see Annie for the first time. "Who's this girl?" She frowned.

"I'd like you to meet Annie Beaumont," I said. "She's my apprentice, and an able one." She was a novice, true, but one who showed great promise in both her manner and her enthusiasm for learning.

Annie greeted Lyda. "I'm pleased to meet you, Mrs. Osgood."

Lyda closed her eyes in response, but Annie didn't appear to mind. I waited to check Lyda until the maid had brought the water. I asked the maid to light two more lamps.

We'd need illumination for the work of the actual birth, and the light from outside was dim, as clouds had blown in on our way here.

When another of Lyda's pains had passed, I said, "Breathe down into my hand, now, Lyda. I'm going to check the opening." I knelt and leaned forward to slide my hand inside her. As I did, my head commenced pounding again and I fought a wave of nausea. This position was a bad one for me. I breathed deeply, concentrating on feeling the size of the entrance to her womb. I slid my hand out and sat back on my heels.

"Thee isn't ready yet, but I'm sure it won't be long." I swayed and grabbed the edge of the bed. My brow was damp with cold sweat, my palms clammy. Lyda and Annie both saw me.

Annie looked at me with alarm. She beckoned to the easy chair across the room. "Come sit here. I'll help her."

I nodded slowly.

"Are you hurt, Rose?" Lyda asked in an odd tone.

"I'll be fine, Lyda." I pushed up ever so carefully and made my way to the chair. "You'll have to help her through the contractions," I told Annie. "Wipe her brow, let her grip your hand. Prop her up a bit more on the pillows, too." I let my eyes sink shut and tried to keep my breath slow and even. I held Lyda, Annie, and myself in the Light, praying for a successful outcome: a thriving baby, a healthy mother, no emergencies to challenge Annie, and a cessation of my headache.

I listened as Annie helped Lyda through several more contractions. I shifted slightly in my seat, hearing Lyda's note rustle in my pocket and idly pictured the handwriting. I froze, the pounding in my head now transferred to my heart. Why hadn't I made the connection this morning? Lyda's handwriting was identical to that on the note Rowena had held.

THIRTY-THREE

My eyes flew open. I stared at my client where she rested in the bed, eyes closed, lashes dark on her cheeks, during a brief respite from the pains.

Lyda couldn't have murdered the much taller Rowena, not in her advanced gravid stage. So she must have abetted Elbridge in the deed. Or put him up to it. And sent him to hit me on the head, too. Thus her odd tone of voice when she asked if I was hurt a few minutes ago. But why try to do away with your midwife when your birth is imminent? I'd think about that later.

Right now I had to decide what to do despite my aching brain roiling with confused thoughts. I had to tell Kevin, but there was no way I could leave the house to find him. I couldn't confront Lyda, not while she was in the throes of her travails. And with my head in this condition, I couldn't very well spare Annie, either. What about the maid? Maybe I could scribble a note for her to take to the police station. But what if she read it? Her first loyalty might be to her employers. Wait. I'd seen a —

Lyda let out a long grunting sound, a sure sign she was experiencing the urge to push. I was going to have to check her again. Women could tear badly if they pushed before the opening to the womb was fully dilated, but usually the urge didn't come until the body was truly ready to expel the baby. I rose ever so carefully.

"Lyda, try not to push quite yet," I said. I perched on the side of the bed next to her, but this time kept my head in an upright position. "I'm going to check you again." Now when I slid my hand in I felt five knuckles-worth of opening. "Very good. Thy baby will be along soon." I wiped off my hand and hurried to the desk under the window even as Lyda let out a long moan. Finding paper and a pencil, I scribbled a note for Annie. I'd seen a telephone downstairs. I prayed it would be in good working order.

Lyda and husband murdered Rowena. Thee must telephone police downstairs. Tell them to find him. Hurry.

I beckoned to her. She scanned my words and looked up, her eyebrows up, her eyes fearful. I held a finger to my lips.

"Go," I whispered. *Please let Elbridge not be about, and let none of the house staff hear Annie using the telephone.* Lyda didn't present a threat to us, unless she had a gun in her nightstand drawer, but her husband would certainly be dangerous if he returned home to find Annie talking to the authorities.

Annie glanced over her shoulder with wide eyes at Lyda, then hurried out the door.

Lyda commenced to make the deep guttural noise of a woman about to give birth. I moved to the head of the bed. My first obligation was, as ever, to produce a healthy baby without harm to its mother.

"Sit up more now, Lyda." I put my hands under her armpits and assisted, but the effort brought on a new wave of pain in my head and nausea in my gut. I blew out a breath and sat on the edge of the bed again, willing the pounding, the sick sensation, to go away. "Bring thy knees up and thy chin down, and give a good push."

She did so even as she cried out, her face reddening with the effort. I felt my own face turn the opposite color, knowing if I looked in a glass I would be pale from pain. When she was spent, she fell back against the pillows.

"It's harder this time, Rose," she wailed. "Why? I thought it was supposed to get easier."

Maybe because thee has a guilty conscience. I palpated her belly again. "I'm quite sure the baby is head down." I gently pressed my fingers in and around the top of the womb. "Yes, this is his rump, not his head. And his back is on top, which is good. I can feel his spine. Maybe he's tipping his face up, though, which presents a larger area to the opening." I made a ring with both hands and placed it back on the crown of my head without touching my wound. "See?"

She gazed dully at me.

"When that part presents at the mouth of the womb, the head is birthed more easily than if this part does." I moved the ring to encircle the top of my head nearest the brow.

"Will my baby still come out?"

"Of course. Don't worry. It just might take a little longer. Thee has only been pushing for a couple of minutes."

Another contraction set in, and another, and another. Still Annie didn't return. Still the child remained inside Lyda. My heart

sank to the cellar. Annie was in trouble. I
knew it.

THIRTY-FOUR

Lyda had been pushing for almost thirty minutes with no real results. I could see the dark-haired head when she pushed, but it retracted between contractions. Lyda grew weary. I myself was becoming ever more fearful, and now felt a portion of desperation about getting this child out.

And still no Annie. Had she been able to call? Had she gone to the police station herself? It was true, I hadn't made it clear she needed to come right back and help me. Worst, had she somehow encountered one of the staff — or Elbridge — and someone discovered what she was up to? If any harm came to Annie, I didn't know what I would do.

But the immediate need was to get this baby out before it started to suffer ill effects from the intensity of a prolonged labor. I opened the tin of lard and scooped out a small amount. The next time the baby's

348

head moved back inside I wiped the inside of Lyda's passageway with the grease. I only used it in extreme circumstances like this one, because there was a slight danger of the lard getting into the baby's nose. But it was a better choice to get the infant out into the world and then deal with a greasy nasal passage than to let this labor continue for much longer. I'd seen babies become distressed after hours of pushing, and the mother's exertion was exhausting for her, too.

I hadn't brought over a cloth to wipe my hand on. I looked around for one, not wanting to stand again unless absolutely necessary. On the nightstand lay a delicate square of fabric. I reached for it, then pulled my hand quickly back as if the cloth were on fire. It was identical to the handkerchief I'd found under Rowena's body. The handkerchief clinched the couple's guilt as far as I was concerned. And it would for Kevin, if he ever got here.

I wiped my hand on the sheet instead. It would need laundering after the birth, anyway. I knelt on the bed. I was just going to have to cope with my head pain until this labor was over. As another contraction set in, I said, "I need thee to hold thy breath and push as hard as thee can, Lyda. Does thee understand?"

She took in a breath and held it, exerting with all her might.

"Good." And it was good. The membranes at her opening bulged around the head. "One more good push."

It worked. The head slid into my hands. I cleared mucous from the baby's mouth with my pinkie finger.

"Now one more," I instructed. "We're almost there."

She let out a yell with her eyes squeezed shut. The door, at right angles across the room from the bed, burst open. I whipped my face in the direction of the door, keeping my hands cradling the infant's head. Annie appeared first, with Elbridge directly behind her. He marched her in and kicked the door shut behind him. He held a cricket bat in the air with one hand. The other had Annie's right arm twisted behind her.

"What is thee doing? Let her go!" I demanded.

He pulled Annie to a stop, his eyes agog at the sight of a head protruding from his wife's private parts. A trembling Annie stared at me. Lyda gave a great deep shout as the baby's body slid into the world in a mess of fluid and blood.

I focused on the baby girl, who was limp

and pale. *No.* It was as I'd feared. I moved her over on the cloth and rubbed her little body with vigor. She hadn't taken a breath. "Thee must live," I whispered. I picked her up by her heels. Sometimes the blood flow to the brain helped get the new life started.

The bat clattered to the floor as Elbridge fell. A thud resounded, and my hand jerked. The newborn took in a breath and let out a squeaky wail, her tiny arms flailing. I offered up a quick prayer of thanks. I laid her down again. Her skin grew pink in front of my eyes. She cried again, this time showing off a hearty set of lungs. She kicked her legs, then grew calm.

Lyda opened her eyes. "What was that . . . Elbridge?" Out of the corner of my eye I saw Elbridge crumpled on the ground on his side. "What's *he* doing in here?" Lyda asked. "And is my baby alive?"

"Thy daughter is well. I believe your husband fainted at the sight of the birth."

Annie cleared her throat. "I had to leave a message for the person you wanted, but Mr. Osgood heard me at the end," she whispered.

"It's the afterbirth, Rose," Lyda called out, her voice creaking as she began to push again.

I had no time to cut the cord. Annie hurried over and held the baby out of the way of the bloody placenta as the slippery mass slid out.

Would Kevin get here before Elbridge regained consciousness? He had to. Lyda wasn't a threat, not in her weakened post-birth state. By the way Elbridge had behaved when he pushed his way in with Annie, though, he would most surely be a danger to us after he awoke.

I took the little girl while Annie brought me the tying cord, scissors, and a bowl. I tied the umbilicus in two places and severed the baby from the placenta, handing her back to Annie. "Clean her up a bit, if thee will."

Elbridge moaned where he lay next to the sharp-cornered bureau, but he didn't open his eyes. I was glad to see the cricket bat had fallen far from where he lay. I had no doubt it had doubled as a murder weapon last Seventh Day night and as the cause of my own wound two days ago. I grabbed the ball of tying cord and hurried to his side. Kneeling very carefully, I bound his hands together. I pulled the knot as tight as I could, then knotted the cord again.

"Rose, what on earth are you doing?" Lyda demanded.

Without speaking I tied his feet together,

too, then pushed up to standing, which made my head commence thudding. I went to wash my hands, still not speaking.

"Why did you tie up my husband?" Lyda was shouting now. "Can't you see he needs help?"

I still kept my silence. When Annie caught my eye and made a small gesture with the baby toward Lyda, I shook my head once, slowly. After I returned to Lyda and confirmed the placenta was intact, I set it aside.

"Let's clean thee up, Lyda," I said.

"All right," she consented. "But only if you help Mr. Osgood. And for God's sake, untie the poor man."

I made no move toward Elbridge. Instead I wiped Lyda's birthing area clean, and I pulled her nightgown down and the coverlet up. I stood with great care and went to wash my hands once again.

"Mr. Osgood, wake up," Lyda called sharply to him "You have a daughter."

His eyes flew open. He tried to push up to sitting, but with his hands tied he only managed to get up to one elbow. "I do? That's splendid, my dear." His voice was thick with grogginess. He blinked a few times. "Say, what am I doing on the floor?"

"I was going to ask you myself," Lyda said in a harsh tone. "What did you think you

353

were doing, barging in here while I was giving birth? It's no place for a man."

He rolled onto his back and winced. "I'm hurt. What in blazes happened to me?" He raised his arms in the air. "And why are my hands all bound up?" He tried to move his legs. "And my feet!" His gaze lit on Annie, who still held the baby. I could almost see the memory creep back into his brain.

"You!" he snarled. "You called the cops on me. I heard you. Why, I . . ."

Annie backed away, shielding the baby. Lyda stared at her.

"You what?" Lyda screeched. "I thought you were a midwife's apprentice, not a secret detective."

"I asked her to." I held up a hand. "Don't blame her for anything. I found thy handkerchief under Rowena Felch's body, Lyda. And thy handwriting is identical to the note her body was clutching. Why did thee have to kill Rowena?" I asked Elbridge, but I was thinking, *Kevin, where are you? Hurry.*

"He didn't want to, but I insisted." Lyda lifted her chin.

"Lyda, don't say such things!" Beads of sweat like nervous pearls covered Elbridge's face. "Don't say anything. Can't you see Miss Carroll here is in thick with the police? We have to get away, now. Help me up."

"Lyda isn't going anywhere," I said. "She just gave birth. Thee has a head wound, Elbridge, from thy fall." And it served him right, too.

"I'll be fine," Lyda snarled. "Get out of my way." She swung her legs over the side of the bed, sitting up.

For the second time in minutes the door burst open. Kevin rushed in, weapon drawn, followed by Guy and another officer, also with arms at the ready. Kevin swept the gun from side to side. He instructed the men to keep watch on Elbridge, then lowered the gun and stepped closer to where I stood.

"So, Miss Rose. All under control here, I see."

THIRTY-FIVE

Kevin kept his face serious, but I caught a wink aimed in my direction.

"I suppose thee could call it under control," I said. "These are thy culprits. Lyda just confessed to forcing Elbridge to kill Rowena." I took in a deep breath and realized my head had stopped pounding, perhaps from the relief of the police taking over this dangerous situation. "If thee examines the handkerchief on the table there, thee will see it matches the one from under Rowena's body."

"Anyone can own a rag like that," Lyda shouted. "Rose, you must fetch me my wrapper." Lyda pointed to the armoire. "I can't be indecent with policemen in the room." She scooted her legs back under the covers.

She had the nerve ordering me around, but I complied. It might be the last act of kindness anyone ever did for her. When I opened the door of the cupboard, the scent of violet flooded my nostrils. I sniffed as I narrowed my eyes and stared at the hanging dresses without seeing them.

"What are you waiting for, Rose?" Lyda called.

I grabbed the wrapper and shut the door. Lyda donned the garment. "Now I'd like my baby." She held out her arms, but Annie only shook her head and took a step backward.

Kevin approached Lyda. "Mrs. Osgood," he began. "Where was your husband Saturday night between dusk and approximately five o'clock in the morning?"

"Why, he was right here with me, Officer. Weren't you, dear?"

Elbridge kept his eyes on the floor in front of him and nodded.

"Lyda, on Monday thee told me Rowena had been bashed in the head," I said. "Thee had no way of knowing the method of death. Am I right, Kevin?"

"Correct. You, Miss Rose, were the only person outside of the police to see it. And we made quite sure not to let the fact slip out to the newspapers."

"Why, I heard it somewhere," Lyda scoffed, tossing her head. "The news must have gotten around town. I think the maid

357

told me."

"I don't believe so." I turned to Kevin. "The armoire is filled with the scent of violet. It was what I smelled on the handkerchief when I first picked it up, but the smell was faint from being out all night and I couldn't place it."

"I'm not the only lady who wears violet!" She again made as if to climb out of bed but Kevin set his hand firmly on her shoulder.

"Lyda, thee helped kill Rowena," I said.

"Mrs. Osgood had nothing to do with it," Elbridge blustered. "She was home the whole night!"

"No, she wasn't." I continued. "Lyda, I smelled the scent of violet when I found Rowena's body. It is thy perfume."

"Rowena must have fancied the same aroma," she insisted.

I smiled sadly. "Frannie Eisenman said Rowena had a severe sneezing reaction to scents. No, it was thee, luring her with the note, pushing Elbridge to kill her." I gazed at Kevin. "I realized a little while ago the penmanship on the note Lyda wrote summoning me to her birth matched the handwriting on the note." I drew the note the driver had brought me out of my pocket. "Kevin, I think if thee compares the writing on this note and the ink on the one summoning me to the carriage house with the note found at the body, they will all match."

He nodded approvingly.

"Oh, and the cricket bat?" I pointed to where it lay in the corner. "If thee examines it well, I believe thee might find traces of Rowena's blood, as well as my own, and possibly strands of our hair, unless Elbridge or Lyda scrubbed it well clean."

"Now isn't that interesting? The murder weapon itself." Kevin rubbed his hands together. "Gilbert, secure the bat, will you?"

Elbridge sank his head into his bound hands with a groan as Guy lifted the bat and turned it over and over, examining it.

I looked at Lyda again. "Thee couldn't stand the fact that Rowena was given thy husband's job."

"Well, it was neither fair nor right. And you don't have proof of anything. This absurdity has gone on too long. Give me my baby." She extended her arms toward Annie again.

I shook my head and Annie half turned away, protecting the child with her arms. Kevin took the note and thanked me.

He addressed Lyda. "We interviewed a witness who placed you both, Mr. and Mrs. Osgood, at the scene of the crime Saturday evening at nine o'clock." Kevin laid a hand on Elbridge's shoulder. "Elbridge Osgood, you are under arrest for the murder of Mrs. Oscar Felch." Elbridge cast an anguished look at his wife.

I handed Kevin my cord scissors. Elbridge didn't struggle as an officer cut loose his feet, helped him up, and ushered him out.

Kevin reached down and lightly touched Lyda's shoulder. She twisted away but couldn't evade his touch. "Lyda Osgood, you are under arrest as an accessory to the murder of Mrs. Oscar Felch. I'll call for a police matron to stay with you until you are recovered enough to be transported to the jail. And until she arrives, Officer Gilbert will guard you. We will find someone to care for the wee one."

"You can't do that!" She gazed at her baby with stricken eyes, as if only now realizing the impact of her crime. She brought her hand to her mouth as tears seeped from her eyes.

"Indeed I can, Mrs. Felch. It's the law." He instructed the other officer to call for the matron. Kevin turned to me. "Thank you," he whispered.

I acknowledged his appreciation with a frown. I was getting better at detecting, true. I gazed at the sweet bundle in Annie's arms. The newborn and her older brothers, nearly babies themselves, would now be no different than orphans due to the desperate, foolish actions of their parents. I'd helped justice to be served, but at a tragic cost. Perhaps I should stick to midwifery from now on.

THIRTY-SIX

Annie took the baby downstairs over Lyda's loud protests. I waited with Guy in Lyda's bedroom.

"You can't take my daughter away from me," she wailed.

"I'm afraid we can, Mrs. Osgood," Guy told her, looking pained to have to say it, being the father of a baby daughter, himself.

Wild-eyed, Lyda threw back the covers and attempted to climb out of bed. "I'm going to get my baby!"

Guy stepped next to the bed and set his hand firmly on her shoulder. "You aren't going anywhere."

Lyda glared at him and shrank from his touch. She abandoned her efforts to escape, though, and turned her back to him, curling into a ball. I hurried to the bed and pulled the coverlet over her silently shaking shoulders.

The nervous maid let us know of the

police matron's arrival nearly two hours later. I left Guy with Lyda, who appeared to have fallen asleep, and went downstairs to meet the female officer. She was a no-nonsense middle-aged woman in a dark uniform dress, a police badge pinned to her bosom. The department employed a few police matrons, specifically to keep watch over female prisoners. We stepped into the parlor where Annie sat with the sleeping infant. After I filled the matron in on the facts of the situation, she nodded.

"How long before Mrs. Osgood can safely be transported to jail?" she asked.

"I'd like her to stay here in bed for two days, if possible. She didn't have a difficult birth, but the process takes its toll on any woman's body, and I don't want to risk bleeding by overtaxing her."

"Very well. It won't do harm to handcuff one of her hands to the bed, I trust?"

"I think it would be a prudent move," I said. "I'll bind her breasts before I leave, because her milk will come down in the next day or two. As for this little one" — I gestured toward Annie and the newborn — "I'll telephone the grandmother who's caring for the older Osgood boys. I expect she might agree to come and fetch the baby." When the matron agreed, I obtained the grandmother's name from the maid and put the call through. The grandmother turned out to be Elbridge's mother, not Lyda's, and she came promptly with a driver and carriage.

"One of my servants recently gave birth and can serve as a wet nurse for the time being." The snowy-haired grandmother cradled her granddaughter, touching her cheek, then looked up again. "I never liked that Lyda. Not good enough for my son by half. And now look what she's gone and done, dragging him into a life of crime, leaving her babies motherless. I hope she hangs." She said good-bye and turned away.

I murmured to Annie, "It's more likely her own son will hang." I let out a heavy breath. "I have to go up and see if Lyda will let me bind her breasts. She might refuse."

Which was exactly what happened, so I abandoned my efforts and told Guy and the matron that Annie and I were leaving. We walked toward town with heavy steps, Annie seemingly feeling the weight of what we'd just been through as much as I was. Another snowstorm appeared to be brewing and my headache was creeping back. Dark gray clouds threatened the sky and I tasted snow in the cold air.

"Annie, thee did well," I told her, slipping

her arm through mine. "Was it terribly frightening, having Elbridge apprehend thee like he did?"

"*Mon Dieu,* yes, Rose." She crossed herself. "He kept insisting we go upstairs, and I kept telling him the baby wasn't born yet and he couldn't. In the end he almost dragged me. I'm sorry to have left you alone, with your headache, and all, but he was so irate I thought it was better to keep him out of the birthing chamber."

"Thee did the right thing. And continued to by keeping the baby in thy arms. Lyda could have used her as a weapon, as a security."

"You mean, threaten to harm the baby if we didn't let them escape, or some such thing?"

"This is a woman who pushed her own husband to murder, don't forget. That's exactly what I mean."

"She wouldn't!"

"Annie, humans are capable of great wrong, even to their own families. I think she might have, and thee made sure she couldn't attempt it."

A wagon laden with pumpkins rattled by on the cobblestones as we approached Market Square, and the Baptist Church bell struck three times. A cry of, "Thief!" went up across the way as four lads ran by clutching small loaves of bread. Smoke danced up from the chimney of a nearby bakery, and the inviting aroma of fresh bread tickled my nose and taunted my stomach. Despite the terrible misdeeds of Lyda and Elbridge, everyday life went on as if nothing truly bad had happened. Merchants sold their wares. Mills and factories beat their industrial rhythms. Children played, women toiled, teachers taught. At least the Osgood wrongdoers wouldn't be attempting any more crimes, ever.

"Luckily for all of us, not all births are so dramatic as this one," I remarked, almost to myself.

"I should hope not."

"Now that we know it was Lyda behind my attack, I can't figure out why she would want to kill her midwife when her birth was imminent." I frowned as I walked.

"She did say she was about to call a doctor when we walked in. Maybe she had arranged for someone else to help her. And then when you survived, she couldn't very well not call you after labor started."

"That's a good deduction, Annie. I think you're right." Maybe Annie would be my helper in more ways than one in the future.

"Rose, I must return to Mrs. Roune's and

see if she has need of me for the rest of the day, even though she said she didn't. Just in case."

"Thee is a conscientious sort, Annie. And I know thee will make a successful midwife." I squeezed her hand.

She said good-bye, trying to wipe the smile at the compliment off her face. I turned toward High Street, but thought the better of it. I wouldn't be able to rest if I didn't know that all the other messy ends of this ball of yarn had also been tidied up, and I thought knowing might help my head, too. I aimed myself in the direction of the police station instead of home.

Five minutes later I sat opposite Kevin in his office. He'd pumped my hand so vigorously when I walked in I thought it would fall off. Now he beamed.

"Excellent teamwork, Miss Rose, wouldn't you say?"

"I suppose. But a few things still puzzle me."

"Such as?"

"For one, what was Hilarius doing on Greenwood Street Seventh Day night if he didn't kill Rowena? He's always maintained his innocence."

"Ah, I persuaded that bird to sing. Remember when we conjectured if Mr. Felch

367

was involved, he must have hired someone to kill his wife?"

"Yes."

"Bauer told me Felch did hire him!" Kevin ended on a triumphant note. "Bauer was supposed to kill her and make it look like a burglary. Felch had given him a key to the back door so he could sneak in and do the deed. But Felch didn't know his wife would be out at a meeting. When Bauer got there, he spied Mrs. Felch waiting in front of her house. He says once he saw her, he realized he couldn't kill her and he hid, thinking she would go inside. Instead he watched the Osgoods kill her."

"With the cricket bat."

Kevin nodded. "He said it happened so fast he couldn't stop them. He watched them drag her under the bush. By the time they drove away and he went to check, she was dead. Mr. Felch had threatened him if he didn't kill his wife, so Bauer figured he'd better stage the break-in, anyway."

"He was terrified to tell the truth."

"I convinced him we'd be lenient if he did. Although he plum made a mess of it, breaking the glass from the inside instead of out."

"Thus the shards on the front stoop." I gazed at the desk in front of me without seeing it. "So his agreement with Oscar was the reason he looked so frightened every time he spoke of that evening. Frankly, Kevin, I'm glad he's innocent."

"It's always good to discover the truth. And now I have Felch in a cell next to Osgood."

I thought for another moment. "I'm relieved Zula is innocent. I'd hate to see a young woman like her be a killer. Not to mention how it would have besmirched the suffrage movement. Can't you just imagine the headlines?" I shook my head, then regretted it as I winced.

"You're not better yet, are you?" He furrowed his brow, looking concerned. "Go on home and take a good rest. And Miss Rose?"

"Yes?"

"I can't be having you helping me with another murder case. It's too dangerous by a long shot. Look at what happened. You were lucky to get away with only a head wound."

"All right, Kevin." Although I couldn't really vouch for what I would do if another murder was committed in our fair town. I'd gotten quite a taste for teasing apart the various threads that knit together a case. Despite the danger, I liked the feeling of solving a mystery, but I prayed it would be a good long time before another murder was committed. Never would be fine, too.

THIRTY-SEVEN

I awoke from a nap at home later in the afternoon to sounds of giggles and scurrying around. I used my chamberpot and rinsed my hands in the basin. Donning my glasses, I opened the door to the hall, my head blessedly free from pain for once. Dark had already fallen outside. Luke sat on the floor reading. He leapt to his feet.

"Rose, did thee have a good rest?" he asked in an overly loud voice.

"What is thee doing on the floor, Luke? And what time is it?" I yawned.

"I'm just reading." He glanced at the ceiling, looking way too innocent for a thirteen-year-old boy.

Or girl, I reflected, remembering my own hijinks at his age. What could he be up to?

"I think it's about five thirty," Luke said.

Betsy ran in. "Granny Dot says tea's on the table. Come on!" She grabbed my hand and led me through the sitting room. The door to the kitchen was closed. Betsy stopped and clapped her hands. "Ready?" Her eyes shone and she bounced in her little knitted house slippers.

"Am I ready for tea? Certainly. Lead the way, miss."

Betsy pulled open the door with a flourish. I took one step into the kitchen and stopped. The room resounded in, "Happy birthday!" and "Many happy returns of the day!"

I swiveled my head from left to right and back. All the other Baileys stood around the table — the twins, Faith, and Frederick, along with Mother. Zeb stood with Faith. David stood beaming, too, next to Annie and Bertie. Small cakes, fruit tarts, a plate holding squares of fudge, and a bowl of peppermint and butterscotch candies surrounded a vase of colorful late asters in the middle of the table. Little wrapped packages filled the few empty spaces. A grateful smile spread across my face even as my eyes filled.

"Is thee surprised, Auntie Rose?" Betsy asked. Luke scooted past us with a big grin on his watchman's face.

I scooped Betsy into my arms. "I'll say. How did thee keep the secret, my sweet?"

"They only told me after thee went to sleep."

Mother nodded knowingly. I laughed and swiped at my tears.

David moved to my side. "Happy twenty-seventh, Rosie." He lightly kissed my forehead.

"Me, too," Betsy demanded. "Don't I get a kiss, too?"

David laughed out loud and complied with her demand. I looked at Annie.

"Did you know about the party this morning?" I asked her. "If so, you're good at keeping a secret."

She smiled and shook her head. "Faith sent me a note after I got home."

"I thank each of thee for being here," I said, looking at each in turn. "I never expected a party. But I needed one about now."

Bertie sent me a knowing look and I reflected it back to her. She'd clearly heard of our harrowing encounter with murderers.

"Well, let's eat," Mother said. Faith poured fresh cider for the younger ones, and Mother served tea for the rest of us.

"Aren't you going to open your gifts, Auntie Rose?" Mark asked, looking wistfully at the gaily wrapped packets.

"I'll do it after we eat, Mark. I shan't forget to call on each of thee to help me open them, all right?"

He nodded, pressing his lips together but unable to conceal his happy smile.

The younger children took their sweets and drinks into the sitting room, Luke carrying Betsy's cider since she wasn't yet adept at walking without spilling.

"Does thee want to share anything about thy suspenseful morning?" Mother asked.

I mused on the prospect as I sipped my hot, milky tea. "I'd rather not just now. Let it suffice that the world has been set right again, thanks to Annie and Kevin."

"And thanks to thee, Rose," Frederick said in a quiet voice. "Dorothy told me of both thy bravery and thy commitment to thy laboring client, criminal though she was. Harriet would have been proud."

What a welcome change in his demeanor. I prayed it would last and also that we wouldn't ever smell alcohol on his breath again. Perhaps starting a Find Frederick a Wife project would be a good effort to begin, too.

"Indeed she would have," Mother added with a soft smile.

"I was only doing my job," I protested. David squeezed my hand and I remembered what I wanted to tell him. "David, I don't know if thee heard Hilarius Bauer is innocent of all charges. He said Oscar did hire him to kill Rowena. When he saw her, he realized he couldn't do the deed, and then saw Elbridge murder her right before his eyes."

"I'm not surprised to hear that Bauer had too big a heart to be a murderer. I'll speak to Father. Perhaps he can find more permanent employment for the man."

"I do hope so," I said. "His mother is quite ill, and he needs the income. Zula Goodwin is innocent, too." I addressed Bertie and Mother.

"Good," Mother said. "The movement didn't need a stain on one of its active members." She dug into her pocket, drawing out a folded letter. "I almost forgot, Allan wrote to thee, Rose. And he added a note to me about Elbridge Osgood."

I raised my eyebrows. "And?"

"Delilah had told us her distant cousin had once been expelled from the cricket league for whacking a fellow player with the bat. He apparently had no control at all over his temper."

"The authorities will be controlling the temper now, and we'll all be safer for it, by gum," Bertie said.

"A truer statement I have never heard," I said. I opened the note from my father, which simply wished me a happy birthday and expressed his love for me. I folded it with eyes once again full, gazing around the table at my family, my beau, my best friend, my apprentice. How fortunate I was, and how lucky, truly.

"I have good news, too," Faith said. "My article on the Amesbury suffragists' demonstration will be published in the *Boston Evening Transcript.*"

"Faith, that's wonderful!" Annie clapped her hands.

"Yes, the reporter we met thought my piece was well done and convinced his editor to include it. They're going to pay me for it, too."

I smiled at Faith's glowing face. "I'm delighted for thee, sweet Faith."

"And there's more. *The Amesbury and Salisbury Villager* wants to hire me. As a reporter! Just as thee used to be, Father."

I'd forgotten Frederick had worked as a reporter in his younger days before he became a teacher.

A beaming Frederick slung his arm around his daughter's shoulders. "Thee is a chip off the old block, as they say."

David stood. "I'd like to propose a toast.

Well, a tea toast." He raised his teacup. "To justice, to love, and to prosperity among us, whatever form it might take."

"And peace among us, too," Bertie added.

Everyone sipped their agreement. I'd be happy to drink tea in support of justice, love, and prosperity for the rest of my life. And above all to peace.

ACKNOWLEDGMENTS

Thanks once again to editors Amy Glaser and Nicole Nugent and the entire Midnight Ink crew for publishing this series. I'm so pleased to have Greg Newbold creating the art for the gorgeous covers.

I'm grateful to author Tiger Wiseman for again opening her Vermont home for a writer's retreat in the summer of 2016. I also wrote furiously for a weekend at the Wicked Cozy Authors annual retreat. These awesome authors — Jessie Crockett/Jessica Estevao, Julie Hennrikus/Julianne Holmes, Sherry Harris, Liz Mugavero/Cate Conte, and Barbara Ross — are the best support group ever.

Rose's mother, Dorothy Henderson Carroll, is named for my paternal grandmother, Dorothy Henderson Maxwell, who was born only a few years after this book takes place. Midwife and mystery fan extraordinaire Risa Rispoli again vetted the birthing details in the book.

Independent editor Ramona DeFelice Long once again gave the book a close edit, and it's a much better book for her insightful comments and questions. She reminded me, after I sent her a manuscript with only one midwifery-related scene, that part of the allure of this series is Rose being a midwife, not just an amateur sleuth. Oops. I fixed that right away. Ramona also hosts a virtual writing champions group every day at seven a.m. on Facebook. That hour of uninterrupted writing every morning, with a dozen other writers scattered all over the country doing the same, is one of my most productive creative times. Thanks, O Champion of the Writing Champions! In addition, I hied off with Ramona, KB Inglee, and author Kimberly Gray to a convent retreat house for some intensive writing, where I polished this book and started another.

The character Frannie Eisenman is a real person in the current era. She won the right to name a character at the Super Sawyer Fund auction, an auction to raise money for a little boy undergoing leukemia treatments. Hope you like your 1888 self, Fran! Ruby Bracken was also a real person, the mother of Moishe Ragieme, who was the high bidder on my naming rights item in the 2015 Rags to Runway auction, which benefits a school in Guatemala. Jasmine is named for the granddaughter of yet another generous charity bidder, Jane Harris-Fale for Opportunity Works. And the name Emily Hersey was a Rubbish to Runway auction winner, won in 2016 by Lisa Losh. The real Emily, Lisa's grandmother, was a long-time Amesbury resident living on Market Street who played piano and raised six children.

Thanks again to Allan Hutchison-Maxwell for reading the manuscript and offering his valuable editorial comments, and to his wonderful fiancée, Alison Russell — historians both — for doing the same.

My Amesbury Quaker family, my Sisters in Crime family, my good friends, my family by blood, my partner Hugh — I love you all and thank you, always, for your support.

I appreciate readers and librarians more than I can express. If you like my stories (please also check out my mysteries written as Maddie Day), a brief review on Amazon or Goodreads really helps an author — as does telling your friends.

ABOUT THE AUTHOR

Edith Maxwell (Amesbury, MA) is the president of Sisters in Crime New England, a member of Mystery Writers of America, and a longtime member of the Society of Friends. She is also the author of the Local Foods Mysteries, the Country Store Mysteries, and the Cozy Capers Book Group Mysteries (the last two written as Maddie Day). You can find her at edithmaxwell.com and blogging at wickedcozy authors.com, killercharacters.com, and midnightwriters blogspot.com.

The employees of Thorndike Press hope you have enjoyed this Large Print book. All our Thorndike, Wheeler, and Kennebec Large Print titles are designed for easy reading, and all our books are made to last. Other Thorndike Press Large Print books are available at your library, through selected bookstores, or directly from us.

For information about titles, please call:
(800) 223-1244

or visit our website at:
gale.com/thorndike

To share your comments, please write:

Publisher
Thorndike Press
10 Water St., Suite 310
Waterville, ME 04901